Adventures in Christianity

The
Trip

Geoff Fredericks
Kathleen Martens

xulon
PRESS

Acknowledgements

All glory goes to the Father! Without His help and the intersession of the Holy Spirit, this book would not have been written.

Co-creating this book was an adventure in itself. We experienced things in the writing of this book that neither of us ever conceived of. Geoff's wife, Sally and daughter, Chandra, thought he had gone off the deep end when he started spending all his time writing. Kathleen's son, C.J., and her friends just shook their heads as she embarked on yet another activity. Thank you to all who supported and loved us anyway.

Thank you to Helena Foutz for editing our work and offering insight and support to our cause. To her oldest daughter, Hannah, thank you for your feedback. Keep reading—it takes you to places you might not get to go otherwise.

Claudia Avalos, you were so supportive in our early efforts. Your excitement kept us fresh and driven. Although our time together was short, it was vibrant and joyful. Thank you for your support and encouragement.

Most importantly, thank you to our Lord and Savior Jesus Christ. Our mutual love for Him is the driving force that continues to move this project along. Many times, in the writing of this book, we were overcome with emotion and stopped and prayed in His name. The power of prayer is an amazing thing. Although we know that, we never cease to be amazed at the manner in which He answers them. Thank you, Father, Son and Holy Spirit.

Adventures in Christianity – The Trip is the first in a series of adventures designed specifically to draw the reader's attention to the fact that Christianity is not about what one does in relation to religion, but about how one relates Christianity and Christian thinking to everyday life. It's the relationship one has with the Creator and what one does when no one is looking that defines character.

Table of Contents

Preparation

The door flew open and Buck came running into the room, his eyes open wide with excitement and his face flushed with color. "Mom, the church elders have decided that the Youth Group's gonna go camping when school gets out! Can I go?" he said excitedly.

Becky paused for a moment and said doubtfully, "I don't know, Buck, I'm not sure we can afford that right now; there's all the camping equipment and food to buy. It's just not in our budget."

Bam! The door of opportunity had been slammed shut before it even got cracked open. Buck dropped his head and tried to suppress his disappointment, as he had many times before, and slowly left the house. He understood but it didn't make it any better.

Buck started walking, slowly and dejectedly. Without even thinking he headed for the church. Buck was a handsome teenager. He was muscular but on the thin side. His brown wavy hair came down to his shoulders and a slightly long rounded nose set between two enchanting brown eyes, which, he was told he inherited from his father. He typically wore t-shirts that were well worn and most of the time holey skater-type shoes and blue jeans that were often tight and short due to his rapid growth spurts. As he walked along he started thinking about his life and wondered again, probably for the thousandth time, what his life would have been like if his father were still alive. Fifteen minutes later he found himself at the Youth Hall.

The Faith Church in Jamestown was where you could find most of the young men fifteen to eighteen years old at any given time when school wasn't in session. It was a safe place to hang out where the people always seemed to make you feel welcome. There's something about a small town church that gives a kind of comfort to your soul.

Dolton looked up as Buck came slowly strolling through the double doors of the Youth Hall and jumped to his feet to find out what was up. Dolton James was a tanned, stocky young man at five-feet ten-inches tall with straight dark brown hair cut very neatly and combed straight back on his head. His dark blue eyes were set neatly under what looked to be manicured eyebrows and over a long slender nose. Dolton had almost perfect posture and usually dressed in new t-shirts, new dark blue jeans and top-of-the-line tennis shoes. Many times Buck found himself a little envious that Dolton was always dressed with new clothes. His mother always seemed to keep him looking his best. This seemed to bother Dolton at times, but they never talked about it.

"Well?" asked Dolton.

"Mom said that we don't have enough money, it's not in the budget," said Buck.

Phil Thomas, or "Mr. Phil" as he was known to the youth, was one of the elders of the church, and could usually be seen sitting at the far end of the hall. He had overheard their conversation. He always seemed to be there; sometimes the boys wondered if he ever went home. He was a tall man and had a soft but authoritative way about him; when he spoke people usually listened. His long, straight, sandy brown hair hung down on his shoulders and blended into his long beard. He had dark brown eyes that sunk slightly back and were framed with crows' feet and scars. He never talked about it, but some people thought that he had been in a terrible accident. His golden brown tan made him look older than his years, but there was no hiding his handsomeness. He motioned the boys over with a wave. Both Dolton and Buck had seen Phil wave them over and under their breath said to each other, "Oh no . . . . We didn't do anything . . . I wonder what he wants."

As they slowly moved over to the other side of the hall, Mark rounded the corner and walked through the doors. Mark Miller, the pastor's son, looked like a smaller version of his dad. He liked to wear t-shirts, loose fitting jeans, and a much worn pair of skater-type shoes. Mark yelled out, "Hey, guys!" which made everyone in the hall look up.

"What's going on?" Mark said with a smile as he stepped between Dolton and Buck.

Phil spoke, "I couldn't help but overhear that Buck can't go on the trip."

"No, no, NOOOOO! That can't be; he HAS to go!" said Mark as he put his arms around Dolton's and Buck's shoulders. "If Dolton and I are going he has to go too. It wouldn't be a trip without him. We're like brothers!" Mark turned and ran out of the hall as he yelled back, "I'm going to go talk to my dad and see if he can help."

Phil got up and put his hands on the back of Dolton's and Buck's necks and said in a deep voice that usually meant something serious was about to happen, "You two need to come with me."

Dolton and Buck walked warily with Phil as he directed them out of the Youth Hall, around the corner and down the outside hall to Pastor Mike's office. As Phil and the boys came into the Pastor's office, Mark was already begging, "Dad! You've got to help figure out a way for Buck to go on this trip!"

Pastor Mike Miller, the spiritual leader of Faith Church, was a kind and gentle man of stocky build and fair skin. His brown wavy hair was usually cut in a businessman-like fashion – short and tight. He was about to tell Mark that there was nothing he could do when Phil spoke up, "I'll sponsor Buck if I can go as a chaperone."

After a short pause and a knowing look between the two men, Pastor Mike told the boys that they needed to wait outside while he and Phil called Buck's mom. The boys paced anxiously in the hall – except Mark who snuck back to the office and pressed his ear to the door.

"What do you think they are talking about?" whispered Dolton.

"I don't know, but I'll be real surprised if my Mom agrees to anything. She can be pretty stubborn – especially when it comes to money. Once her mind is made up it's pretty hard to change it," replied Buck.

"Shh," said Mark pressing his ear even tighter against the door, "I can't hear what they're saying with you guys prattling."

"Prattling? I wasn't prattling, were you prattling?" said Dolton.

"Well, I sure wasn't prattling," followed Buck.

"I'm not even sure what prattling is," Dolton interjected.

"Oh, brother," said Mark as he lifted his ear from the door, resigned to the fact that he would get nothing from his eavesdropping.

After twenty minutes Pastor Mike and Phil came out with long faces, looking sad, and said, "Boys, we're very sorry to have to tell you this, but after talking to Buck's mom, all of you will be going on the camping trip." It took a moment for the words to sink in. Mark, Dolton, and Buck threw their hands in the air yelling and singing in falsetto, "Hallelujah, Hallelujah!"

"Okay boys, okay," laughed Pastor Mike. "Next Thursday night during the Youth Program we'll find out how many kids will be going on the trip, and then we'll figure out where it will be and work out all the details. Make sure you don't miss it." The boys left the office pushing and shoving each other in excitement.

<{{}}><

The next few days Mark, Buck, and Dolton met every day after school at the Youth Hall to talk about the trip and try to figure out where they would be going. Thursday night finally came and they gathered outside the Youth Hall – all 17 kids from the Youth Group were there.

The Youth Program met every Thursday at 6:30 p.m. sharp. Attendance had been declining ever since Bobby, the volunteer youth pastor, had left. He had been popular among the youth but was called on a mission that took him out of the country. The elders of the church had decided that having a camping trip for the teenagers in the Youth Program would help boost morale and increase attendance. Right on time, as usual, Pastor Mike called the kids in and started the program off with music and prayer; then he announced that in four weeks the elders would be sponsoring a camping trip for the Youth Group. Youth, ages fourteen to eighteen, who wanted to go would need to have permission slips filled out and submitted within two weeks. As Pastor Mike gave the announcement, the kids talked with excitement and had a hard time concentrating. At the end of the program, permission slips were handed out and some of the kids came up to Mark to ask him if he knew where they were going on the camping trip. Mark told them, "I'm only the pastor's son. I don't have divine intervention."

Buck was standing with Dolton by the double doors. "I hope we get to sleep outside."

"Maybe they'll take us fishing," said Dolton.

As Buck and Dolton we're talking about their wish list, Mark came over and joined in. "Hey guys, it sounds like were going to have a great trip. Have you heard anything about where we might be going?" Dolton asked Mark.

"No, but it'll probably depend on how many kids'll be going," he replied.

<{}}><

Two weeks had passed and it was the Thursday night Youth Program again, the last night to turn in a permission slip to go camping and the day before school would be out for the summer. There was a lot of excitement during the program; at the end it was time to turn in the permission slips. Pastor Mike had sent Buck and Mark around to collect them and bring them to the front. After a quick count Pastor Mike announced that only seven of the seventeen kids had turned in slips. Kids started talking about why they couldn't go; some were going on vacation with their families, two were already going camping and the others said their parents told them no.

Pastor Mike quieted down the kids and then said, "For those of you not going please don't be disappointed about missing out on this trip. I'm sure this won't be the last trip we ever take. There will be others. Now, those of you who handed in your slips, I need to speak to you before you leave. Thank you all and may the Lord bless you and keep you."

The program ended with a prayer and music. The kids going on the trip moved to the front of the hall. "I would like to have a meeting with all of you and your parents here this

Saturday at 10 a.m. We will discuss the trip and what you'll need to bring," said Pastor Mike.

A hand went up, waving excitedly; a young man of slight build who looked through a pair of thick black-rimmed glasses with dark black hair parted in the middle said, "Sir... sir."

"Yes, Weber," said Pastor Mike.

"My parents would like to know what the trip will cost and what we need to bring," he said.

"Please have your parents come to the meeting on Saturday and we'll have all the details. As a matter of fact, it's very important that all of your parents attend the meeting on Saturday," said Pastor Mike. Pastor Mike then dismissed everyone saying, "I'll see you Saturday at 10:00 a.m. and please don't be late."

Planning

Saturday morning came and almost everyone showed up early. Buck and Dolton arrived at the same time as Pastor Mike, Mark, and Phil. Fifteen minutes later, the double doors of the Youth Hall opened to Weber Deerfield and his parents, Karen and Stanley. Weber would not be hard to pick out of a crowd. He received his height and slim features from his mother, but his black hair, round nose, olive skin, and oddly gray eyes were from his father. As a matter of distinction, both of them had eyes that were hidden behind the same kind of dark, wide-rimmed glasses. Weber always wore the same type of clothing, a short-sleeve dress shirt that he kept tucked in, casual dress pants with a perfect crease down the middle of each leg, a leather belt, and black wingtip shoes. He looked like the type of kid who got picked-on a lot in his early years due to his nerd-like appearance. He was well liked in this group, except for Zach, who picked on him mercilessly. But, then again, Zach picked on almost everybody.

Next through the doors came Dolton's mother, Mrs. James, the richest woman in town. She was a striking woman with light brown highlighted hair and makeup that looked as though she had a makeup artist following her around doing touch-ups before every stop. Her dress, shoes and handbag not only matched but also looked expensive and most likely were.

Following Mrs. James was Buck's mother, Becky Bond, who came in dressed for work, which happened to be at the local restaurant. Becky was a widow who worked hard and managed to raise her son alone. It meant hard times as far as money but she and Buck had a very special relationship and most days the money troubles didn't get in the way. As she entered the room she saw that her son looked happier than she had seen him in a long time; a special sparkle of love appeared in her bright blue eyes that gave her a look of joy, happiness, and peace all at the same time. She loved seeing her son happy; it's all she ever wanted for him. *I'm sure this trip will be good for him*, she thought.

A few moments after Mrs. Bond arrived, Zach and Quinton came strolling through the doors. Zachary Adalick was a well-built young man, streetwise and tough, both due to his last name and the fact that he spent a lot of time on his own. Saying that Zach had attitude was speaking mildly. Every bit of him practically shouted, "Don't mess with me!" Zach was tall for his age, standing six-foot two-inches with sandy blond straight hair that just covered his ears. He had deep-set dark brown eyes and an even tan showed off the white in his almost perfect teeth. His smile, if you were unlucky enough to receive one, usually only showed itself just before he took on a rival. He was mostly seen in a baseball jersey with the number 1 on it, blue jeans, and old-school tennis shoes. Zach blurted out to Pastor Mike, "My parents had to go to work and they want me to take notes. They said if they had questions that they would call you or see you tomorrow at church." Pastor Mike replied with a nod of his head and a brief smile.

Quinton had his hands in his pockets and gave Phil a little wave from his hip and then spoke quietly saying, "Dad went golfing and Mum went shopping and they'll talk to you tomorrow also."

"That's fine, Quinton, thank you," replied Pastor Mike politely.

Quinton Rothford, a child of English parents, was extremely polite and always apologizing for something. Quinton was very thin at five-foot eleven-inches. He had a European look with olive skin and dark brown hair cut neatly in a regular boys' fashion. The cut exaggerated his high forehead and made his ears noticeably stick out. Two very distinguishing features were his cleft chin and bright green eyes that made him look like a movie star. Quinton dressed sharply in polo shirts, belted dress slacks, and penny loafers that each carried a penny for good luck. Quinton possessed what could best be described as a quirk, which was the source of much fun and laughter when the boys were all together. He was always hitting himself. If you gave him a pencil, he would tap it on his forehead; if you didn't stop him he would tap it into a sore. Once Zach gave him a ruler and he hit his chest until the ruler broke. If he didn't have anything in his hands he would hit his wrist on his side or make a fist and beat the opposite shoulder. Every once in a while he would hit himself in the face with an open hand. His quirk always seemed to happen at the most inopportune moment for Quinton. It made him the center of attention, which he always seemed to shy away from.

Some years back one of the children from Sunday school asked him why he was always hitting himself and Mark overheard him say something about 'esseye'. He just figured that he probably meant essay. It did seem that he was always reading; he probably had many book reports to do. Then he heard him explain that "SI" stood for self-injury and mentioned something about insecurities or tragedies. Quinton was a bit of a bookworm. You usually never saw him without a book. He loved to read and would read anything anyone gave him. Consequently, he was much more comfortable talking with adults than with his peers. It made him kind of an outsider, which made him hide in his books more and enhance the problem. Quinton had done a great deal of reading about camping and decided, at the behest of his parents, that he should experience it for himself.

The last to show up was Martha Sue Brown. She came into the Youth Hall slightly out of breath and walked quickly up to Pastor Mike. She was a cute teen with long, light brown wavy hair that gracefully flowed down to the middle of her curved back. Her bangs were not quite long enough to stay tucked back so she was frequently pushing them out of the way and behind her ears without thinking. Although it was a natural movement for her, it was perceived (especially by the boys) as a bit flirty, so she oftentimes caught the attention of many adolescent male stares. Her naturally long eyelashes complemented her beautiful brown eyes, set above rosy cheeks and a button nose. She had full lips, always kept colored cherry-red with a high gloss, that drew the eye of any boy she spoke with if they were not already drawn to how she looked in a pair of belted denims, sandals and a boat-collar, three-quarter sleeve shirt that was always neatly tucked in.

"I'm sorry for coming late, Pastor, but I wanted to let you know that I am not going to be able to go on the trip after all," said Martha Sue.

"I'm sorry to hear that," said Pastor Mike with disappointment.

Dolton and Mark could not help watching Martha Sue's every movement.

"Sorry Pastor, I've to go," she said as she turned and smiled at Mark and Dolton. Their eyes were glued to her as she ran out and disappeared into the sun that just happened to be shining directly into the Hall doors.

"There she goes, off into the sunset," pined Dolton.

"That's sunrise, you dolt!" chided Mark.

"Whatever," said Dolton in a breathy distant voice as he stared in the direction of Martha Sue's departure.

"Man, you've got it bad," grinned Mark.

"Hunh?" he replied.

"It looks like everyone has arrived, so please sit down," said Pastor Mike. He moved to the podium and asked Phil to join him in starting the meeting. Pastor Mike started in prayer, "Please bow your heads for the prayer. Dearest Father in Heaven, thank you for the opportunity to gather this beautiful morning and fellowship with one another as we plan for an adventure with the youth of our community. Be present this morning and bless the planning of this adventure as we attempt to grow in Christian fellowship and love. We ask this through Christ our Lord, Amen."

"Okay, I believe everyone here knows, but just in case I would like to introduce Phil Thomas. He is a church elder and will be one of the chaperones on our camping trip." Everyone clapped and Zach gave a loud whistle. Everyone liked Phil, he had an easy-going way about him; he always spoke with good sense and had a terrific sense of humor that the youth fully appreciated.

"All right, all right now, quiet down," said Pastor Mike over the din. Just as he was about to speak again, Phil leaned over and said something in his ear. After a few moments Pastor Mike spoke saying, "It's just been brought to my attention that only six youth are going on the camping trip and it just so happens that they are all boys. Because of this we have had a proposal by Mr. Phil."

Phil walked up to the podium and said smiling, "I propose that instead of just going camping we go on a back-packing trip." All six boys rose at the same time and began high-fiving each other! Buck looked over at his mother and gave her a 'please can I go' look; she nodded her head.

"Yes!" he said emphatically and smiled back at her.

Dolton headed over to sit in the empty chair next to his mother. As Dolton sat down he was already asking, "Mom, can I go?"

"Yes, Dolton," said Mrs. James in a less-than-excited manner, "you may go." Dolton bounced out of the chair and flew back over to Buck and Mark to make sure that they could go too. Buck and Mark had been watching and knew before he made it back over to them and were already doing crazy touchdown dances.

Weber's parents were in discussion about the change as he came to sit beside his mother. He closed his eyes and started mouthing something that kind of looked like, "Please let me go, please let me go." Weber had never been back-packing before and the prospect of this new adventure was almost more than he could stand. He opened his eyes at the same moment his mother turned around and said, "I guess it would be all right if you went, Web." The good news almost made him fall off his chair!

Zach and Quinton had moved up to the podium together; Zach spoke first, "Pastor Mike, my Mom and Dad'll just need a call. I'm sure they won't care if we changed plans or not."

Before Pastor Mike could reply Quinton spoke from just behind Zach and said, "Excuse me sir, my parents will also need a call."

"No problem," said Pastor Mike to both of them as he noticed Quinton hitting his hip with his wrist. "If I don't get in touch with them today we can get together at church tomorrow." As Pastor Mike and Phil moved back around to the podium, Pastor spoke up, "Okay, okay it sounds like we're all in agreement that the camping trip has now become a hiking adventure. Is there anyone here who is opposed to this change?" The room was silent for a moment, then the boys threw their hands in the air yelling and singing in falsetto again, "Hallelujah, Hallelujah!" and loud whistles rang out once again.

Phil again leaned over to Pastor and said something into his ear. Pastor Mike looked up and said, "We need to take a few minutes' break." The boys were still talking and moving amongst each other and their parents. Pastor Mike and Phil walked out of the Youth Hall. Dolton and Buck went back to talk with their mothers. Weber and his parents were busy talking and Weber's dad put his arm around his shoulders and said, "You're going to have the time of your life, Web!"

Quinton and Zach had moved from their chairs over to the couch to talk with Mark. He was obviously very happy with the change in plans and was waiting for Dolton and Buck to return. Zach asked Mark, "Did you know about this?"

"No way," said Mark, looking Zach straight in the eyes. "I'm as surprised as you are," still smiling from ear to ear.

Quinton said, "I'm sure my parents will let me go."

Zach added, "My folks are okay with anything as long as I'm not getting in their way."

Buck sat down next to his mother, "Mom, thanks for letting me go."

"I want you to enjoy yourself," she said. "It was so nice of Mr. Phil to sponsor you." She paused. "You know, I just can't shake the feeling that I know him from somewhere." She paused again. "Well, maybe old age is catching up with me," she concluded with a smile. "Go and be with your friends." Buck got up and kissed his mother on the cheek then hurried over to join the others. By this time Dolton made his way back to the couch and they started talking about the upcoming adventure.

Fifteen minutes later, Pastor Mike and Phil came hurrying back into the Youth Hall and stepped up to the podium, "Sorry for the delay but I have some very exciting news! Mr.

Phil has procured a donation of all the equipment for us to go hiking!" Before the boys had a chance to shout and dance again, Karen Deerfield stood up and said, "Pastor?"

"Yes?" acknowledged Pastor. "As you know I'm President of the Women's Ministry and our group would like to donate the food that will be needed for the trip." Stated Mrs. Deerfield.

"That's very generous, Mrs. Deerfield; thank you and thank you to the ladies of the Women's Ministry," replied Pastor.

Weber looked up at his mother with shock and amazement that slowly turned into a smile glowing with pride. "Thanks, Mom!" he said as she sat down.

Then quickly and determined not to be outdone, Elizabeth James stood and said over the noise and excitement, "Pastor Mike, I would be pleased to provide the rest of the items for this adventure."

Everyone clapped and excitement continued to spread throughout the room. "Well, thank you too, Mrs. James," replied Pastor, "it looks like we have everything we need as far as provisions go. Thank you all for your generosity and support of our adventure."

Applause followed and Dolton sank into his chair and obligingly clapped. *Why does she always have to be the center of attention? Can't she let someone else have the glory once in a while?* he thought. He started to glare at his mother when Mark slapped him on the shoulder and said, "That's great, this is going to be fantastic!" Dolton looked at Mark with a half smile and said, "Yeah, I can't wait."

"Okay, okay," said Pastor Mike, "I think this meeting is over. Oh, and everyone," he tried to yell over the din, "we'll be sending out a notice in a day or two as to when and where the trip'll be and what the boys'll need to bring. If you have any more questions please come and see me, thank you."

No one got up to leave; the boys were still gathered around the couch and their parents moved slowly towards the podium to speak with Pastor Mike. Becky Bond arrived first. "Thank you so much. I can't tell you what this means to Buck and me."

Pastor Mike turned toward Phil to give credit, "It's our pleasure, Becky." She made a short bow of thanks, "Well, if you'll excuse me, I have to go to work. See you Sunday."

As she turned and hurried out of the Youth Hall, Karen and Stanley Deerfield walked up. "Hello Stanley," said Pastor as he came out from behind the podium and shook his hand. "Hello Karen," giving her a hug.

Stanley spoke in a hushed tone, "Karen and I just spoke with each other and we would like to supply Weber's gear ourselves if it's okay?"

"No problem," said Pastor. Just then Elizabeth James walked up, interrupting in a businesslike voice, "Pastor, we need to talk. Oh, hello, Karen, Stanley," she said as she barely acknowledged either of them.

"Hello Eliza," Karen replied.

Pastor smiled at Karen and then turned to Mrs. James and said, "Would you care to meet in my office?"

"That would be fine," said Mrs. James in that same business tone as she turned to walk out. The Deerfields took the opportunity to excuse themselves. Stanley patted Pastor's shoulder saying good-bye, and they walked over to the couch where the boys were gathered. "Weber, we'll be in the car waiting for you," said Stanley as they made their way for the door.

"Gotta go, guys," Weber told the others and then followed his folks out.

Quinton politely excused himself from the gathering of the boys and said, "I have a few chores at home to do, I'd better go," and left the Youth Hall tapping his side. Zach also used this time to excuse himself, telling them that he had something else he had to take care of, and with a smile he left. Mark, Buck, and Dolton were the only ones left. Mark told them that he had to fold the bulletins for church tomorrow before he could go messing around. Buck and Dolton offered to help, so the three boys left the Youth Hall and headed to the office.

<{()}><

After two days of comprehensive planning, Phil had all the details worked out and he entered Pastor Mike's office. "Excuse me, Mike, got a minute?" said Phil.

"Sure," Mike said.

Phil held out a file folder that he was carrying. "Well, here you go," said Phil as he laid the folder on Mike's desk. "I have here the location of the hike and all the details. The boys. . . ."

"Where did you decide to go?" Mike interrupted excitedly.

Phil gave a little laugh and said with a smile, "Well, I thought that we would start in Yosemite and hike over the glacier and end up in Inyo National Forest. The trip will take about five days; if we leave on a Sunday we should be back on Friday," said Phil.

"Oh, that sounds perfect," said Mike, "the boys are going to love it, God bless."

"I also have the list of equipment that I ordered and the lists of the food and other items that the boys are going to need to bring. It's all there in the folder. I would like to go over the tent assignments with you."

"Sure, what'd you have in mind?"

"Well, I want you and Mark to share a tent. Kind of a father and son sort of thing. I want to put Weber with Zach. I think they will have positive influences on each other."

28

"Or one of them will be seriously injured. Are you sure that's a good idea?"

"Yes, Weber is strong intellectually and strictly routined. Zach is just the opposite, except for the intelligence. He possesses another kind of intelligence that could end up benefiting Weber."

"I see where you're going with this. I trust your judgment. What about the rest?"

"I'll share a tent with Buck."

"Naturally, and Quinton and Dolton? How do you think they'll do?"

"Truthfully, I'm not sure. I just know that the rest of the pairs are right. I'm hoping a higher power will take charge of them. I'd like to go over the rest of the items on my list with you."

"Great!" said Pastor, "but we'll have to go through that later." He continued a little more somberly, "I had a long talk with Mrs. James and she wants to supply clothes, jackets, hats and any other items they'll need for the trip. She also wants to throw a going away party when we leave."

"A party?" said Phil with disbelief. "Well," said Mike, "I had to let her do something; she was insisting on knowing who the anonymous donor of the supplies was and how Buck could afford to go."

"That woman irritates me," said Phil.

"Now, now," said Mike, "whatever happened to Christian charity."

"Okay," said Phil, "the boys are the reason we're doing this anyway."

"When do we want to schedule this trip for departure?" said Mike.

"The weekend after next." replied Phil.

"Sounds good. I'll call a meeting of the elders, set up transportation, and call Mrs. James. Oh, and I am going to need your size and the sizes of all the boys going - and I was hoping that you could call them and get theirs," said Mike.

"I'd be glad too," he replied happily.

Over the next week Pastor Mike and Phil were busy finalizing the trip details. That Sunday, Pastor Mike gave the boys the list of items they needed and confirmed with their parents that they would be leaving the next Sunday after church.

Departure

The Sunday of their departure finally arrived and the church was full; the boys could hardly sit still during the service - they swore the sermon was twice as long as usual. At its conclusion, Pastor announced the bon voyage party for the youth and everyone was invited to join. Everyone exited the church to find tables, chairs, and food set up and music beginning to play.

"I believe that the whole church decided to stay," said Pastor Mike to Mrs. James with a smile. "Yes," she said in a dry tone, "they must all be hungry."

Phil was with Nolan, who was helping pack the van. Nolan Trendovich was a reformed Polish Jew who spoke English without an accent. He was a thin five-foot eight-inch tall man, with black eyes, curly black hair, and usually his beard was two to three days of growth covering most of his face; his most distinguishing feature was his large nose. He was one of the church elders and one of the most caring people you could ever meet. He had two unique character-istics – one was his stuttering. He stuttered terribly, and if you were standing close enough when speaking with him, you were showered with his spray. When he read or sang he spoke well; no one would ever guess he stuttered, but to casually speak with Nolan was to invite a bath of stuttering. Second, he was known to break out in song for no apparent reason. What made it so unusual was that the songs he sang were in Polish – no one knew exactly what he was singing about, but one thing was evident: he really enjoyed singing those songs because he sang them happily and loudly.

Most people in Jamestown knew that Nolan came from a small town in Poland close to the border of Slovakia. In the 30's and 40's, his family used to raise horses and the family farm was host to visitors wishing to tour the countryside. They held many tours throughout their region and he and his brother, Ryan, became famous for their knowledge of its rich history. It had begun to be a very popular vacation attraction until their farm was threatened by the violence that was prevalent in that area of the world. It became so bad that his parents sent him and his brother to the United States for safety. A short while later news came to them that their parents were victims of the violence. Other family members urged the boys to remain in the States and give honor to their family by being successful, which both decided that they would do. Nolan carried his love of the Lord with him through his years of struggle and it led him to this small community and to Faith Church. He labored hard for the church with Pastor Mike in its early days and became one of its first elders. He had been a fixture at the church ever since.

Nolan had been busy collecting the necessary and personal items from the boys before church and was busy packing the backpacks and getting the equipment ready to load; all the while he was singing some happy Polish tune that carried through the parking lot and over to the area where everyone else had gathered. Some even heard his singing over the music that was playing from the bon voyage party.

"Nolan," said Phil, "did you see my compass?"

"Yes," said Nolan, "I pppput it in the sssside ppppocket of your ppppack."

"Great," said Phil.

"You knnnow," said Nolan, "that Mmmrs. Jjjames is a very gggenerous wwwoman."

Phil just looked at Nolan and nodded his head with a smile.

"Ssshe had ttthese jjjackets and ssshirts mmmade up fffor ttthe whole gggroup," as Nolan handed one to Phil.

"Yes, these are nice," said Phil. "They have the church logo on the back and the James family crest on the left front. That logo sure is different," he paused to look closer. "Very unique."

"And the ccchurch llladies sure were nnnice to pppput nnnames on the bbback pppacks, and the fffood ttthey ppprovided," said Nolan.

"Well, there sure is a lot here," said Phil as he winked at Nolan. One by one the boys gathered by the van in excitement asking if there was anything they could do to help. Nolan quickly put them to work placing items next to each backpack.

Pastor Mike was moving through the crowd visiting as many congregational members as possible. He had fallen in love with the community when he first came to Jamestown. It was a lot of work to build the congregation, but every single one of the flock was a treasure beyond any earthly worth. He knew each member by name and always looked forward to events like this so he could have a chance to catch up with them. He came up to the table where the Deerfields were sitting, pulled up a chair and sat down. "Hello Karen, Stanley," said Pastor Mike with a smile, "I wanted to thank you for all your help. You and the ladies did a fantastic job preparing all the food for our trip. Your ministry has been such a blessing to the church and this community."

"You're welcome, it was our pleasure," said Karen. "You know, Pastor, we really want Weber to have a good time and finally interact with others his age."

"I don't know if you noticed," Stanley offered, "but he is a bit of a techno-geek; he doesn't spend much time away from his computer. As a matter of fact, I had to have him fitted with a backpack with solar panels so he can charge up his laptop. He never goes anywhere without it and I really want him to go on this trip. He never leaves home and this should be good for him."

Karen was starting to look like she was going to cry. Pastor Mike noticed this and calmed her quickly by saying, "This *will* be good for the boys. The opportunity to get out and see nature will be a great experience for Weber and all the boys." Pastor stood up shook Stanley's hand, stepped over and gave Karen a hug and said, "Happy tears and again thank you for your help."

Pastor turned and as he did came face to face with the Rothfords, Lloyd and Barbara, Quinton's parents. Pastor Mike greeted them, turned and introduced them to Karen and Stanley. "Please sit down," said Karen to Barbara.

" 'ow lovely of you, thank you," said Barbara in a thick Cockney accent and sat down next to her. "The boys are going to 'ave so much fun," said Barbara enthusiastically, "I even 'ad a dream about it meself last night."

"A dream?" said Pastor.

"Oh yes, Quinton was 'aving fun up until they got to the islands - I don't know what it means 'cause just then I woke up."

"The islands?" asked Stanley, "They're going to the mountains."

"I know," chuckled Barbara, "it was only a dream. Anyway they're going to 'ave so much fun. I almost wish I was going meself!" Everyone laughed and the ladies got up and went to get some food.

Pastor Mike was still visiting tables of people when Becky Bond approached him. "Hi Pastor," she said, "Have you seen Buck? I wanted to say good-bye before I leave for work."

"Yes," he replied, "he's with the other boys at the van. Come on, I'll walk over there with you." As they walked Becky said, "Pastor I can't thank you and the church enough for all you have done for Buck and me."

"You don't have to thank us, you and Buck are part of our family; I just wish there was more we could do. I know it's not easy to raise a child on your own, especially a boy. But you are doing a wonderful job. Buck is a wonderful young man and is definitely headed for great things in his life. Don't worry about a thing; he'll be well provided for on this trip, I promise."

As they reached the area of the van, Buck spotted Becky and came over to her. "Do you really have to go before we leave, Mom?"

"Yes, I can't be late for work," she said as she held his head with both hands and kissed him on each cheek. He saw that she was going to get emotional; her eyes began to fill up as she stared straight into his eyes and said, "I love you. Be careful and do what you're told."

"Don't worry, Mom – I'll be with Pastor and Mr. Phil, plus the guys will look out for me too." Becky squeezed his hand and had started to turn and leave when Buck stopped her, "Mom, I want you to meet Mr. Phil." Phil had been busy helping Nolan pack the van and stood up to find that Buck was standing there with his mother.

"Mr. Phil, this is my mother, Becky Bond. Mom, this is Phil Thomas, the elder who sponsored me."

There was just a moment's hesitation. "Hello," he said, "It's a pleasure to meet you."

"It's a pleasure to meet you too, and thank you; I can't tell you how grateful Buck and I are for your generosity," she said as she looked straight into his eyes. She hesitated. "I'm sorry, but have we ever met? You remind me of someone."

Just then Pastor said, "I guess it's show time! Mrs. James wants to announce her contributions and show off the jackets." At this Becky turned, kissed Buck again and gave him a hug and left for work.

Pastor walked through the crowd towards Mrs. James while Phil made his way over to the microphone where the music had been playing. As Pastor Mike and Mrs. James made their way up to the microphone, Phil stopped the music and asked for everyone's attention and handed the mike over to Pastor. He began, "Thank you all for coming out to support our Youth Group. As you all know, the James family has been very generous in the past and today is no exception. Mrs. James has graciously donated clothes, transportation, and hosted this wonderful bon voyage party."

Pastor lifted a lightweight jacket in one hand and a polo shirt in the other so everyone could view them. The crowd applauded and Mrs. James sported a modest looking smile, though her eyes twinkled with excitement at being the center of attention, and raised a hand to wave at everyone. She explained to the crowd that the jackets were custom-made, lightweight with the church logo on the back and the James family crest on the left front. The polo shirts had the church logo on the back, like the jackets, and the front said "Faith Church, Youth Ministry, Jamestown" and in the middle was a silhouette of a man hiking. Mrs. James insisted that they don their new jackets for a group picture before they left. They put them on with the crowd "oooing" and "ahhhhing" and lined up for the picture. Mrs. James was in her glory; she took a series of pictures before she dismissed them. Dolton looked like he wanted to crawl in amongst the gear in the back of the van.

"Okay boys, it's time to go," said Pastor Mike. They stood outside the van in a semi-circle and held hands. The crowd gathered behind them and placed hands on the group. Pastor looked around and said, "Triple D, would you please give the blessing? Where's Deacon Dave?"

Deacon Dave Dillon was the next senior to Pastor Mike and was in training to become a pastor himself. He had been one of the first friends Mike met when he came to Jamestown. It took him a while to warm up to the idea of God and, as he used to call it "all that Jesus stuff." Once he accepted it, he became one of the community's strongest evangelists. He decided a few years back that he wanted to make the Lord his vocation and began seminary. He came back as a deacon and cut short his education because of family issues, but resolved them and was planning on going back in the spring to finish seminary. He was going to take over for Mike in his absence. Dave was kind of a practical joker and frequently referred to Pastor Mike as "PM". The Pastor, in turn, called Deacon Dave Dillon "Triple D". Pastor Mike never knew what to expect when Triple D turned up.

"Here I am. PM. Look out! Comin' through!" trumpeted Triple D. Just then Pastor Mike saw him and laughed so hard that he almost fell over. The crowd followed suit as they watched him approach. He was wearing a bishop's cope that he had fashioned out of newspaper and what looked like a biretta that bore a striking resemblance to the quilt he had hanging in his office. His hands were out-stretched over the crowd and in one hand he carried a cross that he was certain was the one that hung in his office. "Nothing to worry about, PM. I have everything under control. I'll have this place whipped into shape before you return, or my name isn't Bisho....I mean Deacon Dave!" At this the crowd roared even louder and Pastor Mike doubled over from laughing so hard. After they composed themselves, Pastor asked Dave to come forward to receive a blessing before he made the blessing over the group.

"In the name of the Father, the Son and the Holy Spirit, I entrust to you, in my absence, the care and safety of this flock that I have been called to shepherd. May you be steadfast and sure in your duties and loving and compassionate in your dealings with the children of God who come to this place of worship. Lord, guide this man of God and keep him and all our families safe from harm from any source until we return safely. I ask this through Christ our Lord. Amen," prayed Pastor.

"Amen," murmured the crowd. Deacon Dave and Pastor hugged and then Dave placed one hand on Pastor and the other he held up over the group of travelers and prayed, "Dear heavenly Father, place your guardians in watch over this group of youth and leaders. Keep them safe in their journey and send forward the angels to remove any impediment that would keep them from enjoying the beauty and adventure that you have in store for them. Keep the enemy far from any place they will be and place the hearts and prayers of our congregation with them the entire trip. Give them back to us safely and happy in the knowledge that your world is one of beauty, glory, and love. We ask all this through Jesus Christ our Lord and Savior. Amen."

"Thank you, Triple D. Okay boys, into the van," commanded Pastor. With that the parents came up to them to say their goodbyes, all except Beck Bond who left earlier. Phil recognized the lonely look on Buck's face and handed him the last couple of things to go into the van. It was enough to keep him busy and not let him think about the fact that his mom had already left. As Phil turned around, Stanley walked up to him and offered his hand and asked him to take care of Weber. "You may have noticed that he's not the outdoorsy type," he said.

"Don't worry, Stanley, we'll take good care of them and I'll keep a special watch on Weber myself," replied Phil. "I appreciate that," said Stanley as he reached up to straighten

Phil's jacket collar. "No problem," he said as he turned to load the boys into the van.

The crowd watched with excitement as they climbed into the van. Nolan took the driver's seat, Phil rode shotgun and Pastor climbed in and took a seat behind Nolan. Mark, Zach, and Weber went all the way to the back seat; Dolton, Quinton, and Buck took the middle seats behind Pastor. "Everyone bbbuckeled up?" asked Nolan, "Gggood!" They started out of the parking lot and turned and headed towards the main highway and away from the church as the crowd all waved good-bye; they were finally off!

<{{}}><

As the van approached the main highway, excited chatter ensued from everyone except Dolton who was staring out the window. Mark was turned around in his seat talking to Buck and noticed Dolton. Mark unbuckled his safety belt and rose out his seat slightly and gestured to Quinton; he was confused but traded places with Mark. As Quinton passed, Mark said, "Thanks, I need to talk to Dolton."

Nolan looked back at all the commotion and said, "You nnneed to bbbuckle up." Mark sat down and buckled up, "Sorry, Nolan."

In a hushed tone Mark asked, "Dolton, are you okay?"

"Yeah, it's my mother." He paused. "She always makes such a big deal out of everything. She always has to be the center of attention. It's embarrassing; I hate it," Dolton said, still looking out the side window.

Mark moved closer so only Dolton could hear what he was saying, "I think if it were my mother, I might have a talk with her about it. I don't know exactly what I'd say, but I'd definitely say something since it bugs you so much."

Dolton replied, "That's just it, Mark, I don't know what to say either! One time I tried to say something but she blew me off as if I didn't know what I was talking about. It always seems like she is trying to buy her way into something – people's affections, favors, or just to be the center of attention like she was today. Sometimes, I just wish we weren't rich, and then she would have to be just another person, just another mother. . . . Aw, what's the use." Mark saw the hurt on his face and couldn't imagine what he could say to help his friend, so he just sat there next to him in silent support.

Meanwhile, Buck, Zach, and Quinton were locked into a discussion about what kind of music they liked best. Buck liked some of the rap and R&B but was actually partial to music from the 40s and 50s; romantic stuff, he called it. Zach only liked old school rock & roll, and Quinton stated that he liked contemporary and classical, which really made the conversation animated. Pastor Mike jumped into the conversation declaring that Christian R&B was the best, only to bring in Phil who said he preferred country or Christian R&B. The debate was on.

Apparently Nolan decided that he was happy enough because he started to sing. He was fairly quiet at first but progressively got louder and louder until he started drowning out everyone. When Pastor shouted, "NOLAN!" the van went completely quiet for a second then they all broke out in laughter. When it finally calmed down Phil said, "Aren't we getting on the highway here?"

"Oh!" and with a jerk of the wheel Nolan merged the van onto the main highway on-ramp. Weber and Zach started laughing and then everyone laughed. Dolton seemed to cheer up after that and there were nothing but smiles as they talked about the trip.

Weber pulled out small laptop and began relating the history of where they were going, tips on backpacking, the best way to pack a tent and other comments that soon became annoying but he was generally ignored. Mark and Dolton were talking about Martha Sue; Zach put his head back for some sleep and Quinton, who happened to be by a window, leaned on the armrest and was hitting himself on the chest. With his eyes closed Zach said, "Hey, Tarzan, quit hitting yourself."

Pastor leaned in to talk with Phil asking, "How long is this leg of our trip?"

"Oh, about an hour and a half," he answered.

Nolan spoke up saying, "I tttthought wwwe would sssstop for a rrrrestroom break in about ffffforty ffffive minutes."

"Okay," said Pastor, settling back into a nap. Phil continued to read maps as Nolan drove and hummed Christian songs.

"You know I sit next to her in Math?" said Dolton.

"Duh," replied Mark, "I sit on the other side of you."

"Yeah, I know but you don't smell as good as she does," Dolton retorted.

"Hey Buck, what do you think about Martha Sue?" asked Mark.

"She's all right," he said.

"Buck doesn't like girls," chided Zach with his eyes still closed.

"Oh no, he likes girls all right, he just freezes up when he actually has to talk to one," teased Mark.

"They make me nervous," Buck explained. Quinton was listening and pounding his thigh with his fist. "Hey Quinton, you haven't said much, what do you think about Martha Sue?" asked Mark.

"He doesn't like Martha Sue, he likes Buck's mom," goaded Zach.

All of a sudden, the fist that had been pounding his thigh found its way to Zach's mid-section, doubling him over. There was a split-second of silence from all the boys; nobody moved. No one hit Zach and got away with it.

Zach straightened up as he looked over at Quinton; everybody expected to see that infamous smile of his that he bared just before he pounced. A smile did begin to appear but not the smile they expected. "Good one, Quint. I didn't know you had it in you," smiled Zach as he patted his mid-section.

"All right calm down back there," ordered Pastor Mike.

Nolan slowed down and pulled off the road at a rest stop for a break. When the van came to a stop and Nolan said, "Okkkkay, we'll bbbbe sssstopped for about tttten minutes." Everyone jumped out of the van and walked into the building to use the facilities. As they gathered one by one back by the van, the boys continued talking about what the trip was going to be like. Zach eagerly stated, "I hope we come across some lakes or streams with fish in them. I wanna go fishing!"

"I can't wait to see some deer or a bear," Weber chimed in.

"A bear?" said Zach, "You're crazy."

"Well, not really," replied Weber a bit nervous at the suddenness of Zach's reply, "I just want to see some wildlife."

"Me too," said Quinton quietly.

"I don't think bears are the kind of wildlife we want to hang out with," said Mark.

"Maybe some cuddly squirrels and cute little rabbits," said Buck and they all began laughing, except Weber and Quinton. After a short moment, Weber and Quinton looked at each other and began laughing too. Just then Pastor Mike, Phil, and Nolan walked up to the van and they all climbed in and they were off again.

After about ten minutes on the highway Phil turned around and said, "We'll be going up into the mountains soon; if anyone starts getting carsick let me know right away." Everyone looked back at Weber.

"What?" he said, lifting his shoulders and hands. The van rounded a curve and they started up the grade. The landscape outside had changed from suburban to more rural and was now grassy fields and farmlands, soon becoming large grassy rolling hills. The conversation slowed as they looked out the windows at the terrain that continued its dramatic change. The van's motor strained as the grade got steeper; they could feel the pull as they rounded the curves; left, right, left, right; the boys leaning with every curve. The grassy rolling hills were now changing into rocky, tree-covered, steep slopes; the road wound up the side of the mountain. No one was talking as Nolan maneuvered the van through the winding mountain road, passing thickly treed forests on one side and a rocky sheer cliff on the other.

"Wow!" said Buck as the van took an outside corner.

"Look how high we are," said Quinton with a nervous voice. Weber had put down his laptop when the van started up the mountain and, in fear of falling, had grabbed onto Dolton, who didn't notice until the van took a sharp corner.

"Weber," Dolton said, "What are you doing? You're buckled in."

"Sorry," said Weber a little embarrassed.

"Wow!" said Zach. "Look how thick the trees are getting." The forest was getting denser and the trees were now blocking the sun. This landscape seemed to go on for quite a long time. All of a sudden the trees thinned and cabin-style buildings began to appear in a lush green meadow. The group was approaching a small mountain town with a restaurant, gas station, and three or four small shops. Just after passing the town they saw another large green meadow where a rich brown soil road was cut through the middle of it; the afternoon sun shone bright in the meadow, making the colors dramatic.

As the van passed through the meadow Phil rolled down the front window a bit and said, "Oh my, can you smell that?" The smell of pine trees, damp earth, and grass filled the van. The clear blue sky framed the bright yellow sun and warmed the cool air as it came through the window into the van.

"Wow!" said Weber, "I've never seen *anything* like this before."

Arrival

The boys were still enjoying the changing views when Nolan said, "Hhhere's our ttturn." The van slowed and turned into Tuolumne Meadows Drive and through an opened set of old rusted iron gates. Nolan pulled up to a combination shop and office for the Tuolumne Meadows Campgrounds. Phil said, "Stay in your seats; I'll be right back," and he got out of the van and entered the office. The boys were itching to get out of the van, mumbling and grumbling, trying to talk Pastor Mike into letting them out.

"Please boys, keep your seats," he said calmly. After a minute Phil came out and said to Nolan and Pastor Mike as he took his seat in the van, "We're in Tent Area #1, Space #15." Nolan was humming again and nodded; he started the van and slowly pulled away.

They passed by two ponds alongside which sat a little market that Phil told them was probably the last sign of civilization they would encounter until they finished the trip. Then Nolan turned up a gravel road that led to the camping area. The narrow gravel road wound through the pine trees and, because of all the bumps and tight turns, the van could go no more then ten miles an hour. It seemed to go on forever for the boys who wanted to get out, stretch, and start their adventure. A few minutes later, they saw the sign indicating tent camping to the right and trailers to the left. Nolan turned slowly right and the camp area came into view. A couple of the boys whispered an emphatic "Yes!" as they saw it. The tent camp area opened up through the trees and there were campsites on both sides of the road. Some were barren soil, some were grassy, but all were surrounded by pine trees and had a picnic table, fireplace, and an area for parking a vehicle. All thought this was a great place to start their adventure.

It was about two hours before dark as the van pulled into their camping space. Nolan had just finished humming one of his favorite tunes, but the boys had their faces glued to their windows and were not listening to him. Pastor Mike and Phil were watching Nolan back up the van. The van stopped and Pastor Mike said aloud, "Praise God! We've arrived." The doors of the van flew open and everyone shot out as if they had been cooped up for days. "Wow! This is going to be great!" said Buck excitedly; they all agreed heartily.

"Stay close by, we don't have much time to set up camp before dark comes and I want you all to learn how to do this tonight," instructed Phil.

Pastor Mike and Phil walked to the back of the van and discussed how they wanted to unload and where to set up camp. The boys were milling around the camp area, fascinated with the environment and activity.

"Look how big the trees are!" said Weber.

"Hey look, squirrels chasing each other," said Quinton as he began to follow the two woodland creatures, "And one of them has something in its mouth! I think that one stole his nuts!"

"I think I'd be upset if someone stole my nuts," said Dolton.

"Dolton!" said Pastor sternly.

"I can't wait for tomorrow," said Zach.

"Me neither," said Buck as he walked over to Dolton and Mark.

"Okay boys, gather around," shouted Phil. "As we call your name, come and retrieve your pack and walking stick. Weber!"

As he came forward Weber thanked the men for taking such good care of his pack, "After all," he said as he grabbed it, "I am carrying highly specialized equipment." Zach rolled his eyes. The rest of the boys received their gear without incident, and lastly, Pastor Mike and Phil got theirs.

"Nolan, what's this box and ice chest doing in there? I don't remember packing it," said Phil.

"Oooh! Mmmrs. Jjjames sent dddinner for aaall of us," replied Nolan.

Pastor Mike turned to Dolton and said, "Remind me to thank your mother when I get back, Dolton." Dolton looked down and gave a little nod as he walked away.

Mark went over to his dad and said in a low voice, "Dad, Dolton has a problem with his mom doing stuff like this; he thinks she's always trying to buy her way into everything or show off how much money they have, like the jackets and stuff."

"I understand," Pastor Mike acknowledged in a whisper and a nod.

Phil led everyone over to the picnic tables and told them to put their packs down so they could set up camp before they ate. "Listen up," said Phil, "we have four tents so there are two people per tent. Tent one is Pastor Mike and Mark, the second tent Weber and Zach, the third is Quinton and Dolton, and the fourth will be Buck and me." From the sound of the murmuring Phil could tell that they weren't entirely happy with these arrangements. "Okay, settle down, I have my reasons for putting you together like I did," said Phil.

"Let's get these tents set up before it gets dark. When you're done you're free to look around but don't go farther than the treeline or you might miss dinner."

"Boys, listen up," said Pastor Mike, "Mrs. Brown, Martha Sue's mom, donated some of her beauty products for the trip." Before Pastor could get another word out, the laughter and smart remarks started flying.

"Quiet down," Phil admonished.

"As I was saying," said Pastor Mike, "Mrs. Brown gave each of us a bottle of lotion to keep the mosquitoes away, and you all have one in the side pocket of your pack, so use it."

They all pulled out the lotion and applied it. When they were done, at the direction of Phil, they each found the place in the camp they wanted to set their tents. The equipment was new and none of the boys had ever set up a tent before. Phil instructed everyone to lay the pieces out before assembling them. Five minutes later Phil and Buck had theirs up. It was evident that Phil was an experienced outdoorsman. Zach and Weber had the tent laid out and Weber was trying to interpret the directions for Zach who was obviously not happy with his interpretation, as evidenced by his red face. Dolton was getting upset with Quinton, who kept hitting himself with the tent poles. Pastor Mike and Mark were doing better only because Pastor Mike was putting the tent together while Mark read the directions. Buck went over and started helping Zach and Weber, and within a few minutes their tent was up. Phil helped Dolton and Quinton and in a few minutes theirs was set up too. Pastor Mike and Mark finished within moments of everyone else.

"Well, 30 minutes; not too bad for your first time," said Phil, "We'll all get faster as the days go on."

Nolan, who was busy wiping and polishing the van while they set up their tents, was starting to sing louder and louder when Pastor Mike said in almost a yell, "Nolan! English, please!"

"Sssorry Pppastor." said Nolan. He continued to polish the van and sing but this time at almost a whisper. The boys were starting to leave the campsite. Pastor Mike yelled out, "Be back here in an hour, we'll be eating soon!"

"Okay!" they shouted back and off they went. Mark said, "Hey let's go see what's going on in other camp sites? Let's go check it out."

"If you're thinking of seeing pretty girls, think again. The only girls that come out here all look like mountain men," teased Zach. They started down the road.

The men finished going through the supplies and began setting up the gourmet dinner that Mrs. James had sent along with them. It was an elaborate spread that consisted of meats for sandwiches; three kinds of bread, the finest quality condiments, several kinds of cheese, two kinds of mayo, four different mustards, real butter, and "fixin's" - pickles, tomatoes, onions and lettuce. There was also potato salad, brown sugar baked beans, corn chips and potato chips. In the bottom of the box were the ingredients for making S'mores.

Nolan said "Ttthat Mmmrs. Jjjames is a vvvery gggenerous wwwoman gggiving the way ssshe does: the eqqquipmmment, ttthe party, and nnnow ttthis dddinner. Ssshe rrreally lllikes ttto tttake care of ttthings." Pastor Mike and Phil just looked at Nolan. He glanced up to find them both looking at him. He smiled and said, "It wwwas MMMrs. JJJames that gggave the donnnation of ttthe cccamping equipment, wwwasn't it?"

"No," said Pastor Mike, "Mrs. James' donations came after the camping equipment had been donated. The equipment came from an anonymous donor."

"Well, it wwwas a nnnice gggesture just the sssame. We rrreally have sssome gggenerous folks in ooour cccommunity," said Nolan.

After they finished setting up, the boys came walking back into camp. "Gggood ttttiming; how wwwas it?" asked Nolan.

"I can't believe how pretty it is here," said Buck, "it smells so. . . hey! Is that food I smell?" Zach was already hovering around the picnic table like a vulture. It only took about a half a second for the rest of the boys to catch the scent and head for the table.

"Nobody touch anything!" shouted Phil sounding like a drill sergeant, "Freeze!" he bellowed. "Let's get the rules straight," he said. "It's very important that each and everyone of you do *what* Pastor Mike and I tell you, *when* we tell you and exactly *how* we tell you to do it. That starts right here, right now! This is for your safety, others' safety, and for the welfare of the entire group. It's not too late to send you back with Nolan. This is not a game; we'll be out there in the wild with only each other to depend on; no parents, no neighbors, no civilization; just us. It's vital that you all understand this before we start the trip. Is there anyone who cannot abide by these rules?" There was a moment of complete silence among the boys. "Excellent. Pastor?"

Pastor Mike said, "Why don't we pray before we eat? Phil?"

"I'll say the prayer," said Phil. "Dear Lord, thank You for getting us here to the starting place of our adventure. You promised that once we decided to follow You, You would be with us to the very end of the age. We come before You to ask Your presence and blessing on our trip. Show us the glory of Your hand in the wilderness, the love of Your heart in the wildlife and the strength of Your promise in protection against harm. Bless all who come to this site after us and let their passage be safe. Bless the food You have provided for us today through your faithful servant Mrs. James. Bless our provisions so that we may not be in want on our trip and bring us to a safe and happy conclusion of our trip. We ask this through Christ our Lord. Amen."

"Amen," they all said.

"Before you start eating I want everyone here to know that this food will most likely be the last fresh food we will have for a week, everything else will be freeze-dried, so enjoy!"

To watch them eat you would have thought that they had not eaten in a week. Quinton muttered, "Oh, potato salad," as he heaped it high onto his plate. Mark was piling ham two inches deep onto his plate with no bread. Zach built a sandwich that had everything on it including the potato salad and the beans. Weber had two plates, one was for his sandwich and chips and the other for his potato salad and beans so that nothing touched. Just as everyone had mouths full of food, Buck swallowed and turned to Pastor Mike and said, "Is there anything to drink?"

Nolan jumped to his feet and with a mouth full of chips said, "I ffforgot the sssodas!" Everyone ducked and covered their plates and yelled, "Nolan!" Dolton laughed so hard he fell right off the picnic table. Everyone stared at him for a second and then burst out laughing again. Nolan scurried off to get the sodas. When he returned with the drinks everyone was eating, talking and laughing. As dinner was coming to an end a corn chip flew across the table and hit Zach on the chin. Zach looked up to see an embarrassed Buck who admitted, "Sorry, I was trying to hit Mark."

When Mark heard that, the chips he was holding found their way to Buck's face; and the food fight was on. Food flew from all directions. Pastor Mike, Phil, and Nolan just backed away and let them have fun. After the boys were sufficiently covered, Phil shouted, "Okay, okay that's enough."

As the dust settled from the food fight Weber found himself wearing a piece of roast beef over his forehead that looked like an eye patch. Buck had both kinds of chips decorating his hair and clothes. Quinton was tapping a pickle on the table and Mark and Dolton were still holding food that they were going to throw. Buck, who had started the fight, had come out the cleanest of them all. They were all laughing. "Well, this is a good start for our trip – it's good to see them bond. I have a feeling that they're going to be a family before this trip is over," Phil observed to Pastor Mike.

"Okay boys, let get this mess cleaned up!" ordered Phil.

It took about forty-five minutes to clean up the dinner mess and they found themselves well into the evening. Nolan started packing the van to go. He planned on staying at his brother Ryan's house until it was time to pick the hikers up at the end of their trip. Quinton overheard Pastor and Nolan talking about his plans and said to Nolan, "I didn't know you had a brother here."

"Yyyes," replied Nolan, "Hhhe's my tttwin brother. Wwwe cccame to ttthe States wwwhen wwwe were young mmmen, abbbout yyyour age. Hhhe lllives abbbout aaan hour away fffrom here wwwith his wwwife Iiirene. Iii vvvisit them aaa lot. Iii lllike to ggget ooout into the mmmountains. Iiit's kkkind of like ttthe aaarea wwwe gggrew up in. Iii hhhike uuup here and cccamp, iiit's rrrreally beautiful. Yyyou are gggoing ttto have a rrrreally gggood tttime."

"So, where are you from anyway?" asked Zach.

"He's from Poland. Don't you know anything?" said Weber.

"I know plenty, nerd boy. I wasn't asking you," Zach retorted.

"Yyyes, Iii'm fffrom Pppoland."

"So, have you always stuttered?"

"Zach, that's not polite," Weber said meekly.

"Ttthat's aaall right, Wwweber. Iii don't mmmind aaan-swering quessstion aaabout my ssstuttering. Iii ooonly ssstutter when Iii speak Eeenglish. When Iii ssspeak Polish, Iii don't ssstutter."

"Cool."

As Zach and Nolan continued their conversation, Weber went over to his backpack and opened up the front pouch just under the solar panel. He pulled out his laptop and booted it up. "All right, baby, let's see what you can do," he said.

Quinton saw him take out his computer and came over to see what he was doing. "Who're you talking to?" he asked.

"Aw, no one, I'm usually alone when I get on my computer so I talk to myself sometimes. Makes me feel like I'm not alone," Weber replied.

"So, can you connect with that thing?"

"That's what I'm about to find out. I asked my Dad to set up a satellite connection so I can send him updates during our trip. I'd like to send my folks my first message tonight. Okay, baby, connect!" Weber commanded. "Oh, man! It did it! I'm connected!"

"What a sweet setup!" said Quinton, "Very impressive!"

"Thanks!" Weber said, pleased to have a compliment. He was already getting a little tired of Zach giving him a hard time; it was nice to be around someone who didn't cut him down at every opportunity.

"So, does this give you complete access to the Internet and everything?" asked Quinton.

"Yeah, it's just like sitting on the computers at the cyber café. No limitations. So, do you spend a lot of time on the computer?" he asked Quinton.

"Yeah, I read a lot and love research. Anytime we have papers due, I spend more time doing research than I do actually writing the paper. Plus I read just about anything I can get my hands on. Even e-books. I have over 200 in my collection," Quinton said proudly.

"Cool," said Weber, obviously impressed to find another computer nerd among his companions. "Would you like to send a message to your folks?" he asked Quinton.

"Really? Yeah, thanks!" he replied. They took turns sending out messages to their families and friends.

<{{}}><

Pastor Mike and Phil called everyone over to the outdoor fireplace where they were building a fire with the wood that Nolan had brought. Within a few minutes Phil had the logs placed in the pit and topped with the kindling and tinder; he threw a light on top and set the logs ablaze. Nolan had just finished packing the van and walked back over when Pastor Mike said, "To close off our first night we're going to have S'mores!"

Weber, Buck, and Quinton in unison said, "What?"

"S'mores!" said Mark, "It's chocolate, toasted marshmallows, and graham crackers and they're called S'mores."

Zach spoke up, "You toast the marshmallow in the fire and then put it between two graham crackers and a half bar of chocolate. It's good, you have to try it."

Nolan came around with the toasting wires and passed them out to each of the boys, then handed Phil and Pastor theirs. No sooner did Quinton get his toasting wire than he started hitting himself with it. Phil demonstrated. He laid his graham crackers out and put the chocolate on them and placed them to the side. Then he placed two marshmallows on the end of his wire. He stuck his marshmallows into the fire and started toasting them. Weber, Buck and Quinton watched intently and their mouths began to water. Phil took his marshmallows out of the flames to find they were on fire. The eyes of the three boys were as big as silver dollars. Phil gave the wire a small circular motion and the fire went out. The marshmallows were done and toasted to perfection. Phil set the marshmallows on the graham cracker with the chocolate, sandwiched the rest of it with the last piece of graham cracker and removed the wire, held it up and bowed, "It's that easy." Phil had to do a two-step to the side to avoid getting run over as all six boys went for the marshmallows at once.

Weber, Buck, and Quinton were just in front of Mark, Dolton, and Zach so they grabbed marshmallows first. All three of them set their marshmallows on the wire at about the same time. Phil finished eating the demonstration S'more and went to help the three, "You boys forgot to set up your graham crackers and chocolate." With a small chuckle he quickly put together three sets.

Mark said, "Let us show you how to do it."

"Make way for experts," Zach chimed in. Pastor Mike was now directing Weber, Buck, and Quinton on toasting techniques and after a few minutes they all were eating and enjoying their S'mores.

Quinton stood up and started hitting himself with the wire as he contemplated making another S'more; then grabbed two marshmallows, this time remembering to set up his graham crackers and chocolate before he put his marshmallows in the fire. Weber and Mark were getting up to make another S'more when Quinton pulled his marshmallows from the fire. They were still ablaze when he gave the marshmallows a circular motion, not a small motion but a large jerky circular motion.

All eyes were on the two fiery marshmallow blobs flying through the air as they both found their unintended targets with a smoldering *squish*. The first one hit Zach squarely in the chest, the second landed in Pastor Mike's lap. Pastor Mike just looked up at Quinton and said, "Looks like it was cooked to perfection." Zach looked down and didn't say anything but glanced up and gave Quinton a dirty look and a snarl as he removed the marshmallow from the front of his shirt. They all laughed, no one could help themselves.

Quinton started hitting himself again with his wire as he said, "I am really sorry, Zach, and you also Pastor Mike."

"Don't worry Quinton accidents happen," laughed Pastor Mike.

"Let's have some more S'mores," said Phil.

As everyone ate, Pastor Mike said, "Let's tell campfire stories. Who wants to go first?" No one said anything so he offered to go first. "I have a story about something that happened not too far away in these very woods." Everyone quieted down and paid attention as he started his story.

"It was about fifteen years ago. There were two boys, Bill and John, and their big black dog named D-O-G. They pronounced it Deeogee; emphasis on the O." The boys chuckled as he continued.

"They lived in a forest town, similar to the area we're in. One Saturday afternoon they decided to take a walk in the forest. The three of them walked quite a bit farther then they ever had before when all of a sudden a storm hit and it started to rain. Bill told John that they should go back and John said, 'It's too far to go back, we need to find some cover until the storm passes.'

"The rain was starting to fall harder and harder when they came across an old cabin. It was leaning and moss-covered with a few broken windows and part of the roof missing." Pastor changed his voice as he changed characters. "'Over there!' said John, 'let's go in there.' The rain fell fiercely as the three of them made their way through the tall grass and forest ferns. They were soaked to the skin by the time they reached the cabin. Almost everything in the cabin was broken and covered with a layer of dirt. 'Wow!' said John, " 'I don't think anyone's been here in a long time.'

"Just then a loud crash of thunder went off like a bomb and they jumped. The dog let out a whimper and tried to hide between the boys. 'It's getting dark and the rain isn't letting up,' said Bill.

'Well,' said John, 'we can stay here until it does and then go home.'

In the rubble they found two stools that were broken but sturdy enough sit on as long as they didn't lean too much. As they sat there and it grew darker and darker, Bill said, 'Hey, didn't there used to be a cabin in the woods where a group of people were killed?'

'Yeah,' John replied, 'I remember hearing something about a guy that murdered some people for being in his cabin. You don't you think that this is that cabin?' BOOM! Another crash of thunder sounded and lightning seemed to be striking on both sides of the cabin.

'"Hey! I think I saw someone outside!' said John.

'You think someone else got caught out in the rain too?' asked Bill.

'I don't know,' replied John.

As they watched out the window of the cabin Bill yelled out, 'IF ANYONE'S OUT THERE, WE HAVE ROOM IN HERE!' They only heard the rain. A few moments later, they heard some rustling in the trees and the sound of twigs breaking. They looked at each other as they heard the sound of footsteps. Another crash of thunder sounded followed by a violent flash of lightning. The lightning lit everything up so they looked around but saw nothing. They sat back down in silence. Suddenly there was a loud bang as if something big hit the side of the cabin."

"The dog was so scared that he jumped out through one of the broken windows and ran off into the woods. 'Where's that stupid dog going to?' asked Bill.

'He'll be back,' said John, 'what hit the cabin? Who's out there?' he yelled.

The rain began to let up and Bill said, 'Maybe we should go. The rain seems to be stopping.'

"'No, I think we should just stay here for a few minutes to make sure it doesn't start raining again.' Just then they heard the dog cry out, yelping over and over like someone was beating him. The cries stopped all of a sudden and there was silence. The boys looked at each other and saw panic on the other's face. They didn't know what to think or what to do.

John slowly raised himself to look out the window just in time to see the dog flying at his head! Bill let out a scream as John hit the floor. "'What is it?' said John.

"'Look at D-O-G!' The big black dog was standing in the corner of the cabin shaking uncontrollably. The dog that had been pure black was now pure white.

'Come on!' shouted John, 'Let's get out of here!' John grabbed D-O-G and ran for the door with Bill right behind him. John grabbed the handle and whipped open the door and…"

Just then Nolan slapped Mark and Dolton on the shoulders and yelled BOOOO and they jumped, causing the rest of the group to jump, as well. Except Pastor Mike and Phil, who were laughing and slapping their knees. They had planned the whole thing.

"NOLAN!!!!" yelled Mark, "you nearly made me jump out of my skin!"

"Me too!" said Dolton, looking a little pale. The other boys started laughing nervously.

"Man, you should have seen your face," teased Zach.

"Yeah, well you're looking a little pale too, tough guy," retorted Dolton.

"Ttthat wwwas great Pppastor Mmmike!" laughed Nolan, "bbbut I hhhave to ggget gggoing, my bbbrother is eeexpecting me soon."

As Nolan stood up Pastor Mike and Phil also stood and shook Nolan's hand and gave him a hug. "Thank you, Nolan," said Pastor Mike, "Please drive carefully and thanks again for helping with the trip."

"Okay," said Phil, "we'll see you at the other end of the trail."

"IIl'll bbbe there," yelled Nolan as he climbed into the van. The boys were all standing up waving and shouting good-bye as he drove off into the darkness.

"All right, boys," said Pastor Mike, "I think it's time to get ready for bed. We have a big day tomorrow and we'll need to get an early start." It was obvious that they were not at all ready to sleep but they went dutifully to their assigned tents.

Quinton and Dolton found the night air pleasant so they both lay atop their sleeping bags staring up at the top of the tent for a while. Then Dolton asked, "Are you thinking of that story Pastor told?"

"Yeah," said Quinton with a bit of a giggle, "it was great when Nolan scared you and Mark."

"Yeah, I guess," he replied with a laugh of his own. "I didn't even see it coming."

"You should've seen your faces," said Zach from his tent.

"He can hear us?" Dolton asked Quinton.

"Yes, I can hear you; everybody can. You're in a tent, you dolt. The only thing between you and us is a thin layer of cloth," chided Zach.

"Settle down and get to sleep," ordered Phil.

Zach lay back down with his hands behind his head. Weber propped himself up on one arm and looked over at Zach and said, "Hey, did that story scare you?"

"No," said Zach with the hard guy attitude he was so good at, "Pastor was just trying get us."

"Well, it sounded kind of real to me," said Weber with a little shake in his voice.

"Don't worry, Webinator," said Zach, "it's not. Pastor just made it up, so go to sleep."

Phil and Buck were also lying on their bags talking about the story. "That was a great story and having Nolan scare Mark and Dolton, I almost fell off my seat."

"It was pretty funny," replied Phil.

"Mr. Phil," Buck said in a low soft voice after a few moments, "I don't know if I can ever thank you enough for helping me come on this trip."

"Well, Buck," said Phil, "it really was my pleasure to do this for you. Now go to sleep, we have a big day tomorrow."

"Good night, sir" said Buck.

Pastor Mike and Mark were the last ones to settle into their bags. "G'night Mark, don't forget to say your prayers," said his father.

"You know, you don't have to tell me that anymore. I've been saying my prayers on my own for a long time now, Dad."

"I guess you're right, sorry, force of habit," he replied.

"Dad, was there any truth to that story or did you make it all up?"

With a little laugh Pastor Mike said, "I made it all up and I worked out the scare with Nolan before we started the S'mores. He was supposed to grab one of you when I gave him a signal. Guess he decided to grab two of you instead. Go to sleep now, we're starting early." With a yawn, Pastor turned out the last light and the campsite became dark and quiet.

First Morning

Early the next morning Phil awoke to find he was the first one up. As he stretched he admired the morning. The air was crisp; dew blanketed the ground and the sky was pale blue as the sun began its regular ascent. Pastor Mike awoke a short while later and came out of his tent with a stretch. Phil said, "Good morning, Pastor. Did you sleep well?"

"Not too bad, you?" he replied.

"Not bad. I didn't think the boys were ever going to fall asleep last night."

"I know," said Pastor Mike, "I heard them wrestling around for quite a while myself. Should we let them sleep a little longer?"

"We can wake them in a few minutes and then we'll start getting breakfast going." Pastor and Phil sat for a while commenting on what a beautiful day it was. "It seems perfect that we'll be starting today, a good beginning to our trip. What time should we be ready to start the hike?"

Just as he finished asking the question Mark and Buck came out of their tents. "Good morning!" they said to the boys.

"Better wake the others," said Phil with a smile.

Mark stretched, yawned and said, "Okay," then headed past Buck to wake the others. Mark walked over to Dolton and Quinton's tent, grabbed the tent, shook it, and yelled in, "Time to get up!"

He walked to Weber and Zach's tent, grabbed the tent and was about to shake it and yell when Zach said, "We're up!"

Buck walked over and sat down by Pastor Mike. He looked like he had not slept well. Pastor Mike said, "Have a rough night?" He mumbled something about hard ground. Pastor Mike chuckled and stood up, patted Buck on the shoulder and chuckled, "It's going to be an interesting trip," as he walked away.

Phil began to boil the water as most of the boys were gathering around and sitting down to watch. "Whatsamatter, you never saw anyone boil water before?" said Zach.

"Okay," said Phil, "you'll all be responsible for your own dishes. That means cleaning and packing them back in your packs. We'll take turns cooking. Everyone but Weber will carry the food supplies," said Phil.

"Why isn't Weber carrying any of the food?" said Mark.

Pastor Mike replied, "Mr. Deerfield already had a back-pack for Weber and he's going to be carrying other supplies. The seven of us are more than enough to carry the food."

Everyone pitched in and assembled the plates, utensils, and food. Zach was assigned the chore of dishing out the oatmeal. Mark and Dolton took the water bottles over to the nearest water faucet and filled them up. Quinton mixed up the morning drink. Weber and Buck mixed and cooked the bread.

Pastor Mike and Phil left the boys cooking breakfast and went to register their hike and get the permits. When they returned the boys had breakfast ready. "It smells great!" said Pastor Mike. "Let's pray before we eat." Everyone bowed their heads. "Good and ever-loving Father, bless this, the first meal of our adventure. Make it sustain and strengthen us. We ask this through Christ our Lord. Amen."

The breakfast consisted of oatmeal with butter flavoring, instant fruit mix, and the bread pancakes. As Phil picked up his bread he told them, "The bread is important, it has to be mixed and cooked each morning and evening as needed. The morning quantities also provide the lunch bread if it's on the menu, so be sure to check with me or Pastor in the morning before you start meal preparations so you know how much to make." The boys must have been hungry because the only sounds that were heard were the utensils hitting the bowls and the sounds of nature in the background.

As they ate birds began flying nearby and landed within a few feet of the boys to beg for scraps. "Wow!" said Quinton, "look at that blue jay, isn't he beautiful?"

Weber threw a piece of bread and the bird flew down and grabbed it up and flew off with it. As Mark watched the bird fly off, he looked back to see a squirrel stealing bread from Buck's dish while he was watching the bird. Dolton also saw the squirrel and said, "Hey Buck, your bread just grew legs."

Buck turned around to see that his bread was gone and looked at Dolton as though he was the guilty party. Dolton started laughing and pointed his finger at the squirrel running up a tree. By now everyone was laughing and watched the thief enjoy Buck's bread as he sat on a branch eating his treasure. Buck turned to Dolton and said, "Sorry, man, I thought you were messing with me."

When the meal came to an end, everyone headed to the nearest water faucet to clean their dishes. Buck and Weber took the bread-making dishes and cookware to wash them. The bread mix had dried in the mixing container while they were eating. The cookware was quite a mess, so it took them longer to get everything clean. When they were done they rolled up their sleeping bags and pads and stowed them on their packs and began dismantling their tents. They did this much faster than they put it up the night before.

As they pulled the tents down, Phil reminded them firmly, "Listen up, you need to remember how these tents go together; we'll be setting them up again 8 to10 hours from now! When you're finished make sure you use the restrooms."

By the time the tents were packed and the backpacks were loaded, the boys were anxious to start the hike. Phil went around to each of the boys and helped them on with the packs, adjusted them, and let them know that they needed to remember how it was done.

Phil instructed them again, "Okay, until you get used to these packs use the buddy system to take them on and off. If your feet start to hurt don't be afraid to let Pastor Mike or me know right away. That's an important point, you don't want to have bad feet for this hike. Don't forget, when we break for lunch, remember to change and wash your socks. Everybody got it?"

"Yes." "Yeah, we got it." "Yes sir," they replied.

Pastor spoke up, "Gather around and let's pray." They huddled in a circle and put their arms on the packs of those next to them. "Heavenly Father, bless our footsteps and watch over us. Let our adventure in Your beautiful world be profit for our souls. Keep us clear-minded, keen-eyed, and sharp-sensed so that we may enjoy all You have to offer. We ask this through our Lord and Savior, Jesus Christ. Amen."

"Does everyone have everything?" Phil said as he looked around. "Okay then, grab your walking pole and let's be off."

Phil led the way, followed by the boys and Pastor Mike, who brought up the rear. They walked down the narrow gravel road out of the campground past the little market that was just inside the entry gates.

Phil turned around and asked the group, "Does anyone need to use the facilities before we leave civilization?" They shook their heads and proceeded on.

They turned toward the ponds and up the trail that went between them. A breeze rippled the water and the sun glistened off the two ponds as they walked away from civilization and into the wild. As they passed a carved signpost that read Tuolumne Meadows, Quinton yelled, "Mr. Phil!"

"What? Stopping already?" he murmured.

"Can we stop here so I can take a picture of everyone by the sign?"

"Yes, good idea," he replied. "Let's gather by this post and get a picture," he ordered the group. Everyone stood around the sign.

Pastor Mike was busy putting everyone in place for Quinton when a forest ranger came walking up. "Hi there!" he said, "Just starting out?"

"Yes," said Phil.

"Well, you sure are a nice looking group and you couldn't have picked a nicer day to begin your hike," said the ranger. "Would you like me to take the picture for you?"

"That would be great!" said Quinton. They posed just under the sign, all dressed in matching shirts, cargo shorts, hiking boots, and backpacks; except, of course, for Weber.

"You're a fine looking group. Say cheese!" said the ranger. "Cheese," they replied as he clicked the camera.

"Thank you!" they all said.

"No problem, it's my pleasure," said the ranger as he handed the camera back to Quinton. He waved as he started walking off and said without turning back, "Have fun and be safe."

<{}>\<

It was about eight o'clock when they got back onto the trail. The meadow was wide and long with many small hills and valleys. The grass was tall, green, and fragrant and there was no shortage of bugs to accompany them. The trail led right through the middle it all.

Although it was early in the morning the sun's rays warmed the air. The boys' foreheads became beaded with sweat. When they finally reached the treeline, the change in landscape gave them relief from the heat and bugs of the open meadow, but they soon met with a new group of bugs that made their home in the trees and the pine needles on the floor of the woods. Oddly to them, it seemed there were more bugs in the woods than in the meadow.

Pastor Mike, who took up the rear, watched the boys try to shoo them away with waves of their hands. After a while it looked as though they were trying to direct planes at the airport with their arms flying wildly in an attempt to get the bugs out of their faces. Weber kept hitting his glasses and twice almost knocked them off his face. Pastor couldn't help but chuckle and silently thanked God for the bugs. "Remember," he yelled up to the boys, "you have that bug lotion in the side pocket of your packs. Use it but keep moving."

The pine trees cooled the air a bit more as they went farther into the woods and they found relief from the sun. The day got warmer as the sun rose higher in the sky. While they walked the boys would shift positions and talk to each other. Buck and Dolton couldn't get over how big and beautiful the trees were and pondered the possibility of seeing any deer on this trip. Zach was amused watching Quinton hit himself with his walking pole every other step. Zach dropped back next to Pastor Mike and said, "I don't want to sound mean but if Quinton keeps hitting himself with that pole he's not going to make it to the end of the trail."

"Don't worry, he hasn't hurt himself yet. He doesn't even realize he's doing it," explained Pastor Mike.

"Why does he do that?" asked Zach.

"I asked his folks once and they said they didn't know why. It started a few years ago. It could just be that he feels insecure or inadequate. You know how hard it is growing up."

"Yeah, I guess so," he said.

"I'll keep an eye on him," said Pastor reassuringly.

Meanwhile, Mark made his way up to the front with Phil. "So where're we going and how far is it?"

"I'm surprised no one's asked that question before now," Phil said as he smiled and looked over at Mark. "Well, we have about 35 to 40 miles to walk as the crow flies. We'll be going over a glacier, through thickly wooded ancient forests, meadows that will take your breath away and all types of landscape in between. We've already traveled about three and a half miles. Would you like to see the map?"

"Yeah!" said Mark excitedly. Phil passed him the map and within a minute Mark had passed it back to Phil.

"Thanks," said Mark.

"Didn't understand it?" asked Phil.

"Nope," he replied.

"When we stop, if you like I'll explain it to you," offered Phil.

"Thanks, I'd like that," said Mark and he fell back into line.

The sun was shining bright and there wasn't a cloud in the sky. It was still warm but they were making good time and the songs of nature serenaded them on their way. There were plenty of birds singing and the squirrels and chipmunks played and chirped in the trees above them. They kept careful watch on the travelers.

The smell of pine trees sure is strong, thought Weber as he adjusted his pack for the ninth time, which made him bump his hat. While fixing his hat he knocked his glasses. From the back of the line Pastor Mike could see that Weber was not the only one who was uncomfortable wearing a pack. He yelled to Phil, "Let's hold up here! We need to stop!"

As Pastor Mike passed the boys, he told them to rest a minute but not to take off their packs.

"Is everything okay?" asked Phil.

"No, not exactly," said the Pastor, "we need to let the boys rest a minute and make some adjustments to their backpacks. Some of them are having a hard time."

"Okay. Have them come up one at a time and we can readjust them. We only have about a mile until the lunch stop but we do need to get them adjusted properly."

They called the boys up one by one and adjusted their packs. Buck was first up. As he stood in front of Phil, he grabbed the shoulder straps and tightened them and then checked the waist belt. "Okay, you're good to go now. How are your feet doing?" asked Phil.

"They're fine," said Buck, "Just a little hot."

"We'll be stopping for lunch soon and you'll get a chance to change your socks and rest your feet," said Phil. The rest of the group came up one at a time and Phil checked their packs and questioned them about their feet. It took about 10 minutes to get everyone adjusted, and then they started down the trail again.

The trail was easy to follow and clearly marked. Phil had no problem finding the trail markers. The trail wound in and out of the tall pine trees going uphill more then down. From time to time squirrels, rabbits, and birds could be seen playing or looking for food on the forest floor as the group passed them on the trail. "Hey, Buck!" Dolton called, pointing to a squirrel, "There's the thief's cousin who stole your bread. He's gonna follow you to lunch."

"Not this time," answered Buck.

"Boy, my feet are getting tired," said Weber.

"I know what you mean," said Quinton, "I think my feet could use a break."

"Me too," said Dolton. Just as he said that they turned around a little bend. Downhill, in a clearing ahead, there were two small lakes nestled in between the trees.

"Okay, everyone, it's lunch break!" shouted Phil. "This area is called Twin Lakes. Don't forget you need to change your socks before we start out!"

"Wow," the boys said. "This is great!" said Zach. "Do you think there are fish in there?"

"Probably," said Phil. The boys dropped their backpacks next to the large rocks at the side of the trail and ran down to the lakes. As Mike and Phil stopped at the rocks where the boys dropped their things Mike laughed and said, "I thought their feet were hurting."

Weber and Zach reached the bank of the first and largest lake. Weber said, "These look like ponds, not lakes."

"I was thinking the same thing," replied Zach. Weber was surprised that Zach actually agreed with him on this point. He had never agreed with him on anything before.

"Well," said Phil with a smile as he walked up behind them, "I don't think it would have sounded as good if they called them Twin Ponds."

Zach turned to Phil and asked, "Can we go fishing here?"

"Sure," he replied, "the fishing will probably be best in the large lake."

Weber asked excitedly, "Can I try?"

Surprised, Zach said, "Haven't you ever gone fishing before?"

"Well, I've read about it and my dad put some stuff in my pack," said Weber rather embarrassed.

"Sure! Come on I'll show you how it's done," said Zach, and they headed back to their packs to get their equipment.

Meanwhile Mark, Buck, Dolton, and Quinton had headed over to the smaller lake with Pastor following slowly. "Look, that little stream is feeding the small lake and the small lake is feeding the large one," said Mark. "It looks good enough to swim in."

"Oh yeah!" said Dolton. "Can we go swimming?"

"Well, I think so, we have some time before lunch," said Pastor Mike. Mark, Buck and Dolton took off running back to the rocks where they had left their packs.

"What's the matter?" Pastor asked Quinton. "I think I'll go over and watch them fish," said Quinton as he started off in a slow walk hitting his hip with his wrist. Mark, Buck and Dolton met up with Phil as they were running back.

"Easy boys," warned Phil, "what's up?"

"We're going swimming!" said Mark, out of breath.

"Oh! Great," he said, "so. . . what are you doing over here?" The boys stared at each other for a second and then back at Phil.

Buck said, "You know, we don't have any swimming trunks."

Dolton started to laugh and said, "I know *you're* right." Then they all started laughing.

"I guess you'll have to go in your underwear," suggested Phil, and without another word they were gone.

Pastor Mike walked up to Phil as the boys were leaving and said, "What's going on with those three?"

Phil, still laughing, said, "They're going swimming and forgot they didn't have swim trunks."

"Youth is wasted on the young," laughed Pastor Mike as he shook his head.

Zach and Weber gathered their gear and were at the bank of the large lake trying to decide where the best place to fish would be. The lake had a lot of tall grass growing around it and large boulders that sat at the edge of the bank in three different places. "That group of rocks where the water is flowing in," he pointed, "that'll be a great place to fish. Take off your shoes and socks and let's get going," instructed Zach.

As they climbed onto the rocks Zach pulled out his pole, extended it, ran the line through the eyelets, grabbed a hook and a lead weight, and tied the hook and weight on. He reached into his bag, drew out a plastic worm, and attached it to the hook. All the while Zach was preparing, Weber was watching intently trying to catch every movement that Zach made.

Weber extended his pole, ran the line through the eyelets and was stuck; he couldn't remember what to do next. "Umm, Zach, could you show me how to do that?"

"I thought you said you read all about this, genius," said Zach.

"I did, but doing it seems to be a little bit different than reading or watching," said Weber.

"Okay," he said, "do what I tell you, you've done all right so far. To tie the hook on, put the line through the eye of the hook and bring the line up to form a teardrop. Good, now put your finger through the teardrop and twist five times. Take the end of the line and slip it through at the bottom of the twist and then back up through the hoop at the top of the twist. Now pull the hook at the end of the line to tighten the knot." Weber did exactly as he instructed and held it up proudly. "Good, now take the weight and clamp it on the line about eighteen inches up from the hook and then put on your worm." Zach picked up his rod and reel and cast out into the lake and sat on the rock.

"Umm, Zach?" said Weber after a few moments of silence.

"What now?" said Zach.

"How did you do that?" Weber asked nervously.

"Oh, for Pete's sake!" Zach jumped up so fast that Weber stepped back, thinking that Zach might hit him. "Okay," said Zach, as he reeled in his line and grabbed Weber's pole to show him, "take your rod and reel with one hand, flip back the guide line bar with the other as you hold the line with the hand that's holding the pole. The hand that flipped the bar goes down to the bottom of the handle. You place the pole back carefully, and as you whip the pole over and to the side of your head, you let go of the line and it goes out. Be careful not to hook your face. When it lands, flip the handle so that it trips the line bar. Then you reel in the slack and wait." Zach then reeled in Weber's line handed him the pole and said, "Now you do it."

Weber looked as though he might pass out. "It's okay," said Zach reassuringly, "it's fishing, not a test."

Weber started; he took his rod and reel and did everything exactly as Zach had showed him. He placed the pole back and whipped the pole over and to the side of his head and let go of the line. It was almost a perfect cast! "I did it!" Weber yelled, "I did it!

"Good job, Webling!" said Zach, feeling a little strange, a sense of some unexplained happiness. *Wow, this must be how it feels to be proud*, he thought.

Weber was beside himself, "I can't wait to tell my dad that you taught me how to fish! Hey, you know something? This is the longest conversation we've ever had where you haven't insulted me."

Zach didn't know to react so he just said, "Yeah? Well, don't get used to it. Now we have to be quiet and let the fish come to us. So. . . shut up and sit down."

A few minutes later Quinton walked up and asked, "What's going on?"

"We're fishing," said Weber still excited.

"Can I watch?" said Quinton.

"Sure," said Zach, "just try not to talk too much. It'll scare the fish away." Just then Zach had a strike. He gave the pole a gentle jerk up and the fight was on. In less than a minute Zach had landed the first catch of the day. He pulled it from the water and showed it to Weber and Quinton.

The commotion had drawn the attention of Phil and Pastor Mike and they were making their way over. Phil said to Zach, "Nice catch!"

"Thanks," he replied proudly.

"I hope that you're on a catch-and-release game because we don't have time to cook them this time."

"Oh, okay," said Zach, a little disappointed as he lowered the fish back into the water.

As Zach and Phil were talking Weber got a nibble. "Uhhh, Zach? ZACH!" said Weber louder, "What do I do now?"

Zach turned and said, "Give it a jerk up!" Weber did as he was told and he watched the line move about in the water.

"Okay, SpiderWeb, you've got 'em hooked, pull up slow on the pole and then reel it down slow." Again, Weber did as instructed and after a minute or two the fish could be seen close to the surface of the water.

"Now," said Zach, "reel down to about two feet above the water and lift the pole and the fish out of the water." Weber did it and out came the fish wiggling on the end of his line. Weber was ecstatic with excitement.

"Alright now, Webbidy, swing it over here," said Zach.

Just as Weber started to swing the fish around, Quinton moved in for a closer look. He stepped unevenly on a rock and tripped. His arm hit the fish right off the line, and back into the water it went. The look on Weber's face said it all - shock, sadness, then mad as he turned to Quinton, who was beside himself with embarrassment. "Oh, Weber! I am so, so sorry. Was that your first fish?"

Weber just stared at Quinton with his mouth clenched tight. Zach, Pastor and Phil couldn't help themselves and broke out laughing. Pastor Mike said laughing, "You wouldn't've been able to keep it anyway ."

Zach then walked over to Weber, put his arm on Weber's shoulders and said, "That was a good catch, SpiderWeb."

Weber's face lit like a light bulb with happiness and pride. "It was big, wasn't it?" They laughed even harder.

"Zach," said Phil, "I think you've got a fishing partner. He even has a story about the big one that got away!"

While Zach and Weber were fishing, Dolton, Mark, and Buck made it over to a sandy area at the water's edge of the smaller lake where Dolton was stripping down to his underwear, trying to beat Mark and Buck into the water. "Last one in has to ask Shelly Dayton for a date," said Mark. Dolton started for the water one step in front of Mark and Buck. They all dove in and swam out a ways. Dolton was the first to surface.

"Well," he said, "looks like both of you will have to ask Shelly out." They laughed.

"I wouldn't mind asking out Martha Sue," said Mark almost too quiet to hear.

"Yeah!" said Dolton, "She's my kind of girl!"

"Oh, she's okay," said Buck.

"Okay?" shouted Dolton and Mark together. "She's the prettiest girl in town!" said Mark.

"Yeah, are you blind?" agreed Dolton.

"Well, you guys can fight over her but she just not my type, okay?" said Buck as he splashed Dolton.

"Good enough" replied Dolton as he splashed back, and the fight was on.

After having their fun swimming, they decided to get out and dry off before getting dressed for lunch. As they laid in the sun on the rocks drying themselves, Mark said, "Man, I sure am glad we got to do this."

"It's better then just hanging around like we do every summer," agreed Dolton.

"Well, I can't even believe I am here in the woods with my two best friends swimming in a lake, on a hiking trip, in the mountains! Wow!" said Buck. "I wish we could do this every summer."

The sun felt warm and pleasant as a slight breeze came across the meadow to help dry them off. All that could be heard was the breeze rustling the tall grass around the lakes and the birds singing from the tall trees at the edge of the treeline. Just as they were about to doze off, Phil called for them, "It's time to fix lunch. Come on, boys!"

Phil and Pastor Mike had left the boys fishing and headed back to get ready for lunch. Phil pulled out the stove and the pot and Pastor got the food out of the packs for the meal. "First trail meal, spaghetti with meat, leftover bread, juice, and trail bars for dessert, right?" asked Pastor.

"Yeah, what'd you do, memorize the food list?" asked Phil.

"Yes!" he answered emphatically. "That way I don't have to carry another piece of paper. You gave me so many I just wanted to lighten my load."

"Oh. . . and that one piece of paper has made all the difference in the weight you're carrying," chided Phil.

"Well, you know me," teased Pastor, "less is more. Cleanliness is next to godliness. A stitch in time saves nine."

"My, aren't we full of clichés," Phil chuckled. "Let's set up the cooking area over there away from the trees."

Zach, Weber and Quinton packed up their fishing gear and arrived just before Buck, Dolton and Mark. "What's for lunch?" asked Zach.

"We're going to have freeze-dried spaghetti and meat with bread from this morning and fruit juice and for dessert, a trail bar. So...let's get cooking," instructed Phil.

"Mmmmm, that sounds yummy," said Dolton sarcastically.

"I'm glad it sounds so good, Dolton. You can get the water on the stove and everybody else get out your utensils," said Phil.

"Gimme your water, guys," Dolton urged. As he got the water jugs he emptied most of them into the pot for the spaghetti – the rest was poured into the container for the juice.

Zach and Buck got their things together quickly, so Phil asked them to go get water. They gathered up everyone's water bottles and started down to the lake. Weber came up asked if he could mix the juice. "Sure," said Phil as he watched Zach and Buck head off to the lake. Then he noticed that neither of the boys had a filter with them so he called out to them and ran to meet them. "Buck, Zach! Hold on! You boys will have to filter that water or we'll all be sick as dogs by the end of the day."

"Filter water? How're we supposed to do that?" asked Buck. Phil led them back to the backpacks and pulled out a filtering unit from his pack. It was a silver tube with plastic hoses coming out of opposite ends and a pump handle on the top. "Put this end into the water bottle and this end into the lake water," said Phil indicating which end was which. "Make sure you don't put this end into the mud at the bottom of the lake or you'll break the filter. Try to find a place where the mud isn't stirred up too much. Once you have it all in place, begin pumping here," he said showing them the pumping action of the filter. "This will ensure us of good water to drink on our way."

He handed Buck the filter and pointed them to the lakes. Phil sat down next to Weber and noticed that Mark and Quinton were just sitting down, doing nothing. He sent Mark and Quinton down to the lake to help Zach and Buck with the water bottles. Meanwhile, Buck and Zach had found a place at the far end of the large lake. Buck lay down on his belly on a rock over the water. He was leaning in pumping water into the filter and asked Zach, "So, how was the fishing?"

"It was great!" said Zach, "The Webmeister hooked his first fish, and I got two before we had to quit. How was the swim?"

"It was nice and cool. This place is unbelievable. This was such a great idea!" said Buck.

"Yeah, I'm having a pretty good time so far," Zach confessed. When Mark and Quinton reached them, they teamed up and finished the filtering of the water quickly.

When they returned from the lake, Dolton was stirring the spaghetti. The smell seemed to fill the meadow. It made them all aware that they were hungry again. Pastor Mike and Phil were sitting on the grass looking at the map and talking about their timeline. Weber had finished mixing the juice and was sitting on a rock with his laptop. Zach and Buck passed out the water bottles and sat down next to Dolton. Quinton made his way to Weber.

"Hey, how're you getting power from that thing? Did you bring a ton of battery backups for it?" asked Quinton.

"No, my backpack has solar panels on it, so while I'm walking I'm charging up the battery – no need for extra batteries," Weber explained.

"Cool! You e-mailing your folks again?"

"Yeah, I want my dad to know that I caught my first fish!"

"Excellent," said Quinton, "would it be all right if I got on for a bit when you're done?"

"Sure, no problem. I'm almost done. There," said Weber as he handed his laptop over to Quinton.

"Thanks. You want me to shut it down when I'm done?" he asked.

"Yeah, thanks. I'm gonna go see what's taking Dolton so long. I'm hungry," said Weber as he headed off to the cooking area. It wasn't long before Quinton finished and came up behind him and thanked him for the use of his computer.

"Okay, the spaghetti is done," shouted Dolton just as Weber finished putting away the laptop.

Pastor said, "Great, let's pray." Everyone gathered around in a circle and bowed their heads. Pastor Mike said, "After I say this prayer we're going to start something new. When it's time to pray we're going to hold up a thumb, and the last thumb up is the one who gets to pray." They all looked at each other and smiles started to appear on their faces as they realized what that meant. No one wanted to pray out loud so each was sure that his thumb would be the first one up. Pastor Mike continued, "Shall we pray? Dear Lord, we give you thanks for the beautiful way you have sent us off today, and for the food you have provided us with, prepared by the hands of your humble servants. Let it strengthen us for our journey ahead. Amen."

Everyone filled his dish, grabbed a piece of bread, poured his drink, and sat down in a circle – hardly a word was spoken. The fresh air and exertion had made them very hungry. About the time plates were becoming empty Dolton said to Weber, "I heard you caught a fish."

"Yep, I caught a big fish," said Weber.

"How big was it?" asked Buck.

"It was about this big," replied Weber holding his hands apart about eighteen inches. Everyone laughed.

Zach said still laughing, "Yep, he's a fisherman all right."

After Lunch

Lunch was over. They all cleaned their dishes and, since Dolton cooked, he cleaned the main pot. As they packed up from lunch, Pastor Mike announced, "Mr. Phil says that we have quite a walk to get to the treeline before dinner, so make sure that you change your socks and are aware of your feet - and don't forget to drink water. Who still needs to wash his socks?" All the boys raised their hands. "Okay, get that done now, we need to be on our way," Pastor demanded.

With the boys down at the lakes washing their socks, Pastor and Phil packed up the rest of the gear. "Sure is a pretty area we stopped at," said Pastor.

"Beautiful," answered Phil, "Just wait until you see what's in store tomorrow. When we crest the glacier you won't believe your eyes."

"Can't wait," said Pastor.

The boys returned with the washed socks and hung them to dry on the outside of their backpacks. "Okay," said Phil, "let's get our packs on and get going. Use the buddy system to get them on." The boys started to get into their packs.

Zach mounted his by himself with no problem so he started helping the others. After Phil got his pack on he went around and checked everyone to make sure that each was adjusted properly. "Okay," said Phil, "we're good to go."

Pastor moved to center of the group and said, "Let's have a quick prayer. Good Shepherd, be with us on this leg of our journey and keep us well and in the right path. We ask this through Christ our Lord. Amen."

"All right," said Phil, "grab your walking poles and we're off."

They headed back to the trees and continued on the trail. Almost immediately it seemed that the trail became a little more difficult to walk. It gradually rose and the incline became steeper. Phil could be seen from time to time checking his compass and map. He was constantly watching for the trail markers. As they hiked, the flora became a little denser and the trees seemed to grow a little higher. The tops of the trees sheltered the forest floor from most of the sunshine so the heat of the day didn't seem to matter. After a while, conversation waned. With the weight of the packs and the change in elevation, some panting could be heard as they caught their breath from time to time.

Weber reveled in his thoughts about his fishing achievement. *I still can't believe that I actually caught a fish.* Buck was walking next to him and had never seen as many gorgeous views in his life. He couldn't keep his eyes from constantly looking around. Every once in a while he lost track of what he was supposed to be doing and bumped into Weber – a couple of times knocking his glasses off. The pine trees now outnumbered most of the other trees and were growing closer together. From time to time the group would pass small clearings with short grass. The sun shone through the trees in small individual rays that lit up the grassy area it reached with brilliant green and yellow colors. That was the only direct sunlight they saw because of trees made a roof at the top of the forest.

"Hey, Zach," said Dolton, "I don't think you washed your socks good enough."

"Why not?" Zach asked cautiously.

"Cuz the flies are buzzing around 'em," laughed Dolton.

"Maybe it's because I smell so sweet. Or. . .it could be that they're running from you," he replied slyly as he turned around and grinned his infamous menacing grin.

"Easy, man. I'm just joking with you," he said, as he backed away a little not wanting to be the recipient of the wrath of Zach.

"You know what they say about paybacks," warned Zach as he turned around and continued hiking at his normal pace. Dolton kept his distance and left him alone - for now. Dolton had always been a smart aleck. He had a quick wit and was never at a loss for words. Sometimes it got him into trouble, but it was what his closest friends found the most enjoyable about him.

Mark and Dolton walked side by side on the trail and now talked about how great the trip had been so far. Dolton was still anxious to see some wildlife – something other than the numerous birds, chipmunks, and squirrels they had already seen. Quinton walked behind Pastor Mike and hit himself with his walking pole every other step as he looked around. Unexpectedly, Phil raised his hand for everyone to stop. Mark and Dolton, who had been talking, almost walked into Quinton and Pastor. Weber and Buck almost did the same to Mark and Dolton.

They stopped at the edge of a clearing where the sun shone through. Phil put his index finger to his lips to motion for quiet and then pointed. Zach, who had been following Phil, was already staring at it. They quietly gathered around Zach and Phil as he pointed. Then they saw it in the distance, blending into the background: a deer—a buck with a large rack of antlers. It was looking straight at them. Without making a sound, Quinton retrieved his camera and took two photos before the deer moved. The buck turned in the thick brush and in two leaps vanished into the pine trees and was gone. Wows were exclaimed.

"Did you see the antlers on that deer?" exclaimed Zach.

"Yeah," said Quinton with excitement, "I got a picture."

"Did you see how large it was?" said Pastor Mike.

"Okay, boys," said Phil, "if we keep our voices down when we're walking we might see more animals. Keep your eyes open." The group started back up the trail walking in pairs. Weber whispered to Quinton, "Hey, could I get a copy of your pictures when we get back home?"

"Sure," whispered Quinton with a bit of excitement in his voice, "I'll e-mail them to you."

Pastor Mike moved up to speak with Phil, "How far are we going this afternoon?"

"Well," said Phil, "we need to get to the treeline tonight, so that tomorrow we can go over the glacier and back into the trees before dark."

"Oh," said Mike with a blank expression. Phil gave a little laugh and said, "We have another two to three-hour walk, if we don't stop."

"Great!" said Pastor sarcastically, "For a minute there I thought we had a really long way left to go."

"Hang in there, Mike, enjoy the beauty around us and we'll be there before you know it," encouraged Phil.

The boys walked quietly, looking into the forest for more signs of wildlife. The sounds of footsteps and the thuds of the walking poles, birds, and the soft rustling of the trees were the only sounds they heard after their talk had been exhausted. They walked the rocky dirt trail that wound upwards through the pine trees in silence, enjoying being outside and together.

"Hey, what's that?" asked Quinton upon hearing strange sounds in front of them.

"That would be another group of hikers coming up. We are going to have to share the trail, boys. Make a single file line so we can let them by," shouted Phil to the group. "Good ear, Quinton."

The boys fell into a single-file line and greeted the other hikers as they passed. "Is that going to happen a lot on our trip, Mr. Phil?" asked Quinton.

"Oh, I expect we'll run into people every now and then. This is a popular trail among hikers," replied Phil. They continued down the trail two-by-two.

Treeline – First Evening

Without warning Phil stopped. "Okay," he said, "we're here." The boys walked past Phil out of the trees and stopped. The looks on their faces said it all. The site before them was awesome! A mountain of rock that reached far up into the sky with a trail that zigzagged up the side that seemed to go on forever. All at the same time they turned around and looked at Phil.

Even Pastor Mike was in awe. "We're going to climb that?" he said.

Phil smiled and said, "Yep, and we're going to do it in one day."

"No way!"

"You've got to be kidding me?"

"I can't climb that!"

The boys were shocked; they had known that this was going to be an adventure but they weren't prepared for this. "Come on boys," said Phil, "you're not afraid of a little mountain are you? This trip is going to prove that you're men, not boys. Have faith – if you have faith the size of a mustard seed you can do anything you put your mind to. Besides, if I didn't think you couldn't do it we wouldn't be here."

Pastor Mike spoke up and said, "Phil is right, all you need is faith." Everyone stood silent for a moment, still in shock, looking at Pastor Mike.

"All right, let's set up camp," said Phil still smiling. That seemed to bring everyone out of their trance and they followed Phil back into the trees and found an area that was perfect for their first real night in the wild.

The area was mostly flat dirt ground with few rocks. Trees framed the camp area. The boys unloaded the tents and each pair started to work on setting up their tent. In less than 10 minutes the tents were up and Phil said proudly, "Well, I can't believe how fast you all did that. You remembered how to put up your tents—congratulations!" Then he asked everyone, "How are we doing on water? Give me a tally."

Zach spoke up first, "I have half a bottle."

Pastor said, "Three-quarters full."

Buck said, "Half."

Weber said, "Half."

Quinton said nervously, "About a quarter."

Mark said, "A half."

Dolton said, "Not quite a half."

"Ok," said Phil, "we need a group to go back to the little stream and fill everyone's bottles and the collapsible jug."

Mark, Buck, Dolton, Zach, and Pastor Mike said that they would go for water and gathered up the bottles and started back down the trail. Phil started looking through the food trying to decide what they were going to have for dinner. *I should have memorized the meal plan, too*, thought Phil. Weber grabbed his backpack and headed out of the treeline to set up his laptop to try and send an e-mail to his parents. Quinton stood watching Phil with his arms crossed, tapping his arms with his hands, when Phil looked up and said, "Hey

Quinton, how would you like to help me figure out what we going to have for dinner?"

"Yeah," said Quinton excitedly. Quinton pulled open a backpack and started searching. Within a few seconds he brought out a bag marked Beef Stroganoff. "How about this?" he asked.

"That's a great idea," said Phil, "and we still have bread. Here's some rice mix that will be good too. Okay, good job. Let's get everything ready before they get back with the water." As Quinton and Phil set up for dinner Weber had found a large rock to set up his laptop and backpack and was busy trying to get a signal to send his message.

<{{}}><

"Stanley, Weber is sending another e-mail, come here," urged Karen.

"Read it out loud," said Stanley as he prepared dinner.

"Dear Mom and Dad, You would not believe what we did and what we saw today. Aside from catching my first fish, we walked eight miles in one afternoon. I can't believe I actually did it! And we saw a deer with a huge rack of antlers – he just seemed to appear and then disappear into the forest. When we stopped to set camp tonight we saw where we will be hiking tomorrow. I've never seen anything like it before! The mountain just keeps going up and up and the trail looks like a rocky zigzag. Mr. Phil says we'll be going over a glacier tomorrow. I'm not too sure about that, I don't have an ice pick or proper ice boots for it, but he seems confident that we all can make it so I guess I shouldn't worry. I don't know what we're having for dinner but I'm so hungry that I'll eat anything tonight. I'll type you again tomorrow when we stop for lunch. Sorry Mom, but I'm not missing you too much. I'm having too much fun. I promise I'll miss you next time. Okay? Got to go now, they're coming back with the water and I'll be eating soon. Love you, Weber."

"Sounds like he is having fun, Karen. There's no need to worry," said Stanley.

"I'm not worried, I just miss having him around. . .and I hope he doesn't get hurt. . .or get too tired. . .or. . . ."

"Karen, he's fine," said Stanley soothingly. "Phil loves those boys, he's not going to let anything happen to them, especially Weber. I asked him to keep special watch over him before they left and I know he's the kind of man to do it."

"You're right, honey. I don't know what I was thinking." Karen shut off the computer and walked back into the kitchen.

<{{}}><

Pastor Mike and the boys walked back about a quarter mile to the small stream they had passed and filled the bottles through the filter and pump. Zach was pumping as the others took turns kneeling down next to him with their bottles. Mark asked, "Hey, man, how'd you like the trip so far?"

"This is the best thing I've ever done, I love it out here," said Zach emphatically, "I hope I can do this again."

"Well, we're not done yet," said Mark as he took the bottle back from Zach and left. Buck was next, he knelt down and gave his bottles to Zach.

"Isn't it beautiful here?" asked Buck.

"Oh yeah! There's nothing like this in Jamestown," said Zach.

"I can't believe I'm here," said Buck as his bottle filled, "sometimes it feels like a dream."

Pastor spoke up, "Yes, it's great to be out with Mother Nature experiencing all this. The smell of the pine trees, the blue of the sky, the sounds of the creatures—all made by the hand of God. It's incredible!"

"Kind of makes you wonder what's over the mountain, doesn't it?" replied Zach. Pastor was a bit surprised at this comment. He had never heard Zach talk about the future in any manner before.

"Hey! That reminds me of a song!" said Dolton.

"Oh no, not one of your songs," sighed Mark.

"What's wrong with my songs?" said Dolton trying to sound hurt.

"C'mon, give me your bottles and try not to sing 'til I'm done," said Zach.

"Here, give them to me, Dolton. Zach and I have it from here," said Pastor.

While Zach and Pastor finished filling the containers Buck, Mark, and Dolton investigated the banks of the small stream. Dolton and Mark threw rocks into the stream while Buck was scheming to throw a large rock in the water right by them. As Buck turned the rock over to get a better hold, something caught his attention. He rolled it over into the water and reached into the depression and poked a shiny object. It was stuck but with a little coaxing he popped out. He couldn't believe his eyes. It was gold! He struck it rich!

"Hey, guys!" he shouted, "Look what I found!"

Dolton and Mark quit what they were doing and ran over to see what he was talking about.

"Whoa!" said Mark. "Is that gold?"

"I. . .I think so," Buck said and dipped it into the water to wash it off.

"Can I see it?" asked Dolton. He held out his hand and Buck gently placed it in his palm. They couldn't take their eyes off the treasure.

About the time Pastor and Zach finished filling the containers they heard the commotion and went down to see what was going on. Buck, Mark and Dolton were gathered into a tight circle. Pastor broke between Mark and Buck and saw Dolton standing with his hand out and the gold nugget shining in his palm. Pastor asked, "Whatcha got there, Dolton? Is that gold?"

"Where did you find it?" said Zach.

"Under a big rock at the side of the stream," said Buck excitedly.

"Is it real?" Zach wondered aloud.

Everyone stared at each other for a second. No one had considered that it might not be real. Pastor said calmly, "We should get back before Mr. Phil starts to worry."

They rounded up the water containers and headed back up the trail to the treeline. Dolton gave Buck back the nugget. He stared at it for a moment then placed it into his pocket and started off with the others.

Back at camp Quinton and Phil had already picked out the freeze-dried dinner, set up the cook area and were waiting for the others to return. Phil had found a place on a large boulder, put his feet up and had just started to relax when he heard a noise and turned to see the group come back. Phil sighed and hopped up to meet them.

Buck passed the others and went right up to Phil, reaching into his pocket to retrieve the piece of gold. "Look, Mr. Phil, look what I found under a rock," he said with hopeful anticipation as he handed it to him.

The boys gathered around Phil as he turned it over a few times and then handed it back to Buck and said, "Pyrite, it's pyrite. It's fool's gold."

Every single shoulder in the group sagged at the news. Pastor Mike noticed and asked, "Are you sure, Phil?"

"Yes, I'm afraid so. It's still a nice find. Just think how exciting it would have been if it *had* been real," said Phil, catching on to Pastor's inquiry. "Sorry, Buck, sorry, guys" he said and patted Buck on the back as he walked off to begin cooking.

"I thought I'd really found something," said Buck as he threw the rock up and caught.

"So did I," replied Dolton, "I thought you hit the mother lode."

"The mother lode," repeated Buck, "yeah, the mother lode."

"The mother lode, what a load!" chided Mark as he pushed Dolton who fell into Buck and pushed back. They had the beginnings of a wrestling round.

"Looks like you need to cook off your frustrations," Phil said loudly, indicating for them to come over.

Phil put them to work and left Pastor Mike cooking with the four boys. "Where're you off to, Phil?" asked Pastor.

"I need find a place for the Bearmuda Triangle," he replied.

"Bearmuda Triangle?" they all said at the same time.

"You'll see, finish up what you're doing and I'll explain after dinner," he instructed.

Quinton was the only one finished with his duties so he followed Phil. "So, what's the Bearmuda Triangle?" he asked.

"It's an area that we don't camp in, we store the food there at night to keep animals from it. It's important that the areas we cook and clean or sump in are away from the camping area. We don't want any bears bothering our food or us. At one point of the triangle is the cooking area. Another point is the cleaning or sump area. The last point of the triangle is where the food is stored. We don't camp in this area because when the bears come looking for food, they'll look in the triangle first. That looks like a suitable place for it," he said pointing to a clearing a ways from the camp area. "Now all I have to do is find a rock to counterbalance the food and remember how to tie the knots," said Phil.

"I'll find a rock," said Quinton, and took off. He didn't start looking for the rock right away though. He found Weber and told him that Phil needed help remembering how to tie knots.

A few moments after Quinton took off, Phil had second thoughts about letting him go get the rocks. When he didn't return quickly, he was concerned that he might hit himself with them and get hurt. But Quinton showed up a few moments later, unscathed, with two rocks that he thought might work.

About the same time, Weber showed up with his laptop. He had found a website that showed how to tie knots, "Here you are, sir," he offered.

"Thank you, Weber, that will be quite helpful," said Phil appreciatively, then he turned to Quinton and said, "And thank you, too." Quinton turned red with embarrassment. If he hadn't been holding the rocks he might have hit himself. Quinton hurried quickly away to the cooking area.

Phil and Weber sat down on the ground and looked at the knots that they would need for the nightly setup. "Good job on finding this information. It sure is handy to have it at your fingertips," Phil complimented.

"This is the kind of research I was already doing in elementary school. I've had a lot of practice. There isn't much I can't find through the Internet," replied Weber. They chose the most suitable knots and proceeded to set up the rope and rocks.

The water on two little cook stoves had come to a boil and Buck and Pastor were cooking Beef Stroganoff and Rice Pilaf. Zach, Dolton, and Mark were making some bread when Quinton walked up and asked, "How's it going?"

"Great," said Buck.

"Mmm, that smells good," said Quinton enthusiastically.

"Wanna see something cool?" said Buck and reached into his pocket and pulled out the pyrite. Before Quinton could say anything he handed it to him.

"Wow!" said Quinton excitedly. "Is this real gold?"

"No," said Buck a little disappointed, "it's pyrite. Mr. Phil said it's fool's gold."

"It's beautiful just the same," said Quinton, "Where'd you find this?"

"Under a large rock by the stream when we were filling the water bottles," he replied.

"I hope I find one," said Quinton handing it to back Buck.

"Well, here," said Buck after a moment, "in case you don't, take this one," and he handed it back to Quinton. Quinton was stunned; he didn't know what to say. The others were listening and looked up with amazement at Buck's generosity.

"Uhhh, thank you," said Quinton; knowing it was inadequate, he reiterated, "Thank you!"

"Oh, that's okay," replied Buck, "I like sharing with my friends." The stunned look slowly transformed to a smile. Quinton had never had a person call him a friend, let alone give him something to solidify a relationship.

"Wow, Buck, you're giving away your fool's gold?" asked Mark.

"That was very nice of you," said Pastor Mike. "It represents friendship and shows compassion and true Christian giving."

Buck turned red. "We're all friends here," said Buck.

"Don't take this wrong Buck," said Zach as he stood up, "I didn't know that I was one of your friends, I thought we were more like, umm, acquaintances."

"No," Buck said to Zach with authority. Everyone watched and listened. "As I've been getting to know you, and Quinton and Weber, you've all become my friends, along with Mark and Dolton. I hope you consider me your friend."

Zach stood staring at Buck in awkward silence for what seemed like quite a while. *Oh, I hope he doesn't hit him,* thought Quinton. Then he stepped forward and with a smile he said, "Yeah, I think we are friends." He put out his hand to Buck who took Zach's hand, and with a hearty handshake said, "Friends." The smile that had faded from Quinton's face during this exchange had now returned even bigger than before and he joined in saying, "Friends."

"How 'bout we finish up cooking dinner, fellows," said Pastor, and they all agreed whole-heartedly. *Lord, thank you for touching the hearts of these boys as you bring them into family with each other,* prayed Pastor silently.

The boys went right to work in finishing up the dinner and Pastor Mike found a rock to sit on and meditate about the day. Phil finished setting up the Bearmuda Triangle and saw Pastor sitting on the rock and took a seat next to him. Over the next few minutes Pastor Mike brought him up to speed about the first evidence of the boys' bonding. After Pastor had given him the update, he nodded, smiled and simply held up his thumb and said loudly, "It's time."

The boys saw that the men had their thumbs up and although at first they had forgotten, like light bulbs going on, the boys' faces lit up as they understood what that meant. The last to raise his thumb was Quinton. *I can't believe I have to be the first one to pray,* he thought, *now they'll know I'm a geek for sure and it'll be back to teasing the freak.* Nervously, he began, "Lord, thanks for getting us this far and keeping us safe. Thanks for friendship and fresh air and beautiful surroundings and…"

"Thank him for the food already, I'm hungry," whispered Zach.

"…and thank you for the food. Amen"

"Thank you, Quinton, let's eat," said Pastor Mike. The boys didn't wait for the invitation; they had already begun digging in. In a blink of an eye everyone had filled their plates and all were eating as though they hadn't eaten all day.

The sun set as dinner came to a close. Everyone pitched in, doing his own dishes and cleaning up the cooking area. By the time they finished and Phil had hung the food up for the night, the group had settled down around the lanterns to relax and talk about the day's events. Phil explained the Bearmuda Triangle to the group and told them that they would all have to learn how to do it before the trip was over.

After a few moments, Mark moved over and sat by Phil. "Excuse me," said Mark, "Uh, what would be the protocol for going in the woods?"

"Going in the woods?" said Phil.

"Yeah, you know, *going* in the woods," Mark said with his teeth clenched in almost a growl.

"Oh," said Phil with a knowing smile.

"Gentlemen," said Phil, "it has been brought to my attention that there was something we have not covered that each of you need to know. In your backpacks you each have a roll of TP, the biodegradable type. I have a shovel. If you need it, take it and return it when you're done. It's dark now, so take a friend and scout out your area. Don't go too far off the trail and *definitely* not too close to camp."

Mark stood up and walked over and picked up the shovel. Buck stood up and said, "I'll go with you." They both stopped at their backpacks and off they went.

Dolton sat there only a second before he couldn't help himself, "I have a feeling that shovel is going to be busy tonight." Everyone started to laugh.

Zach said while holding his stomach, "My system isn't used to that freeze-dried food yet," as a loud gurgle came from his stomach.

It took about an hour before everyone had taken his turn and was back sitting around the lanterns relaxing. Mark sat up, turned to Dolton, smiled, and said, "Play us a song, I know you brought it."

"Brought what?" said Phil.

"Dolton here plays the harmonica," said Mark.

"And he's good too," said Buck.

"How come I've never found out about this?" said Pastor Mike.

"He doesn't think he's very good," said Mark.

"Go get it and play something," said Phil and the rest of the group started chanting "Play us a song, play us a song."

Dolton tried to shrink and leaned over to Mark and said under his breath, "Pay back man, pay back," and got up and walked over and pulled the harmonica from his pack. He sat back down, blew into the harmonica and asked, "What would you like to hear?" Before they could say anything he began playing some rhythm and blues. Then he started to sing and played some more and sang again. He played a heavy-duty R&B riff and while Buck was clapping to keep the rhythm he sang again. "C'mon you guys, sing with me," Dolton said without missing a beat; by this time everyone was clapping to the beat and singing along. They sang it all again and clapped and laughed to the end of the song.

"My goodness," said Pastor Mike, "well done! I had no idea that you were musically talented."

"Thank you," said Dolton.

"Play us another please," said Pastor Mike.

"Oh, okay," said Dolton. He started into another song, but this time everyone became quiet. Dolton stood up and started playing up towards the sky. As Dolton played Phil turned down the lanterns and they all sat back to watch and listen.

Pastor Mike became lost in his thoughts, drifting back in time, back before Mark was born and his wife Sara was alive and the only things in his life that mattered were his wife and the Lord. He missed her so much; he could feel the tears welling in his eyes as he thought about her. A tear rolled down Pastor's cheek just as Mark looked up at his father. He knew that his dad had been taken into thought about his mother again. Mark put his hand on his father's knee and looked at the star-filled sky and listened to the beautiful music Dolton was playing. He played as though he were alone, playing a solo to God himself. *Lord, thank you for moments like this,* prayed Pastor silently again as he pondered the heavenly choirs and what the music there would sound like.

Pastor was not the only one who had been taken away in thought. Phil seemed deeply pensive. Everyone had leaned back to enjoy the music and the clear star-filled sky. Dolton finished and everyone was quiet. No one moved for quite some time. A single clap from Weber and the trance was broken. Everyone started to praise Dolton.

Zach got up and walked over to him and said, "Man I didn't know you could play like that. I don't think I've ever felt that way about music."

"Dolton, that was heavenly, thank you for sharing such a beautiful part of you with us," said Pastor.

Dolton started to turn red and replied, "Thank you, thank you everyone."

"Ok," said Phil gently, "I hate to break up this concert, but we have a big day tomorrow and we should get to bed."

They all began to get up and Mark asked, "Dad, can I sleep outside under the stars? It's a beautiful night and not too cold." The rest of the boys chimed in wanting to sleep outside also. The men looked at each other and Phil said, "It is perfect for it."

"I guess so," said Pastor Mike. The boys cheered and headed to their tents to get their sleeping bags. It only took a few minutes for the boys to lay out their bags. Mark, Quinton, Weber and Zach stepped off into the treeline before climbing into their bags. The men moved their sleeping bags outside and joined the boys after turning out the lanterns.

When the lights were extinguished, the stars in the night sky came alive like sparkling diamond lights scattered throughout the blackness of the heavens. The moon was nowhere to be seen on this night, which allowed the Milky Way, the Big and Little Dippers and other constellations to be seen. They pointed out all of them that they knew and then started making up their own. The night sky was so clear that Mars could be seen as a pink glimmering star. The sounds of nature were all that could be heard for the longest time as they lay in their sleeping bags admiring a sky they had looked at a thousand times but never appreciated before. The crickets, frogs and an occasional owl were the music of the night now; no one could say a word.

Quietly, Pastor Mike said slowly, "As I lay here looking out into our sky and up towards Heaven I can't help but think, some people don't believe in God or a maker of all this; Heaven and Earth. I wonder. . .that if our planet is this beautiful, how much more beautiful is heaven." He paused for a while, "It makes me feel small as I look up and see the wonders of the universe and how I feel blessed to be allowed to be here and experience this." They lay there in silence for a while. "Dear Father, for the beauty of this night, the music you have blessed our ears with and for each other, we thank you. Good night, Lord, please bless our sleep." Everything and everyone was quiet and still – there were only the noises in the forest.

"Amen," said Quinton.

Second Morning – Switchbacks

Phil awoke just before daylight and crawled from his bag and was greeted by one of the most beautiful sunrises he could remember. The sun had just begun to color the sky with soft pastel blues, pinks and oranges. The clouds hovered harmoniously over the top of the glacier reflecting the colors and painting the sky with abstract objects. He stood, stretched, and took in the brisk clean morning air and silently thanked God for such a beautiful start to the day. He walked over to the cooking area and put water on for coffee. Just about the time the coffee was ready, Zach, Buck, Weber, and Pastor Mike awoke.

As they stretched and admired the morning they gathered around the coffee pot and got their first drink of the day. Phil was starting his second cup and Mike, his first, when they heard a blood-curdling scream! They all jumped up and ran over to the sleeping area to find Quinton standing up in his sleeping bag watching Mark stomping on his like a mad man doing a rain dance.

"What in the world is going on?" said Pastor Mike, out of breath from the shock. Mark stopped and jumped away from his bag. Mark turned to find all seven looking at him as though he was crazy.

"Mark," said Phil, "are you okay?" Mark had looked back at the bag and said in a very high and shaky tone, "There's a. . .there's something in my sleeping bag!"

Phil reached behind his back and pulled out a knife; he then walked past Mark and placed his booted foot on the top opening of the bag and bent over and hooked the zipper with his knife and slowly started to unzip the bag. Phil slowly moved his foot to the zippered edge of the bag and with a wave of his hand cautioned Mark to back up with the others. He then motioned to Buck to fetch a walking pole. Buck returned quickly and carefully passed the pole to Phil, who stepped off the sleeping bag and took the walking pole, hooked the top layer and flipped the bag open. Everyone except Dolton jumped back as a snake came into view. All eyes were on the snake. Everyone was still - except Dolton, who started to chuckle. They all turned to look at Dolton. Phil reached down and picked it up; it was a rubber snake.

"Dolton, you jerk!" growled Mark, but Dolton was laughing too hard to see him move in.

Pastor stepped between them and said, "Now, boys." Pastor Mike turned to Dolton and, attempting to be stern, said, "Dolton that wasn't a very nice thing to do!"

"Well, I know," said Dolton still laughing. By this time the rest saw the humor and began laughing too. Dolton leaned around Pastor, faced Mark and said, "I am sorry— man I apologize Mark. I put it in there last night and then forgot about it. I really am sorry."

Phil, who had kept a straight face, started smiling and said, "I'll keep this," and headed back over to the cook area.

Quinton said with a smile, "I thought I was the only one that screamed like a little girl around snakes." Everyone laughed, even Mark.

"Let's go cook breakfast," said Pastor.

Dolton stepped towards Mark and said, "I wasn't trying to scare you to death, I just wanted to make you jump."

"Oh, you made me jump all right," said Mark as Buck came between them, put his arms on top each of their shoulders and walked them to breakfast saying, "You guys!"

They gathered back at the cooking area and helped Phil prepare the breakfast, which consisted of hot cereal, freshly made flat bread, and juice. When it was all done, Phil stood up from cooking the hot cereal and said, "It's ready," and held up a thumb. Thumbs started popping up; Zach was the last to raise his.

"Looks like you got it, Zach," said Pastor Mike smiling, "are you okay with it?"

"Yes," he said confidently, "it's no problem. Dear God, thanks for the fun we had this morning and thankssss for the food."

"Zach!" Phil admonished.

"Okay, sorry. Thank you God for the food and keep us safe today. Amen"

"Thank you Zach," said Pastor Mike. "Fill up your plates, guys, we have a challenging morning."

"Hey, Mark," said Dolton, "would you passss me the ssssalt?"

"I don't think that's funny," retorted Mark.

"Oh no, it'sssss very funny," Zach teased.

"Don't be upsssset, Mark. We all get ssssscared ssssome-timesss," hissed Buck.

"Yeah, right," Mark conceded and decided to laugh it off.

Buck asked Phil, "Are we going to be able to get to the top of that mountain today?"

Phil replied, "We're not stopping at the top except to look at the glacier, then we're going over the top and into the treeline on the other side. We have to traverse the switchbacks for the bulk of the morning."

"Switchbacks?" they murmured.

"Switchbacks are the trails that zigzag up the steep inclines of the glacier. They're the only way to get up to the top and down the other side. It's going to be the hardest part of our trip. It's very important that when we break in the middle of the day you change and wash your socks. When we get to the higher altitude the air will become thinner and breathing will become a little more difficult. It's important that you let me know if any of you are having problems during the hike. It would be fatal to faint and fall off the trail on this part of our hike. Does everybody understand that?"

They all nodded, so he continued, "Okay, let's get cleaned up and packed up so we can get to the top and the other side before dark. One person from each tent go back and pack up the tents and gear and the other one do KP."

The group got right to work and had everything cleaned and packed in record time. It was apparent that the boys were eager to get going. Phil had been studying the map while they were preparing for the day so he was the last to finish packing as they gathered into a circle.

"Let's pray," began Pastor Mike, "Almighty Father, guide us this day on the treacherous part of our journey. Keep our feet steadfast, our senses sharp, and our energy new. We are glad to know that whatever the circumstances we can count on You to guide us and take care of us. In all things we give You thanks and praise. In Christ our Lord, Amen."

"Okay," said Phil, "grab your walking poles and let's get started."

They moved onto the trail just outside the treeline in the view of the rocky mountain. The switchbacks that led up the jagged slope looked like a spine. As they started up the rocky trail the boys tried to get comfortable in their packs. The trail gradually rose as they walked towards the start of the steep switchbacks. Walking at such an incline made their packs settle in different place on their backs. Phil heard them talking about their packs and stopped at the beginning of the switchbacks, turned around and said, "Okay, gentlemen, make sure you have your packs sitting comfortably and your shoes tied snug." They made the necessary adjustments and everyone nodded his head to acknowledge readiness so Phil turned and led them up.

The trail was steep as they went back and forth up the switchbacks. The trail narrowed, allowing only one person at a time to hike it. The rocky dirt path had jagged rocks on both sides and was so steep that at any time the person ahead of you could be two feet or more higher, depending on how far they were in front of you. Each step felt like climbing stairs, because they had to pick up their legs every time they stepped; with every step they carried the weight of their packs - and it felt like it. The group was eager at first because this was an adventure unlike anything else they had experienced. But as the air became thinner, the cool damp smell of trees and grass at the treeline was now being replaced by the smell of dried rock and dust that was being kicked up by the person in front. An occasional grunt and heavy breathing could be heard from the group. From time to time, Phil would turn around and check on them. *So far, so good,* thought Phil, *but we still have a long way to go.*

It didn't take very long for conversation to completely stop. As the air got thinner and the packs got heavier, everyone conserved his energy for the hike.

Pastor gazed at the back of Mark, who was right in front of him, and began thinking about his wife, Sara. It was a sad remembrance that she never got to hold her son. The complications during birth that ended her life also prevented her from holding the object of her joy. He remembered just how joyous and blissful she was when they found out she was pregnant and then so peacefully happy during the pregnancy. One time she told him, "If this is how it feels to be pregnant then I want 12 children." They laughed and loved and planned their family. They had their whole lives ahead of them. How happy they would be and how blessed they were to be able to start their family.

Mike never talked too much about Sara to Mark and he now thought that he should. The boy had the right to know everything. He had a very hard time talking to Mark about her, not because he wanted to keep anything from him, but because his heart shattered when she died, and every time he spoke about Sara, he couldn't help himself, he cried. Sometimes even just thinking about her made him tearful. Though he loved his son with all his heart, he didn't want him to see his father so weak. It was tough enough growing up without a mother, he didn't need to know that his father wasn't strong. At that moment Mark stumbled, and it brought Mike back from his thoughts as his son caught his balance and continued walking. *He has turned out to be such a fine young man. Sara would have been so proud,* he thought. *I'll talk to him about his mother before the end of this trip.*

Quinton was, by far, the most animated of the hikers. He would take out his camera every 15 to 20 minutes and take four pictures of the mountains and valley below. Buck asked him why he did that and he explained that by taking the four pictures always left to right he could capture everything as a panoramic view of the ascent. Between every shot he would hit his head with the camera. Then, while he was hiking, he would hit himself with his walking stick. It wasn't boring watching him.

Everyone was breathing very hard and Phil called a rest break so that they could all catch their breath. No one talked during the break. It only lasted ten minutes but no one complained as they began again, as the main concentration was on climbing the switchbacks.

As Phil hiked up the trail, his thoughts were on Buck. Oddly enough, Buck had no idea that their lives were inexplicably linked from well before his life ever began—indeed, before his mother and father ever knew each other. Phil had made a promise, and he felt compelled to make good the promise now more than ever. He would have to speak with Pastor about it before he did anything.

Zach, who was probably in the best physical shape of all the boys and had a faster, stronger step than most of the group, always seemed to be close to Phil's back, as if he wanted to pass him. Phil was deep in thought when Zach tapped Phil's shoulder and said as he pointed, "What's that over there?"

Phil's thoughts were brought back to the matters of the moment and he looked at Zach's find. "It's a spring. It's from an underground stream. Looks as though it surfaces for about twenty feet before going back underground. Good eye, Zach," said Phil. "Let's stop." The group was ready for their second break. This was a hard climb and a good opportunity to fill their water bottles. Phil put his directly in the spring and took a good long drink before returning it to the spring to fill it again.

Quinton said, obviously winded, "Excuse me, sir." He politely addressed Phil as he caught his breath. "Don't we need to filter this water?"

"No," said Phil, "in this type of spring the ground filters it for us, so it's not like getting it out of a stream where animals leave their feces and other types of harmful elements enter the water. This is the most safe of all the water we'll find out here." The group spread out along the spring, filling their bottles before tasting it like Phil did.

"Wow!" said Zach. "This is great!" after taking a large drink.

"It almost has a sweet taste," said Buck. They all agreed and proceeded to fill their water bottles to the top.

"Okay, we need to keep moving," said Phil. "I don't believe we're far from the top. "

The group started off again with a little more vigor. The altitude was affecting everyone and breathing was growing more labored. Buck took up position behind Quinton. He watched him hit himself with his walking stick every other step. Then Buck started thinking about his mother; he worried about her. She worked so hard to keep them going and she deserved to have so much more than she did. He wished that he could just go to work to help her out but she insisted that he concentrate on school. She told him that he would be working for the rest of his life so he should take the opportunity to enjoy school. But that didn't stop him from working odd jobs here and there, although it never seemed enough to help out, and she refused to take his money. He thought that if he saved enough he could do something for her, but when she saw what he was doing she insisted that he keep the money for emergencies or college, even though money always seemed to be a problem. But while it didn't keep them from being happy, it kept them from doing a lot of things they dreamed of. His father died about a year after he was born and he and his mother lived on what she could bring in from the jobs she worked. He hated seeing her work so much, but she never complained. He often prayed that he could make enough money some day so that she wouldn't have to work, if she didn't want to. *Maybe some day....*

Mark, who followed Buck, was also deep in thought. He thought about his dad and how cool he was and how lately he had been considering following in his footsteps and become a pastor himself. He had to remember to actually tell him that he had been thinking that. *I'm so blessed to have a father that I love and get along with so well.* A lot of Mark's classmates had trouble getting along with their fathers, and they always seemed to talk about them like they were the scum of the earth. They were always fighting with them and getting into trouble. He was sure that it was just a phase; he remembered his father saying that once when he had asked him about it – but it still bothered him. He never fought with his father and secretly found that remarkable. They had disagreements, but his dad always seemed to respect him for it and he knew that his dad loved him anyway.

He did worry about him, though. There were times he would become pensive and then a bit blue for a while. Mark was sure that these were the times he was thinking about his mother. He was very careful not to ask too many questions about her. He learned early on that it would make him cry and then he would be embarrassed and go off to write another sermon. Mark didn't quite understand why he would be embarrassed when they were family, but accepted it and tried to work around it. Family, he thought, is the one place you never have to be embarrassed. In a family you are loved just because. He was sure that one day they would be able to talk about his mother without his father getting too upset. *I hope that one day we can talk and laugh about her.*

Quinton was having the hardest time with the altitude. Aside from the thin air, every other step he was hitting himself with the walking stick and using more energy. The extra expenditure made him feel a bit nauseated. He was very anxious about getting his pictures, so his mind would go back and forth from wanting to take pictures, breathing, not getting sick, breathing, would he make it, breathing, would he ever do a trip again like this, wanting to take pictures, and breathing.

Weber, the smallest in the group, was starting to lag behind. Zach looked back after seeing the look of concern on Phil's face when he turned to check on the group. Zach slowed down to let Weber catch up. "Do you want me to carry your backpack awhile, man?" offered Zach, "Are you okay?"

Weber looked gratefully at Zach and slowly nodded his head yes, indicating that he was okay. After seeing Weber's reaction to Zach's question, Phil stopped the group and told everyone, "Take a knee, get out your water bottles and drink slowly." Everyone knelt and half of the group, including Pastor, looked like they were going to throw up. Their faces were white and sweat dripped from their foreheads even though the temperature had dropped as they had climbed up the mountain.

"Thanks, Phil," said Pastor in a labored voice, although he was not quite sure that Phil heard him.

When he caught his breath, Phil said, "Everyone give me your attention. We are almost to the top, is there anyone who needs help?" No one said anything as Phil scanned the group. "Okay, you have all demonstrated great strength of character and tenacity up to this point in our trek today. Let's show this mountain that we have the strength and faith to conquer it and that with faith like ours we could move this mountain."

They all stood up, straightened their packs, and started off. They had walked another 30 minutes when an excited voice from the group shouted, "Look!" Quinton had looked up between breaths and viewed the pass at the top of the mountain. He had made it—they had made it! The adrenalin began pumping in all of them and gave them all just the boost they needed.

They continued through the pass where the trail started to level out and become wider. The pass was about 100 yards long and 50 yards wide, covered with icy snow, and the trail cut straight through the middle of the glacier. As they reached the halfway point of the pass they came to a sign. It read,

Summit Glacier
Altitude 12,045 feet
Now Leaving Yosemite

"This is a glacier?" said Weber disappointedly, "I thought it would be different, like a lot more snow and ice."

Phil smiled and said, "Really, if you think about it, glaciers are frozen water that either melt very slowly or never at all. I think the important thing here is not the glacier but the fact that you boys, I mean, *young men*, climbed a mountain and are standing on a glacier at the top, having conquered it."

They stood there thinking about what Phil just said and began to feel proud of themselves. Pastor Mike smiled and gave Phil the thumbs-up sign. "I know it's past lunch time but I think I would rather start down than eat lunch now," said Pastor Mike. "What do you guys want to do?" It didn't take anytime to think this one over, everyone voted to leave.

"Okay," said Phil, "I think before we start out of here we should pack our bottles with glacier snow first." They spread out to pick an area of clean snow. Zach cleaned an area and scraped up some snow and popped it into his mouth. "This is good," he said, his voice muffled. Everyone tasted the glacier and proceeded filling their bottles without wasting time and gathered back onto the trail. Quinton was starting to feel better and took a few pictures before the group started off again.

The trail down the back side of the mountain was nothing like the steep rocky face with its switchbacks. It was rocky but not as steep. The rocks were smaller and the trail down to the treeline looked closer than on the other side where they had camped the night before. The descent down the trail seemed to be going more quickly than the ascent up the other side. Going downhill was much easier as they moved back into air that had more oxygen in it. The treeline on this side of the mountain was not as lush as it was on the other side; the trees grew much farther apart and, the further down the mountain they went, the more grassy patches between the rocky areas and trees there were.

They were silent and observed the changing landscape. Just as they entered the treeline they spotted the first wildlife of the day. A very large bird, an eagle or maybe a condor, none of them really knew for sure, was circling above. It had a wingspan that could have been easily six feet across. They all slowed down to watch its magnificence and collectively they came to a complete stop. It glided in a circle and then a figure eight before flapping its wings twice and gliding off over the trees.

"That was beautiful," Zach said in awe.

"Yeah," the others replied. Quinton slapped himself on his hip and said, "I don't believe it! I should have taken a picture." Phil just smiled, turned, and continued walking.

The trees got thicker and the trail slightly wider as they hiked along. The grass around the trees was tall—about two to three feet high—and the smell of its dampness hung in the air. Over a small rise, the trail turned and they saw that they were headed through a swampy area where the trees had thinned and the tall grass covered the ground on both sides. As they hiked through it, glimmers of standing water could be seen occasionally between the blades of grass.

"Thank goodness the trail is elevated," said Dolton, as the group walked at a steady pace.

"Kind of looks prehistoric," said Weber in a shaky voice.

"I wonder if there are any snakes here," teased Dolton making sure to speak loud enough for Mark to hear.

Within a few hundred feet they walked out of the swamp and directly into a forested area where the pine trees were so big and thick that their foliage seemed to take up 75 percent of the sky. The ground was covered with pine needles; the smell of the trees was very strong. The trail blended into the rest of the surrounding ground area and Phil scanned the trees for trail markers; within a few seconds he spotted one. Zach, who was still behind him, observed him closely. The downward trail became clear again and easy to follow. Phil constantly checked the trail, with compass and map.

As the hikers came to a clearing, Phil called to everyone, "This looks like a great place to break for lunch."

The boys unloaded their packs and stretched their backs. Dolton remarked, "I'm starting to feel like a turtle."

Weber said, "Boy, are my feet tired."

After hearing Weber's comment Phil reminded them, "Don't forget to change your socks after lunch."

Mark, Buck and Quinton walked over to a large boulder next to the trail and climbed up to view the clearing. "Wow!" said Mark, "I've never seen such a cool looking meadow! It looks like a painting or something. Hey, you guys, you have to come and see this!"

The rest of them joined the three on the boulder and they looked out on the meadow in awe. It did look like a painting. The brilliant green grass carpeted the meadow, with a few colorful flowers dotting it here and there. The trees formed an almost perfect circle framing the meadow with their tall brown trunks. It was an exclusive hideaway created by God just for them. They stood for a while in silence admiring the beauty.

Phil said quietly, "Everyone close your eyes; listen closely and tell me what you hear." They all closed their eyes and listened to the sounds.

"I hear crickets," said Weber.

"I hear the leaves and the grass moving," said Quinton.

"That's good, what else?" asked Phil.

"I hear the breeze blowing and I smell the pine trees," said Zach.

"If you're quiet and you listen to nature it will touch your senses and you will know why God blesses us," said Pastor Mike.

"What do you mean?" asked Buck.

"God wants us to enjoy all of His creations, to see the earth the way He made it, not just to feed on the animals and abuse the land, but to take from it gratefully and give back to it, the same way He has given to us. God gave us a beautiful world to live in and the beauty is all around us – we just have to take the time to enjoy it. That's the blessing," said Pastor Mike.

They stood there for a little while longer admiring the view when a man came walking up the trail. "Hey, there!" he said.

"Hello!" they all replied, a little startled to hear an unfamiliar voice from behind them.

"How are you fine folks doing today?" Everyone stared for a second and then Pastor Mike said, "We're great, thank you," as he continued to look at the stranger.

"You're the first people I've seen today and I was starting to think that I wasn't going to see anyone," said the stranger. "How rude of me," he said, "my name is Noah Kinkade." He walked up to Pastor with his hand out.

"Pleasure to meet you, Mr. Kinkade," said Pastor Mike grabbing his hand with a hearty shake, "let me introduce my group. This is Phil Thomas, my son Mark Miller, Weber Deerfield, Zach Adalick, Buck Bond, Quinton Rothford, Dolton James, and I'm Mike Miller."

"Please, call me Noah. Well, you're quite the group," said Noah. "It's nice to see young people out enjoying nature. You all couldn't have picked a nicer place to stop and rest," said Noah.

"We're stopping for lunch," said Pastor Mike, "would you care to join us?"

"Oh, that would make my day," said Noah excitedly.

As they climbed down off the rock Zach said under his breath, "That guy looks homeless."

"Even more of a reason to ask him to join us for lunch," said Phil.

Noah Kinkade

As the stranger walked over to set down his equipment everyone stared. Noah Kinkade was a tall, thin man, but sinewy. He carried two homemade walking sticks that he had fashioned from ski poles. His hair was long and dirty brown - it may have been blond at the beginning of his trip but it was difficult to tell now, being that he was so weathered. He had blue eyes, a pointed nose and an established beard that was probably a couple of months old. He looked to be in his early forties, as gray hairs were already making an appearance in his beard. He had extremely large feet for a man of six-foot five inches.

"I'd like to thank you all for letting me take bread with you," said Noah.

"It's not a problem, we're glad to have you," said Pastor Mike.

As Phil retrieved items from the packs he directed the boys in preparing the lunch feast of freeze-dried vegetable stew, flat bread, granola bars for dessert, and flavored water. Noah actively participated in the food preparation, much to the surprise of the boys. When they were done they all gathered around the food prep area.

"Would you mind if I gave a blessing over the food before we eat?" asked Noah. "Please, be my guest," said Mike, a little surprised.

They all gathered into a circle and joined hands for the blessing. Noah lifted his eyes up toward the sky. "Yahweh, Abba, Father, Alpha and Omega, we thank you for the trails you have led us on and the intersecting of our paths this day. In your infinite wisdom you can see that at this moment in time we need each other to receive the blessings that we have to give one another, fellowship, sustenance, education, guidance, and the love that your Son left for us to share with one another. We especially thank you at this time for the food you have given us to share this afternoon. Bless it as you did the meager fish and bread among the thousands. Let it be more than enough to feed our bodies and sustain us through this day. Guide us on our journeys and protect us from the wiles of the dark lord. With happiness, thanks and love we ask this though Christ Our Lord. Amen," prayed Noah.

Everybody said, "Amen."

"Let's eat," said Zach emphatically.

"Yeah, I'm starving," replied Buck.

Noah was curious and asked, "Are you all Christians?"

"Yes," said Pastor Mike, "these boys are part of the youth group at our church; Phil is an elder and I am the pastor of Faith Church in Jamestown."

"Jamestown," Noah said, "didn't you say one of these young men was named James?"

"Yeah," said Dolton hanging his head, obviously embarrassed by the recognition, "My great great grandfather named the town after our family."

"Well now, you're a very lucky young man to belong to history like that," said Noah excitedly. "You know my family has history too and for a long time I was ashamed of it. I just wanted to be like my friends. I really didn't want the legacy my folks were giving me. I didn't want to stand out. I didn't want their money. I didn't want to be part of their notoriety. All I ever wanted was to be was like everyone else. . . until they passed away, that is. It was then that I was made painfully aware that I was the end of the line of my family. While my folks were alive I had many opportunities to prepare myself for life and a future to keep the family history and line going. I'll tell you the truth: I would love nothing better than to have a wife and child to pass my family's legacy on to. But I've been very blessed and the Lord has led me in a different direction. What I'm saying is you were born into your family for a reason. God was the one who put you there, not your friends, you. You are the only one who can do what God wants you to do and he gave you your family for a reason. But there I go, I'm rambling now. Guess it's been too long since the last time I met someone on the trail," he laughed.

"How come you're out here hiking when you have all that money and could be living in comfort?" Dolton asked.

"Well, money and comfort are two different things," said Noah. "Money is a tool. You can use it to buy things. Comfort is different for everyone. I just happen to be most comfortable when I am hiking trails. I took this trip as a way to reflect on my life."

"How long *have* you been hiking trails?" Zach said judgmentally.

"That's not polite," instructed Pastor Mike.

"Oh, that's okay," said Noah, "I probably look like quite a sight, like I'm some kind of street person with no resources. I've been hiking for quite some time and I'm not the prettiest thing to look at. Actually, I'm halfway through California. I started at the Mexican border and'll end in Canada. I have a few more months left to go."

"A few months?" Zach asked.

"Yep. The trail I'm following is called the Pacific Crest Trail and it goes from the southern border of the United States in California to the northern border ending at Canada. It's quite a journey. . . not too many people can make it. But with the grace of God, I'll make it this time—this is my second attempt."

"Are you a Christian?" inquired Mark.

"Yes I am," said Noah emphatically, "I found the Lord a few years ago and I wish now that I had found Him sooner. I believe that this is why I'll make it all the way this time. The last time I tried this He was not my guide."

"How do you get supplies and food, sir?" asked Weber.

"Wow, you are very polite, thank you. That's a good question," said Noah. "There's a stop in Tuolumne Meadows—that's where I'll pick up my supplies."

"It looks like you're going to need shoes," said Quinton, staring at Noah's feet. "Do you go through a lot of shoes on a trip like this one?"

"You young men have very interesting questions," said Noah with a little laugh. "I'll go through two or three pairs of footwear."

Phil asked, obviously curious, "You said that you tried this trip once before."

"Yes," responded Noah. "I tried and failed because I didn't plan properly and I had the wrong guide. This time I have the right Guide," he explained as he pointed upward, "and I spent a year planning ahead. Whatever I need is already waiting for me at predetermined destinations (shoes, food, etc. . .) usually at post offices. The next post office stop is at Yosemite Mountaineering in Tuolumne Meadows."

"Hey, that's where we started from!" exclaimed Weber as he bumped Quinton's drink, almost spilling it.

"Weber!" yelled Quinton, "Be careful!"

"Weber?" said Noah, "There's a place called Weber Lake approximately one mile directly north through the woods and over a ridge. There's no trail from where we are now, but there is one back down the trail from where you came."

"That's okay," said Phil as he cleaned up from lunch. "We need to keep going—we have people waiting for us to take us back home at the end of this hike. Our timetable is strict."

"Well," said Noah, "you have some mighty pretty country to see this time of year. Based on the fact that you're on this particular trail, I assume you're following the trail that leads through Inyo. Let me tell you folks to be careful when you get there, the trails aren't marked well and the bears can be a problem. Oh, and be real careful around the Thousand Island Lake area. People have been known to have things happen to them around there. Even the Native American Indians have a word for it. They call it *Jamlo Awing*; that means Devil's Play."

"Native Indians? Out here?" asked Quinton.

"Sure. They're called the Miwoks. Don't worry, they're not the kind that scalp you," laughed Noah.

"Devil's Play," pondered Dolton aloud. "What kinds of things happen and weren't you concerned about that at all?"

"Well, to answer the first part of your question, weird things happen although I haven't heard of anything unworldly, if that's what you're getting at. The answer to the second part of your question is no. I travel with the Lord and He offers all the protection that I need. There is never reason to be afraid when you walk with God."

After Noah finished his meal he went to each of the boys and shook their hands and told them to be safe, and to enjoy the hike. Noah then went to Pastor Mike and Phil and shook their hands, "Thank you for letting me share the midday meal with you. Take care, be safe and take care of these young men; the trail is a little harder from here on. Go with God, my brothers."

"Thank you, Noah, it's been a blessing meeting you," said Phil still shaking his hand.

Pastor Mike said quickly, "Would you like to pray with us before you go?"

With a big smile, Noah said, "Can't pass up an opportunity to pray."

"Gather 'round, we're going to pray before we start off again." They assembled into a circle and joined hands. "Dearest Father, among the blessings You have afforded us thus far on our journey, You have seen fit to bless us with another in the fellowship with our brother in Christ, Noah Kinkade. We thank You for crossing our paths and allowing us the opportunity to see that You are everywhere. Keep our new friend safe on his journey and continue to bless his life with the wonders that are only You. If it is Your will, bring him back to us after a time so that we can, once again, share a meal in Your name and bless You together with one another. Watch over our group and see us safe to our destination tonight. Thank You for the wonders that You have given us so far. Truly You are the creator of all that is good and beautiful. We ask all of this in Your Son's most holy and precious name, Jesus Christ. Amen."

After the prayer Noah slipped on his pack, put a walking stick in each hand and started to leave when Pastor Mike stopped him. "Noah, this may be a silly question, but do you have a Bible with you?"

"I did, but it was ruined at Jamlo Awing," said Noah.

Pastor Mike reached into his pack and grabbed his Bible from a pouch and handed it to Noah. "Here, take this Bible," said Pastor Mike, "and if you're ever in our area please stop and stay, our information is on the inside cover."

Unspoken joy consumed him and Noah's eyes glistened as he took the Bible. He slipped it into the pocket of his cargo shorts. "I can't thank you all enough for your time, the meal and your company. May God bless you all," and with that Noah was off, raising an arm with a thumbs up he walked away up the trail in the direction from which they had just come.

"Boy, oh boy," said Weber, "that was cool."

"Yeah," said Quinton as the other boys nodded their heads, still watching Noah walking up the trail.

"Okay, let's get our packs on," said Phil, "we have some serious ground to cover before dark."

After a few minutes they were all geared up. "Okay," Phil said, "Grab your walking poles and let's be off." Phil led them down the trail from which Noah came. It was wider so the group started to walk side by side again. They talked about Noah. "I can't believe how cool he was. He was so interesting," said Mark.

Zach confessed, "I thought that he was just looking for a handout, but man, was I wrong. I judged him without knowing him first."

"Yeah, I did too," said Dolton. "He turned out to be a cool guy. He sure knew a lot about hiking. . . and to top it all off, he's a Christian."

"Do you think that we'll ever see him again?" asked Quinton.

"I hope so," said Pastor Mike, "he knows how to find us."

<{{}}><

Hmm. . .thought Stanley as he looked at his watch. I'm sure they've already stopped for lunch. It's not like Weber not to check in. I'm sure he's having a good time but let's just see what he's up to. Stanley rolled his chair over to his computer. He pulled up the satellite link and connected to the tracking program. He typed in the tracker ID and waited for the program to locate it. He brought up the visual and then zoomed in on the group. *There he is. They're right on schedule. . . but, no e-mail. He must have had an interesting morning if he forgot to send an e-mail. Who's that man – I don't recognize him. Must be another hiker they decided to have lunch with. As long as Web's okay, I guess.* He watched them a little longer and when they finished lunch and held hands in a circle to pray he decided to sever the link just in case someone was monitoring what he was doing. *I'm glad I decided to use the visual tracking – it's good to actually see that Web is okay,* Stanley concluded. *I better get back to work.*

<{{}}><

The hike was no less beautiful than the meadow they had viewed just prior to lunch. They all commented on how great the air smelled, how colorful the trees and sky were and many other observations about the flora and fauna they encountered. After a while, though, Phil noticed that the group behind him was slowing down and he had to wait for them to catch up. Weber was walking with a bit of a limp; Buck, Dolton, Zach, and Mark walked like they had rocks in their shoes. Phil continued on and then turned to check the group again and took a second glance to confirm what he saw and he stopped the group.

"All right," said Phil, "I guess I know who changed their socks and who didn't."

Weber spoke up, "Sir, I changed my socks but my left foot still hurts."

"The five of you take off your boots." Weber had his off first so Phil and Pastor Mike started with him. "It looks like you haven't been keeping them tied tight enough so we're going to apply this moleskin; it should help." After they got the moleskin applied to Weber, Phil and Pastor looked at Mark, Dolton, Zach and Buck's feet.

"You need to start watching out for your feet," said Phil sternly, "they are what will be getting you out of here." Mike said, "If you don't start taking care of them we'll have a serious problem," making certain to talk loud enough so everyone could hear. Phil applied moleskin and had them put on fresh socks and told them wait to put on their boots while they rested for a few minutes.

The area where they stopped to rest had large rocks at the side of the trail under the canopy of pine trees. After the ailing feet were attended to, Pastor Mike walked to the other side of the trail and sat on rock by himself. Mark came over after putting on his boots and sat next to him.

"Dad," said Mark, "I'm sorry about my feet, I forgot cuz I was so interested in Noah."

"I understand," replied Mike, "I'm not upset about that, I was just thinking about your mom and how proud she would have been of you and the way you have turned out." Mark was shocked to hear his dad talk to him about his mom; he didn't know what to say. In all the years he was growing up his dad never initiated talk about his mother. He looked at his son with great pride.

Mark looked into his Dad's eyes and said gently, "Dad, I know you miss her, and I know that it's been hard on you raising me all by yourself. But Mom is in Heaven and I know she's looking down and I'm sure that she is as proud of you as you say she is of me."

Mike reached over to Mark and pulled him close, tightly embracing him as only a father hugs a son. "You have no idea how much like her you are," whispered Mike. Mark had heard his father's voice break before when he talked about her but never like this. He couldn't help but be moved too.

The others were staring when Phil cleared his throat just loud enough so that only the onlookers could hear. He gave them all a look and a shake of the head indicating the need for some privacy. They moved in the other direction and left the two alone.

After a time Mike released Mark and took him by the shoulders and faced him, "Mark, I know that I have avoided talking about your mother all these years and for some reason God has given me the strength at last and has placed it in my heart to let you know that whenever you are ready I'll tell you anything you want to know about her. I just ask that you be patient with me, I can't guarantee that I won't get emotional. I loved her very much and was never prepared to go on in life without her. You remind me so much of her, your patience, your love and compassion and sense of humor. Mostly though, it's your eyes. When your mother looked at me she looked past the physical being and went right to my soul. You have that same way about you and it touches me every time you do it."

Mark stared at his father, surprised to hear him say these words and touched that his father shared his feelings with him at last. He felt the tears of love forming in his own eyes and hugged him hard and quietly said, "Thank you."

They sat in their embrace for a while and then looked at each other and started to laugh. "I love you, Dad," Mark said. "I love you, Mark," replied Mike. They started to dry their tears and noticed the rest of the group was trying to look like they weren't watching or listening. Pastor started to apologize, but Phil cut him off, "In a couple of minutes we should be pressing on," he told the group with a smile and wink to Pastor. Everyone sat quietly in awkward silence.

"Okay," said Phil after a few minutes, "boots tied properly, everyone!" He waited until they were ready. "Okay, grab your walking poles and let's go."

The boys moaned when they got up but they donned their packs and started walking. It was hard to walk with the extra weight and their feet hurting but they didn't complain. They agreed that they would all change their socks from now on though. Pastor Mike passed up the boys to talk with Phil. "Thank you for handling the boys the way you did."

"No thanks necessary," said Phil, "it's you I should thank."

"I don't understand," said Pastor.

"Well," said Phil, "I have a promise to keep to someone and I need to take care of it as soon as possible. When you talked to Mark the way you did it confirmed that now is the time, but I just don't know how."

"I'm sure that when the time is right the Spirit will guide you," said Pastor. "You've remained in prayer about it this long; I doubt the Lord will abandon you now in your hour of need."

"I know that, I guess I'm a little nervous."

"Nervous?" teased Pastor, "Not the Phil I know." At that Pastor let Phil walk ahead and he slowly dropped back to the back of the line checking each of the boys as they passed him.

The trail started to level off, rolling softly up and down, twisting in and out between pine trees. From time to time a squirrel or two would pop its head up to see what all the commotion was. Buck and Dolton came up alongside Mark and asked if he was okay. Mark told them that he would talk to them later. He wasn't quite ready to talk about it yet. Quinton, who was usually hitting himself with his walking stick, was now walking normally. He was deep in thought about their last stop and the problem that his friends were having with their feet. He was trying to remember something that he had read not too long ago about cures and remedies that could be found in the forest.

They had only walked an hour but because of their sore feet they had not covered a lot of distance. Phil stopped for another short break and to talk to Pastor. Phil waved Pastor up to the front and they walked away from the group. Pastor said, "Phil, I don't know how much farther we can make them go."

"Well, we need to find a place to make camp for the night as soon as possible, then," Phil said with a worried tone,

"This will put us quite a ways off our schedule. Somehow we'll have to make up the time tomorrow when their feet are feeling better. It'll be quite a push."

"I know," replied Pastor, "but these fellows have shown a lot of tenacity up till now. I have no reason to doubt that they're up for the challenge."

The men returned to find them sitting quietly, resting against their backpacks, not talking, listening to nature. Phil motioned to them and said, "Okay, let's go." They dutifully got up and only moaned when they realized the full weight of their packs and bodies on their feet.

They hiked along and soon they peaked a large rise and the trail went down very steeply. At the bottom, the trees thinned and they entered into the most beautiful meadow yet. It was kidney shaped with dark green thin-bladed grass about six inches tall moving with the wind and little pink and white flowers that looked like polka dots scattered throughout the meadow. The trees that surrounded the meadow were varied, giving the effect of two separate sections. There were pine trees on the side that they had just come through, and on the other side was a mixture of pine and oak trees. A winding stream running through finished the picture, gave it a serene, calm feeling.

The group stared at the beautiful site. "We find ourselves stopped and staring again at the wonders of our Lord," Phil said. "Thank You, Father, this is perfect." Phil turned and began scouting out a campsite. He stopped at a clearing next to the stream for cooking that was adjacent to a smaller clearing next to it that was just right to set up the tents. "Okay, men, tents over there and cooking area over there," he directed. The group split up into their pairs and set up their tents in record time. Pastor and Phil set to work getting dinner started and sent the five with sore feet to the stream to fill up the water bottles and jugs. He also directed them to soak their feet in the cool stream after they collected the water. When they reached the stream Weber wandered farther down stream to put his feet into the cold water and laid back on a rock and closed his eyes in exhaustion.

Quinton's Cure

No one noticed that Quinton had disappeared. He walked around the edge of the clearing and into the wooded area where the stream entered behind the clearing. "I know it's here, I can find it," said Quinton, "I'm certain I can." He talked to himself and checked the ground around the trees. He walked quite a distance away from the others, but he was determined to do his part and kept on undaunted by the distance he needed to go to complete his task.

"There it is!" he exclaimed, "The moss, the healing moss that I read about a few months ago! I just know this will help!" Quinton quickly gathered up as much moss as he could carry and headed back to camp.

The others at the stream had finished filling all the containers and were now soaking their feet.

"Boy," said Mark, "my feet are sure sore."

Weber whimpered in agreement. Zach said, "I don't see any blisters but man my toes are killing me."

"Me too," said Dolton, "these dogs are barking."

That comment made Buck laugh, which started the others laughing too. A call from the cooking area made them pull their feet out, put their boots on, and take the water back. They came limping into the camp, set the water down, and sat down around the cooking area.

Pastor looked around and asked, "Where's Quinton?"

"We thought he was here with you," said Buck.

"No," said Phil, "we thought he had gone with you." For a split second there was panic and everyone started to get up to look for Quinton. Weber pointed and said, "Well, there he is!"

They turned to see Quinton coming into camp with his arms full of something. He entered the cooking area and said with a smile, "I found it!"

"Found what?" said Pastor looking a little confused.

"The moss," replied Quinton.

"Uhh, what do we need moss for, Quinton?" inquired Phil.

"I read about this moss when I was doing a report a couple of months ago. It's found in this mountain range, and was used by the Indians to cure sores and bruising. So I went to get some for your feet," he said directing the last sentence to the injured as he placed the moss down next to the cooking area.

Phil said, "You know I've heard about these healing practices myself, I'm sure this will be helpful. But that doesn't excuse the fact that you went off into the forest alone. You know the rules."

Quinton hung his head and his wrist began hitting his hip again, "I won't do it again, I'm sorry."

Just then the water began to boil and Phil turned around and continued the food preparation. For dinner that night, there was chili with meat, rice, bread, and juice. The hungry hikers looked on as Phil cooked. They were, again, like vultures that hadn't eaten in weeks, hovering as the food cooked.

No sooner was the food ready than Pastor and Phil stood up with their thumbs in the air, but as they looked back the rest of group was sitting there with thumbs already raised high. They all started laughing and Phil said he would say the blessing. "Dear Father, You have once again led us to a place of beauty to rest. Please bless this food to nourish our bodies. Heal the injured and replenish our energy this evening so we may sleep in the quiet knowledge that you are watching over us and guiding every step. We ask this through Jesus Christ. Amen."

As soon as the "amen" was out of Phil's mouth they began gobbling up their food. The only sound that could be heard was the scraping of utensils against the plates.

As Mark finished shoveling in the last forkful of chili, he said with a mouth half-full of food, "That was great. What's for dessert?"

Pastor stared at Mark in disbelief. Phil smiled and reached into one of the food bags and brought out a trail bar and tossed it to Mark in one motion. Zach, Dolton, Buck, and Quinton were watching this and said in unison, "Can I have one, too?" Phil again reached back into the pack pulled out five more bars and threw one to each of them. As he started to throw one to Weber he put up his hand and said, "No thank you sir, I'm getting full." Phil looked at Pastor and with a head nod inquired if he wanted one. Pastor shook his head no and kept eating. Phil slipped the bar into his pocket and continued to eat his dinner.

When everyone had finished eating they started to clean up. Phil glanced at Quinton, who just happened to be looking in Phil's direction, and said with a nod of his head, "Come here, Quinton, tell me about your moss remedy." Quinton smiled, jumped up, and proudly set himself down by Phil. As they finished their dinner dishes, the rest of the group sat around or propped themselves on large boulder-size rocks and listened to Quinton.

"Well," Quinton began, "I had to do a paper for history a couple of months ago and I didn't want to do just any old report, so I started to research California Indians. There are a lot of them, so I thought I needed to do something different. Something that maybe even the teacher wasn't knowledgeable about. I like it when I know more than the teacher. Anyway, I found out about tribal Indians called the Miwoks. I was really surprised when Noah mentioned them this afternoon. I didn't know that there were others out there who even knew they existed. They are such a small band of Indians."

"Focus, Quinton," Phil said. "Get to the part about the moss."

"Oh, yeah. Well, I researched the Miwoks and was most interested to find that they had knowledge about natural healing. Most Indians do, but they had knowledge about common items found here in California. So I researched a little more and found out all sorts of common vegetation that heals, like this moss. It's called sphagnum moss. It's usually found at the base of short trees. This is different from other mosses because of the way it processes the oxygen from the air and nutrients from the ground. It usually shows up in clean soil near where heather is.

"Those flowers in the meadow are heather, so when I remembered that they grow close to each other I thought I could find some and help you guys with your feet. All you need to do is wrap them up in the moss for the night and you should be fine by morning. I know lots about healing plants and stuff. It's kind of a hobby."

"Man, you've gotta be the smartest person I know," said Zach.

"So, did you get a A on your report?" asked Buck.

"He gets A's on all of his reports, he's a brainiac," interjected Dolton before Quinton could respond.

"Maybe we should call him 'Doctor'," said Mark. Recognizing that Quinton was finished, Phil stood up and paced for a while; he stopped in front of Pastor. "You know," he stroked his beard with one hand with the other tucked under his arm, "this just might work. We'll give it a try."

"Cool!" said Zach.

"Great, I need all the help I can get," said Dolton. Quinton was beaming, sitting tall with a big smile on his face.

"Okay men, take off your shoes and get ready for Dr. Quinton's miracle cure," ordered Phil.

Pastor collected some tee shirts from each of the boys' packs to help hold the moss. One by one Quinton and Phil applied moss and a tee shirt wrap to their ailing feet.

"How are we supposed get to our tent?" asked Zach.

"Yeah," said Dolton, "we can't fly."

Quinton instructed, "It's okay to walk on the moss, by walking on it it'll juice up."

"Juice up," said Weber and Mark together, "that's gross."

"Okay," said Pastor, "everyone is exhausted and we all need our rest, so let's get to bed."

Pastor, Phil, and Quinton walked over to the tent area and turned around to watch the others make their way to their tents. They hobbled at first; the moss made squishy noises when they first walked on it, which made them make funny expressions with every step. They couldn't help but laugh at the funny sight, which in turn made the hobblers laugh, too. Finally everyone made it to their tents and the lights went out. The forest sounds and the snoring were the only things that could be heard.

<{()}><

"Stan, I didn't hear from Weber all day today. Did you?" inquired Karen.

"No, but I looked in on him this afternoon. Would you please pass the carrots?" he replied.

"You looked in on him?" she asked.

"Yes. Thanks. While I was packing Web's stuff for the trip I used a tracking device I got from The Company. I planted it in his computer. So, this afternoon, when I didn't get an e-mail from him, I used the satellite tracking program, located his signal, and saw him having lunch. He's fine, Karen, don't worry," he explained as he helped himself to the carrots.

"You planted a tracking device on him?" she inquired further.

"Sure, this was his first trip and I wanted to make sure I could keep an eye on him."

"Well, then, great minds think alike," she commented.

"What do you mean?" he asked, now curious.

"I planted a tracking device on his glasses before he left," she informed him.

"You did? Why you little vixen," he said playfully. "You haven't lost your touch."

Third Morning – Giant Forest

Morning came and Pastor and Phil were up about thirty minutes before everyone else and were almost through their first cup of coffee, talking about the trip when Buck, Zach, and Weber strolled into the eating area.

"Morning," they said, one by one as they hobbled in. With a frown on his face Zach asked, "How long do we keep this stuff on our feet?"

With a chuckle Phil said, "You can take it off and we'll see what they look like."

Dolton came hobbling in, sat down next to Zach, and started to say good morning when just behind him came Mark. He was mad and holding something in his hand and said, obviously irritated, "Here Dolton!" and threw the thing he was holding at Dolton. "Nice try but the snake thing won't work twice."

Dolton jumped as the snake bounced on his lap and landed on the ground. Everyone stood up and moved back as they saw the snake. Phil reached out and grabbed one of the walking poles and gave it a poke. It didn't move; he waited another moment and bent over slowly and picked it up and looked at it.

"Well, it's dead, thank goodness," said Phil, holding the snake as it drooped limply over his hand.

No one spoke and all eyes turned to Mark. He turned white at the announcement that this had been a real snake, then his eyes rolled back and he passed out. Dolton roared with laughter and almost fell to the ground himself. Pastor and Phil ran over to attend to Mark and revive him.

The rest of them watched the scene and tried hard not to laugh. Zach, who was closest to Pastor and Mark, reached over and took a bottle of water and dumped it onto Mark's face and he came to. Mark sat up almost hitting Pastor Mike's head, and they all laughed even harder.

"It's okay, Mark," said Pastor, "You're okay." He helped him to his feet and sat him on a large rock.

"The snake," said Mark fearfully, "it was real!"

Phil tried not laugh, "You must have smothered it last night."

Dolton said between laughs, "I swear I didn't put that in your sleeping bag."

"Yeah, I know now," Mark replied weakly.

"You should have seen your face," laughed Weber. "Your face was whiter than my sheets," laughed Buck.

"Yeah, man, I almost soiled myself," roared Dolton. With that even Mark and Mike began laughing and the color finally began returning to Mark's face.

Phil took the snake out of the area and they finally started to settle down. Quinton said curiously, "Let's see how the treatment went."

Zach had been halfway through the removal of his wrappings when the commotion started and now he finished the unveiling. "You know," said Zach, "I just realized that my feet didn't hurt when I got up today."

"Neither did mine," said Dolton still removing his foot packs.

Zach stood up, looked at Quinton, and said with surprise, "Man, my feet feel great! And look, no sores!"

The others were now looking at their feet in amazement; they were healed the same as Zach's. Phil, who was sitting next to Weber, grabbed one of his feet and started inspecting it; sure enough there were no signs that there had been anything wrong. The treatment worked!

"Doctor Q's miracle cure really worked!" shouted Dolton in surprise as he stared at his feet.

Zach smiled as he stared into Quinton's eyes – no one knew what to expect when Zach smiled because he did it so seldom but he said, "Thanks, Doc." Quinton was so surprised by his smile that he didn't know what to do or say, but after a seconds of staring at Zach he understood that Zach's smile was an expression of acceptance and all he could do was smile back.

Mark, Dolton, Buck, and Weber all started chanting, "Doc, Doc." Phil and Pastor Mike both laughed and let the boys cheer on, "Doc, Doc."

After a minute Phil got up and put his hand on Quinton's shoulder and said "Good job. Okay, it's time to get breakfast going. Go down to the stream and wash that stuff off your feet, wash your old socks and put your new ones on. I'm sure I don't have to remind anyone about that anymore."

They were all in agreement about that and everyone jumped up to get going. The oatmeal was ready before they got back so they all helped themselves to the morning meal. "Hey, who's praying this morning?" asked Dolton.

"I'll take care of that this morning," said Zach.

"Really?" asked Pastor, a little surprised.

"Sure. Okay, you wart hogs, settle down so we can pray. Father, thanks for the food we'll be eating here this morning. And thanks for the cure you sent us for our feet last night through Doc. Amen."

Dolton, who was the most skeptical about the remedy, could not believe how well it worked and kept feeling his feet. Weber kept standing up and sitting down, making sure his feet were all right. Mark and Buck were yawning between bites of their oatmeal. About halfway through breakfast, Dolton, who was sitting next to Mark, picked up a piece of rope and wiggled it in Mark's lap and yelled, "SNAKE!" Mark jumped up and flew off the rock and dumped his oatmeal on Phil. Dolton roared with laughter again along with the other boys.

Phil shook his head, obviously displeased and said, "Think that's funny, do you Dolton? I think for that little stunt you can do everyone's dishes."

Dolton calmed down and said, "Yes sir."

Pastor said softly, "I think you owe somebody an apology."

Dolton turned to Phil with no smile on his face and said, "I am sorry, Mr. Phil," and then turned to Mark saying with half a smile, "I apologize."

Mark just stood staring at Dolton for a second and then smiled, "You know that there is a payback coming." Dolton grinned largely, holding back a laugh.

While Dolton did dishes the rest of the group packed up the rest of the gear. Mark, Buck, Zach and Quinton took the water bottles to the stream to be filled and Weber set up to send an e-mail. Pastor and Phil waited for Dolton to finish dishes that needed to be packed.

Dear Mom and Dad,

Sorry I didn't write yesterday but we had a very busy and exciting day. I made it over the switchbacks okay, but on the way down my shoes were bothering me so the rest of the hike that day was a little uncomfortable. Quinton found some healing moss that some of us wore to bed last night. When we woke up our feet were all healed. It was pretty amazing. Quinton knows a lot about healing. He really seemed to enjoy that part of the trip yesterday. Oh, I almost forgot. We met another hiker yesterday just before lunch. His name is Noah Kinkade. He was a very interesting man. He is hiking the Pacific Trail, I think that's what he called it. It goes from the southern border of California to the northern border of Washington. He has already been hiking over a month and has a couple more to go! It was amazing to hear his stories. And get this, he is a Christian too! What are the odds that you would hike in the wilderness and meet up with another Christian? We did okay last night, but this morning Mark found a live snake in his bag. He thought it was another joke that Dolton was playing. Yesterday morning Dolton put a rubber snake in Mark's bag and Mark almost fainted. Well, this morning a real snake made its way into Mark's bag and died in the night. When Mark found out it was a real snake he fainted. I never laughed so hard in my life. It probably wasn't nice of me to do that but it was so funny. We all laughed about it later so I know that Mark's all right.

The scenery out here is so incredibly beautiful I don't think that I can describe it with words. Quinton, who we are calling Doc, is taking a lot of pictures. When you see them, I sure hope you can tell how great it has been so far. Well, Dolton is almost done with the dishes so we'll be pushing on soon. I'll e-mail you again later. Hope I can still get a signal later.

Love you, Weber.

<{}}><

Dolton, Pastor and Phil were finishing up just as everyone was wandering back. "Okay," said Phil, "let's mount up."

As the group climbed into their packs there were a few moans. "Does this feel heavier?" asked Mark.

"Yeah, I think so," said Buck.

"It feels about the same to me," said Zach undaunted.

Pastor said with a laugh, "They're actually getting lighter; it doesn't feel like it though."

"Everyone in their pack?" asked Phil, "Make sure you have them adjusted and your boots are tied properly, we don't want another problem like yesterday." He waited until everyone was ready. "Okay, grab your walking pole and let's be off."

It was a beautiful morning; the sky was a gorgeous baby blue with small fluffy white clouds floating sparsely in the sky. The mountains in the background were a hazy purple as the morning mist blurred the detail. There was a slight breeze that carried the morning freshness with it and kept the air cool. The group crossed the small stream and followed the dirt trail through the grass to the trees on the other side of the meadow. Just inside the woods the trail turned and followed the edge of the meadow paralleling the stream. The hikers adjusted their gear as they tried to get comfortable in their packs again after the long hike the day before.

As they rounded a large pine tree the trail brought them back to the stream where Phil stopped the group. "Wow! Look at that!" said Pastor. Up ahead was a six-foot cascading waterfall that filled a small pool before running off downhill. The area was surrounded by bushes, small flowers, and red berries. The morning sun peeked through the pine and glistened off the waterfall highlighting the spray as it hit the pool. There were dozens of little rainbows; it was as though they had stepped into a dream.

Phil walked over to the bushes and plucked a handful of berries and returned, handing each person a few. "Here, wash these off with some of your drinking water," he said. They washed off their berries and popped them into their mouths.

"Mmm, these are good," said Quinton.

"Yeah," said Mark, "better than anything I've tasted from the store."

"Are these okay to eat?" asked Weber as he stopped chewing.

"Yes," said Phil, "These are wild raspberries."

Quinton pulled out his camera and shot a few pictures.

"Let's go," said Phil after Quinton was done and he started off. Zach reached out as he passed the bushes and picked as many berries as he could get. The trail and the stream forked away from each other and the trail started to gradually head uphill. The trees were getting thicker, blocking the daylight from the forest floor.

Buck, Dolton, Mark, and Zach were talking about Doc when Weber dropped back to join the conversation. "Yeah, ole Doc really saved us back there," said Mark. The others agreed. Weber chimed in, "I didn't realize he knew that much about horticulture."

"Horty whaty?" ask Zach.

With a chuckle Weber replied, "It's knowledge about plants and trees."

"Oh," said Zach, "do you know about this stuff?" The others looked at him as they walked and waited for him to answer.

"No, but I can look it up when I need to reference it," said Weber.

"I didn't realize how much I didn't know until this trip," said Dolton. The others agreed saying, "I know what you mean."

"Hey Doc!" called Zach, "Whatcha walking so fast for? Slow down a bit."

"Has anyone noticed that he isn't hitting himself this morning?" noticed Mark.

"Yeah, that's true," said Dolton.

"Hey, yeah," agreed Buck, "I wonder why."

"Hey guys, what's going on?" asked Quinton as the others caught up with him. Just then Zach looked up the trail at Phil.

"What's bugging him?" he wondered aloud. They picked up their pace and caught up with him.

"Everything okay, Mr. Phil?" Zach asked.

"I'm getting worried because I haven't seen a trail marker in quite a while. Let's stop to check the map and compass." They stopped and Phil confirmed that they were going in the right direction. "I'm pretty sure we're on the trail so let's go a little further," said Phil, "and keep your eyes peeled."

It wasn't long before they spotted the trail marker; the heavily dappled sunlight made the markers hard to see. Phil breathed a sigh of relief. After another hour of hiking, the trail opened up into an area where the trees started to thin and the sun shone through. The warmth of the sun felt good and they found themselves looking up, drinking it in as they walked.

"You know," said Weber, "that area back there was kind of spooky."

"Yeah," said Buck, "it reminded me of Pastor's story."

Mark joked, "I was waiting to see the cabin." Just then a loud screech sounded right over their heads and they jumped saying, "What was that?"

Pastor, who had been following close enough to hear their conversation said, "It's okay, it was just a bird."

"Man, what kind of bird makes a sound like that?" asked Buck.

"Keep your eyes sharp and you'll probably find out," replied Pastor. As they continued hiking they nervously scanned the forest from side to side. They heard the same loud screech several more times but never did see the bird. After about an hour of watching the forest Phil blurted out, "There it is!" They flinched and ducked. "There it is," he said again, referring to the trail marker.

Pastor laughed at the sight and Phil turned around to see what was going on. The young men were embarrassed and looked away but Pastor was still smiling.

The forest continued to thin and the trail became clearer, ascending more than descending. As they crested another ridge and came out of the trees, a two-hundred-foot rock mountain lay before them. Phil stopped and they gathered on the ridge to view the magnificent site.

"Look," said Weber with excitement, "on that big rock about a fourth of the way up, it's a goat." They focused their eyes to get a look at it.

"No," said Phil, "it's a Big Horn Sheep and, look, it has a baby with it."

Quinton immediately went for his camera.

"Wow," said Zach, "look how easily it goes from rock to rock."

"Yeah, and the baby is keeping up with her," said Buck excitedly.

They stared at the sheep and Quinton got pictures until they heard Pastor say, "Whoa!" They turned to see what made him say that. Their eyes followed the trail from the top of the ridge down a steep rocky hill to a flat area before the forest, the likes of which they had not encountered as of yet. "Wow!" they said in unison. From where they were standing and the angle of the ridge, the top of the trees below formed what looked like a thick forest-green carpet stretching out as far as they could see, with rocky mountains skirting the sides. Even from this angle they could tell that this part of the forest was old.

"Well, men, how are your feet?" said Phil loudly. "Is everyone ready?" Still in awe, they nodded their heads slowly up and down. So Phil set out and led them down the hill. No one spoke as they headed down the steep, slippery trail. They all had trouble keeping their feet firmly planted. At one point Weber slid right past Zach, who was able to catch him just before he landed face first on the small sharp rocks covering the trail. Weber was not the only one who had trouble. Mark's foot slipped on a rock, and if not for his dad grabbing his pack, he might have gone off the trail and into jagged rocks alongside the path. They slowed the pace even further coming down off the ridge. Once they reached the bottom, Phil called for lunch break.

The bottom of the hill was vastly different than the top. It was similar to the stop at the treeline near the glacier, in that the base of the hill was covered with decomposed granite, except the rocks were small instead of large and there was a gradual slope to the trees instead of a leveling out. The trees were extremely tall and it was as though a line had been drawn, with rock on one side and trees on the other and neither one crossed the line.

A fallen tree just off the trail is where Phil took the group to set up for lunch. They climbed out of their packs and started setting up the food. The talk among everyone was not about the sheep or the forest before that, but the descent they had just made and how dangerous going up it would be. "I don't know how Noah does this by himself," said Dolton remembering their new friend's adventures.

"That's right," said Weber, "he's all alone."

Pastor smiled and said, "He's not alone. Don't you remember he said this time he walks with the Lord?"

"That's right," said Quinton, "he said that the first time that he didn't and he failed, and he knew that this time he would make it."

"Remember that faith can move mountains and your trust in that faith has a protection that comes with it," said Phil. "Believe and have faith in the Lord and He walks with you."

"Amen to that! Thank you Phil," said Pastor. It gave Mike a warm feeling to know that his work with this community was fruitful. It was some time ago when he had come to Jamestown to start his ministry. He remembered how happy he was to find that a building had been donated to start the church. The James family owned an old one-room building sitting on a piece of property at the edge of town. It had been abandoned for quite some time until he was led to it. It was originally the James' family store. When they built their new grocery market downtown some years back they donated the old wood building to the church until funds could be raised for a proper church. It stood abandoned for a while until he arrived. With hard work and some tender loving care, he changed it into a place to worship. Over the years, the church grew to three buildings. The original church building was now the Youth Hall. He knew it was wrong but he was proud of how the openness and simplicity of the hall lent itself perfectly to the various occasions of the church and community and had remained unchanged since its conversion.

Mark was just a baby then. Without the help of the towns-people, he never would have been able to get the church started. He had to do most of the work himself because funds were low. Mike remembered how grateful he was to his father for teaching him carpentry when he was young. *I wish I could have done the same for my son,* he found himself thinking. *No time to for regrets, he has turned out to be a fine young man. Sara would have been proud.*

<{{}}><

Let's see what they're up to this morning, thought Stanley. He pulled up the tracking program and found them at the bottom of a very steep incline at a treeline of a forested area that looked very thick and lush. *I can't imagine Weber climbing that*, he pondered. *He looks well enough, again, nothing to worry about. Karen will be happy to know he's fine.*

There was a knock on his door. "Mr. Deerfield?" the voice said.

"Yes," he replied.

"You're needed in cryptography."

"Thank you, I'm on my way." He shut the program down and thought to himself, *I'll check in on you later, son.*

In an office on one of the top floors of The Company there was a message being delivered. A man dressed in a black suit knocked on the door and walked in without waiting for a response to his knock. He slipped a piece of paper in front of the man sitting behind the desk at the far end of the room, turned around and left as quickly as he entered, making no sound except the opening and closing of the door. The man behind the desk read the note. It said, "PSAT2302 accessed 13:12 ID C19S358D49 at 8266 Elv 37 18 42.84 N by 118 57 40.10 W in SE dir." He put the note to the side and continued what he was doing prior to the interruption.

<{{}}><

The view from the bottom, looking up at the ridge they had just hiked down and the mountain behind it, was fantastic. The sunshine made it look like it had three or four colors of purple with spots of light gray where large shards of rock protruded out of the side. They were rather quiet as they ate their lunch and gazed at the beauty around them.

Most of them had finished eating, and were either changing their socks or relaxing enjoying the view, when a fast moving bird dove over their heads from the trees and into the rocks alongside the trail from where they had come.

"Whoa!" they yelled as they all ducked. "What is that?!" exclaimed Buck.

"It looked like a falcon," said Zach. Everyone turned and looked at him in disbelief.

Zach, aware that they were staring at him, said in an even tone, "I've seen one on TV."

The falcon came out of the rocks with its prey in its talons and took flight, heading back over the forest and out of sight. At this Phil said, "We should be going too." So they cleaned up and packed their things and climbed into their packs. With the group standing ready, Phil said, "Poles in hand, packs on, okay, let's go." And back to the trail they went.

The transition into the forest was like stepping through a doorway into a different world. The pine trees were like giants at least three hundred feet tall and the grass and shrubbery also seemed to be giants themselves. The trail that previously could support two people had now narrowed, allowing only one person at a time to pass. Tall grass and shrubs lined the trail, making it hard for the hikers to walk without getting their packs caught up in it.

"I know I'm the littlest one on this trip but I *really* feel like a shrimp in here," said Weber.

"Don't worry, little man. I'm feeling a little small compared to these plants, too," said Zach, trying to comfort him. The pine trees were spread just far enough apart that a few rays of the sun could be seen in the moist air. The long shadows gave the tall grass and shrubbery an ominous look as though something was there, just out of view, watching them.

"I don't know if I like this," said Weber in a nervous tone of voice.

"Yeah, I feel like we're being watched," said Quinton.

"Me too," said Mark. Buck nodded in agreement.

Shortly into their hike a large tree, about the width of a train, had fallen along the path blocking easy access. Phil stopped, waited for everyone to catch up, and then climbed up atop the tree. He then crawled to the other side and slid off. "Okay," shouted Phil to the group, "smallest first and Pastor last."

As they went over, each one stopped or hesitated on the top. From there they could see the vastness of the forest over the top of the grass and shrubberies. It was immense. On the hike, up till now, the tree trunks in the forests they hiked through may have been the width of two people, but here the entire group could stand by one tree trunk and in that picture there would only be one tree. This forest gave everyone the feeling that they had shrunk.

When Dolton got to the top of the fallen tree, he said, "Man, now I know what it's like to be an ant."

When it was Quinton's turn to cross he knelt atop the tree, took three pictures and mumbled, "These aren't going to do." He pointed the camera down and took two pictures of the group on the ground next to the fallen tree.

"Come on," yelled Zach and Dolton.

"You're not working for a hiking magazine," added Dolton.

After they all had come over the tree, they continued their hike. It wasn't long before they came across another tree lying across the path. It was longer and higher than the last one. The group stopped and Phil instructed the group. "Okay, get your packs off. We're going under."

It was quicker to get everyone and the gear under this tree than to go over it, though some of the boys didn't like it. It was evident that nothing had passed that way in quite some time. Their faces broke through some spider webs, which surprised and startled them.

"Aww gross! I think I ate a bug," coughed Dolton.

After climbing back into their packs, they were off and moving. They walked for about a quarter of a mile when they came across a tree standing next to the trail that looked like it had been hit by lighting. The tree was split straight down the middle with burn marks on both sides and, strangely enough, that didn't kill it. Both parts of the tree were still alive and green. Quinton said, "Let me take a picture." There was a stump close by, so he gathered the group and positioned the camera on the stump, put the camera on timer, and got the shot. "This is like something out of a movie. No one will believe it!" he mused.

Hiking the trail was getting harder; the shrubs closed in tighter and hung up on some of their packs. Weber seemed to get hung up more than the others and Zach had to keep untangling him. They fought shrubs that varied from five to six feet tall for quite a while, and then the trail finally opened up and a ditch appeared. They were stopped again.

"Well," said Phil, turning to the group, "it looks like we have to choose. The 'log walk' over or the trail down and up. As Phil was talking, Zach walked across the log as if it were nothing. "Come on," he said, "it's no problem."

Neither Weber nor Quinton liked the thought of going across. "I think I'll go that way," said Quinton, pointing at the ditch. Weber wasn't keen on that way either and asked nervously, "Is there anything down there that bites?"

"I don't know," said Phil.

In the meantime, Mark, Dolton, and Buck had scrambled across the log and stood on the other side with Zach. "Come on, you guys," they said to the other four.

Pastor turned to Phil and said, "I'll go with these two." Phil nodded and spun around and walked casually across the log to the other edge of the ditch. Pastor said, "Let's go, boys," and Quinton started down the embankment with Weber and Pastor following.

When they reached the bottom, the grass was taller then they thought and for a while it looked like Quinton and Pastor were the only ones down there. The soil beneath their feet wrapped up over the tops of them; it was like walking on foam. The side of the ditch where the rest of the group was waiting was a little steeper but there were rocks and roots sticking out, almost like footholds, which it made it easier for them to climb up. Phil reached out his hand to help Weber and the other boys came over to help Quinton and Pastor. "Whew," said Pastor, "I am glad that's over with." Quinton and Weber agreed.

They continued on the trail, which had gradually widened but narrowed again to a two-person walkway. The trail was pretty clear, so Phil motioned for Pastor to come up so they could talk. Phil spoke quietly, "I need to talk to you about something that has been on my mind." The trail started to narrow even more so Phil let Pastor walk in front as they talked so their conversation wouldn't be overheard. Fortunately, being down in between the tall grass and shrubs, voices didn't travel well, so they were able to converse freely.

"Pastor," said Phil, "you know my history and who I am. I've been thinking. . . ."

"I know you have," replied Pastor.

"Well, you know that the terms of my promise aren't supposed come about until next year and I was thinking that waiting a year may not be the best thing to do. My instinct tells me that things are happening now and if I wait it may be too late. They have served me well in the past and I can't ignore them."

Pastor continued walking and responded, "I know. You have been gifted with discernment and insight, as well as a host of other gifts. It's important that you take everything you are in doubt about to the Lord. He's the only one who can give you clarity. Whatever you decide to do and whenever you decide to do it, I'll back you up all the way. You have been there for me during some of my darkest moments, and I couldn't call myself your friend if I didn't do the same for you."

"I can't tell you what that means to me, Mike. Thank you. I'll be taking this to our Lord, you can be sure. There are still a few issues I wanted to talk over with you though." They continued to talk as they hiked.

Dolton's Adventure

At the back of the group Dolton was having problems with his boots. He stopped and yelled to the group, "Hang on, I think my boot's come untied." He stopped and knelt down to fix it. Buck, who was the next one in front of him didn't hear him and kept on walking. Dolton looked up and saw the group still walking and thought, *I'll just tie up this boot and catch up.* But when he bent over his pack almost knocked him over. So he took it off and proceeded to fix his boot.

Pastor and Phil were still talking when they arrived at the place where the trail forked. Pastor was in the lead and the men focused on their conversation. Phil missed the fork.

Dolton finally got his boots tied and climbed back into his pack and started off after the rest of the group.

Pastor and Phil finished conversing just at the point that the trail came together at the end of the fork. Now that he realized that he should have been paying more attention, Phil turned to check the group. "How's everyone doing?" he yelled with his hands to his mouth. They were pretty spread out by now and he wanted to get a head count. "Do we still have everybody?"

From the back Buck said, "Hey! Dolton's missing, pass the word up!"

They passed the word up to Phil.

"Did anyone see him leave the trail?" yelled Phil.

"No," they all replied as they passed back the question.

"We'll just wait then," said Phil, "he's probably just lagging behind."

"How about that fork in the trail?" asked Quinton, who was still far enough behind not to see that the trail had already come together.

Phil turned to Pastor and said, "He may have taken the wrong fork. You stay here with the others and I'll take this one and either he'll catch up or. . . ." He paused a moment and reconsidered.

"I'll walk thirty minutes and come back. That gives us an hour to find him." He quickly left down the trail they had not traveled.

"Relax boys," said Pastor, "Mr. Phil will find him."

Dolton hurried down the trail calling out, "HEY GUYS, HELLO," when he came to the fork in the trail. "Oh, no," he said starting to get nervous, "which way do I go? Maybe I'll try eenny, meany, miney, moe. No, that won't work. Oh man, my mother couldn't even buy my way out of this one." As he stood there trying to figure out what to do he said a little prayer. He started to drip nervous sweat and said to himself, *well, left looks good* and he started off.

He walked the trail for a while and noticed that there were no footsteps like there were on the other trails they had hiked. He got even a little more nervous when the spider webs kept hitting his face. *I don't think spiders make webs this fast. I think I took the wrong trail. I should probably turn around and take the other trail,* he thought. But when he turned around to go the other direction he realized that he didn't know how far back to go to get to the fork. *I guess this means I'm lost. Oh man, how are they going to find me,* he worried. He stood for a while and tried to remember what Mr. Phil told him about getting lost in the woods. He was too nervous to remember what he was told and the nervousness started turning into panic.

Don't lose your cool, Dolton. Stay where you are until you can think straight. Think, you dolt! Okay, when in doubt work it out, say a prayer, and clear the air. Oh, good, I'm rhyming. Prayer can't hurt, though. He closed his eyes and prayed. *Dear Lord, clear my head and point me in the right direction.* When he opened his eyes he was surprised to find that he felt better and decided to keep going in the same direction he had been going down the path. Fifteen minutes later he saw Mr. Phil coming toward him down the path. They both ran to each other and embraced, Dolton almost kissed him he was so happy to see him. "I had to stop and tie my boots. I looked up and everyone was gone. I took the wrong path. I thought I was a goner," said Dolton, "thank God."

"Come on," said Phil, "let's get back to the others. We'll have been gone for almost an hour and I know they're worried." They both hurried off down the trail towards the others. Dolton was too shook up to talk so they hiked in silence.

As they came into view Pastor let out a "Praise God, you found him! Dolton, are you all right?"

Before Dolton could speak Phil said, "He's fine, he stopped to tie his boots and fell behind. When he arrived at the fork in the trail he took the other path. I met up with him there. He might still be a little shook up, Mike, so I think we'll rest a moment before we continue."

Pastor nodded his head in agreement. They were all trying to talk to Dolton when Pastor shuffled past. "Dolton," said Pastor, "do you need to sit?"

"No," said Dolton, still looking flushed. "I'm sorry I worried you," he said as he hung his head, "I had to use some of that faith you've been teaching us about though," and he raised his head up to look at Pastor.

"Obviously it worked. I must admit that I put a bit of faith into action, too. I am just glad you're okay," said Pastor as he patted him on the shoulder. The rest of them came up asking him if he was all right and saying, "Glad you're okay, good to have you back." Phil made his way to the front and after a few minutes said, "Okay, grab your poles and let's go," and they started off with Pastor bringing up the rear.

"So, Dolton," Zach asked, "what were you thinking when you realized you were lost?"

"Well, I didn't know I was lost until the spider webs kept hitting me in the face," he responded.

"Didn't you think it was weird that you couldn't hear us?" asked Buck.

"It's hard to hear in all this bush anyway. I just figured I'd catch up with you eventually," he explained.

"Didn't you get scared?" Weber inquired.

"Yeah, I have to admit I got a bit scared for a while. Heck, I even rhymed to myself."

"What did you say?" asked Weber.

"It's silly," said Dolton.

"Aww, c'mon. You've already admitted you were scared. How silly could it be?" encouraged Zach.

"Well," started Dolton, "I was having a little trouble thinking straight and I said to myself 'when in doubt, work it out; say a prayer and clear the air.' I didn't mean to rhyme; it just came out that way. Now I can't get it out of my head."

"When in doubt, work it out; say a prayer and clear the air. I kind of like that," said Zach to the surprise of everyone.

"Hey, Buck," ordered Zach, "You need to be in charge of Dolton's boots from now on. Make sure he has them tied up properly before we leave."

"Oh yeah," laughed Buck, "this coming from Weber's keeper."

"What am I, a monkey?" snickered Weber.

Well, they're back to normal, thought Phil and he breathed a sigh of relief.

The giant trees seemed older the deeper they got into the forest. There was mossy growth hanging from them and very little direct light got through to the forest floor. The temperature and humidity were rising and the trail continuously twisted and turned. They hiked like this for over an hour. Then without warning the trail headed straight up a steep incline. It took a long time to climb up the trail. The incline seemed to go as high as the large trees themselves and then, again without warning, they came out of the forest and climbed another ridge, this time to view the vast giant forest from the other end. Phil stopped the group and looked back on the giant forest and said, "As extraordinary as that was, I'm glad we're out of there."

"Amen," said Dolton. "If I never see that place again it'll be too soon."

Everyone laughed and said, "I hear that," and "I know *you're* right."

They turned and climbed off the ridge and headed directly into another forest. This one was not as old or dense as the one from which they just come. There were various kinds of trees and the sun could be seen to shine on the forest floor, even from this point. The trail descended slightly and wound through the trees. By now all the hikers were on the watch for the trail markers.

After another hour of hiking they arrived at an area that Phil decided looked like a good place to camp for the night. "This looks good," said Phil. "It's going to be dark soon."

Pastor held up his hand, "Shh," and everyone hushed for a moment, "Do you hear that?" he said quietly.

"It sounds like running water," said Phil quietly. Phil walked in the direction of the sound. The rest of the group dropped their packs and followed. It wasn't long before they spotted a small stream and access to it where the stream fell off a small overhang and down thirty feet to a stream that entered the forest below.

"Good job, Pastor," said Phil, "now we have water."

The site below was no less beautiful than anything they had seen so far. The forest stretched on for miles rolling up and down with large mountain peaks on both sides. Phil said firmly, "Now that's what I call a forest." They all agreed. "Okay, let's go back and set up camp," he instructed.

They dutifully returned and began getting their gear out. "Let's get the camp set up here and the cook area over there. Without a word spoken, the tents and cooking area were set up again in record time. Phil turned to Dolton, who was the closest, and handed him the water jug to fetch some water. The look on Dolton's face was one of panic; he thought for a split second that he was to go alone. Zach saw this and spoke quickly, "I'll go with you, Dolton." Buck and Mark who were a little slower on the uptake said that they would go also. The four of them gathered up the bottles and jug and wandered off to the stream.

Weber wanted to send a message and asked anxiously, "Can I go to the clearing, sir?" Before either one could remind him that he needed a buddy, Quinton said, "I'd like to go too if it's okay." Phil and Pastor both smiled and Pastor said, "Yes." The boys hurried off to get Weber's equipment and headed for the clearing.

Trouble Begins

"I think it's amazing that your computer has never lost its charge and can always seem to find a satellite connection. I understand the solar panel on your pack but I can't figure out how you can seem to get the connections whenever you want," said Quinton.

"Well," explained Weber, "since my dad was the one who set up the computer he's really the person to ask. I think that there's a program on there that finds the satellites and accesses them. I'm not really sure how that part of it works, but I'm glad it does. I'd really feel lost without my computer. It's kind of like my right arm."

"Yeah, I know what you mean. What does your dad do, anyway?" asked Quinton.

"He is a cryptographer at The Company," he replied.

"I thought only the government had cryptographers. What kinds of things does he decipher?"

"I'm not really sure, he rarely talks about work. I know he's really smart because he's the head of his department, but that's all I really know. Let me get a letter off to the folks and you can have it."

Weber finished his letter, the longest one yet; there was so much to tell them.

"Sorry I took so long. Our adventures keep getting better and better."

Weber moved over so Quinton could do his research.

"So, what are you looking up?"

"Well, I wanted to research more of the plants in this area just in case something happens again."

"Yeah, that was a good call last night. It was amazing that it worked overnight. Even the best stuff from the pharmacy doesn't work that fast."

"That's because most of the elements that work synergistically with the main element are processed away when man gets hold of it."

Weber was trying to keep up with Quinton's research online but was having trouble reading that fast. "Man, Doc, you must be a computer yourself, how fast do you read?"

"Pretty fast. I started reading when I was three and never stopped. Besides, my favorite thing to do is research. Hey! I think you got a response to your e-mail already. Here," as he got out of the way for Weber to read his mail.

"Dear Web,

Glad to hear that you are having a good time. I know the country is beautiful out there, just be sure to use caution. I'm glad that Dolton is all right. That must have caused quite a scare among your group. Based on your location and the direction you are going you may have some trouble with satellite links in the next day or so. Don't worry, your mom and I have things covered. We'll keep an eye out for you. Till next time,

Love, Dad

"I wonder what they mean that they'll keep an eye out. Oh well, maybe they're getting old. Here, Doc, you can continue your research."

"Thanks. Hey, here comes Mr. Phil."

"Hey, Weber, you got a minute?" asked Phil. They stood there talking while Quinton continued his research.

<{{}}>\<

I'm glad I was still here to send Web a response. Karen'll be glad to know that we corresponded in real time. He looked at his watch. *There is still plenty of daylight; I wonder what they're doing now. Think I'll look in on them.* He started up the programs again and locked in on the group. *Wow*, he thought, *that sure is beautiful country. They couldn't have picked a better place to settle down for the night. Hey, there's Phil. Wonder what they're talking about. Looks like the rest of the group is doing well.* He looked at his watch again. *Time to get home for dinner.* He shut down the program and closed up his office and started off for home.

In the office on one of the top floors of The Company the man behind the desk was staring at his computer screen; he had shadowed Stanley's computer and was watching intently. After Stanley shut down the program, he accessed the program again on his own computer and continued watching the group carefully. He zoomed in on Weber and the man that was talking to him; he looked vaguely familiar. "Who is that man?" he pondered aloud. "I know him." He watched more closely. "I recognize that limp." He zoomed in closer and stared until they were done talking. He followed the man as he walked away. "I don't believe it," he said. The man behind the desk picked up his phone and made a call. Then he created a new confidential file on his computer and called it "Shepherd." Less than five minutes later three men dressed in black suits were in his office. "Gentlemen, sit down. We have some planning to do. A lost sheep is finally coming home."

<{()}><

Pastor and Phil had just sat down to relax when Zach and Buck ran back into camp. They were slightly out of breath. Zach said in a puff, "That stream is so shallow that we're having a hard time getting water." Phil smiled and laid back on the rock he was sitting on and said, as he put his hands behind his head, "Well, take the shovel and dig a hole next to the stream and once it clears draw the water from there." Buck got the shovel unhooked and they were off again.

"Man, I can't believe we didn't think of that," said Zach.

"Yeah, that's why he's the boss," said Buck.

"I know *you're* right. Mr. Phil sure knows a lot about this outdoors stuff. Where do you suppose he learned all this stuff?" Zach mused.

Weber and Quinton had finished their research and were going to shut down and return to the camp area when Weber had a thought. "Hey, Doc, let's find out where we are and how the rest of the trip is going to be."

"What do you mean?"

"I mean that since we have the computer and satellite links we probably have some kind of GPS hooked into this thing. Let's use it to find our location and what kind of terrain we're up against for the rest of the trip."

"All right, nerd boy, let's get crackin'."

"You got it, egghead."

The men were relaxing when Pastor noticed that Phil was deep in thought and had a worried look on his face.

"Phil," said Pastor, "looks like you need to get something off your chest. Like to talk a little more?

Phil looked up, his expression unchanging said, "Yes, I would."

"Would you like to pray and give it over to the Lord?"

Phil paused, "I think that's what I should do." They rose and stood together.

Pastor laid a hand on Phil's shoulder and started to pray. "Father, of all the burdens that we choose to carry we have one here that we are ready to give to you. Look into the heart of your servant Phil and relieve the one that he brings to you this evening."

"It's a heavy one that I've carried for far too many years. My indecision about what action to take is more than I can bear alone and I come before you, humbled and grateful, to lay this at the feet of your Son, Jesus. I come to you heavy laden and look for rest from this burden. Take into your hands what was yours to begin with and give me the clarity of mind I need to deal with this situation." Phil paused.

"We ask this through your precious Son's name, Jesus Christ. Amen." Mike concluded.

"Amen," responded Phil and he leaned his shoulder into Mike's and embraced him. "Thanks Mike, you always know the right thing to do. I feel better already."

Mark and Zach were kneeling by the newly dug hole filling up the bottles and Buck and Dolton were standing behind them handing them the empty ones. Buck said, "Hey, Dolton, I'm sure glad that nothing happened to you back there in that giant forest."

"Me too," said Dolton with a little shake in his voice, "I thought when I got to that fork that I was in trouble."

"What were you really thinking and how did you know what to do?" asked Zach.

"Well," he replied, "I was pretty scared and I actually thought of a lot of things. At one point I thought that I should turn around and take the other fork, but when I actually turned around the place looked even more foreign than the direction I was already taking. I really didn't know what to do so I prayed. It was the weirdest thing, after I said a little prayer I just kept walking and a little while later I saw Mr. Phil walking in my direction."

"Wow," said Mark, "I probably would have been scarred stiff."

Zach let out a little chuckle. Mark, offended by his attitude, said, "Not everyone here is as tough as you are Zach."

The two stood up and were about to square off when Buck spoke up, "Hey, it's okay to be tough," as he looked at Mark and then at Zach, "but it's also okay to be scared too."

"You're right, I know," said Zach as he stretched his hand to Mark, "I've just never had friends like you guys before."

Buck smiled as they shook hands and patted Zach on the back softly. With full containers they started back to camp. Mark and Buck lagged behind a bit. Buck leaned over to Mark and asked quietly, "Do you think Dolton knows that both trails came together?"

"I don't think so," said Mark, "but he did what I would have done, pray."

By the time Pastor and Phil finished praying and set up the stoves to cook, the four arrived with the water. "Just in time," said Pastor, "we're ready to start cooking." Phil started whistling as he put the water on to boil.

"How come you're so happy?" asked Mark.

"Oh, I just got a weight off my shoulders," Phil said with a smile. They glanced at each other and noticed Pastor was smiling too; like the cat that ate the canary. Buck helped with the food preparation.

"Why don't you fellows sit this one out? I'll cook tonight," said Phil. They didn't have to be told twice. They found comfortable places to rest and took advantage of the time. Mark's curiosity was too much so he got up to see what Weber and Quinton were up to. In the meantime, Pastor jumped in to help cook and dinner was ready in no time.

"Should I go get Weber and Quinton?" offered Pastor. "Why don't we both go," suggested Phil, still glowing.

They arrived to find them huddled around the laptop. Mark heard the men arrive and turned around excitedly, "Look what Weber found on his computer!" Pastor and Phil leaned in and Weber pointed at the screen, "Look, the GPS on my computer tells us where we are. We're here."

"Where's here?" asked Pastor. They stared at the screen, which showed an enlarged map with a dot in the middle indicating their location.

"Zoom in, Web," Quinton instructed. Weber zoomed in and the name of the location came clear.

"It's called Devil's Play," said Pastor.

"Devil's Play. Hey, that's what Noah was talking about, only he called it Jamlo Awing, right?" said Quinton.

"How did you remember that?" asked Mark, a bit surprised.

"I remember lots of stuff," he answered shyly as he began hitting his leg with his wrist again.

They stared at the screen in silence realizing the significance of the information just shared. Then Phil said, "We should go, dinner's ready." Everyone started back except Weber and Quinton. "I'll help you pack up, Web," offered Quinton.

"Thanks Doc, see you two back at camp," said Phil.

When Weber and Quinton came into camp Mark informed them, "We held up thumbs already and I'll be saying grace."

"Really?" replied Quinton, recalling that he had never heard Mark pray out loud before.

Pastor directed them, "Let's gather holding hands tonight."

Mark waited until everyone was ready before he began. "Most Gracious and Loving Father, we thank you for this adventure and all the blessings that have come from it so far. Generous Creator, we thank you for making our friendship through this journey blossom and flourish. Sustainer of Life, we thank you for the nourishment that you have provided for us to keep us strong in order to complete the tasks you have put before us. Please look down on this ragtag little group and continue to shower us with the blessings of your love, guidance and strength. This we ask through Christ our Lord. Amen."

"Thank you, Mark," Pastor said proudly.

About halfway through the meal, Weber cleared his throat nervously and said, "Mr. Phil?"

"Yes Weber," he replied.

"Well, you know I looked up something about the area we are in, Devil's Play. It was the name given by the Indians that lived in this area at one time. Noah warned us about Jamlo Awing. I think it's the same place. Maybe we should find another path and go around it."

Pastor interjected, "You know, Weber, just because someone had a hard time in this area doesn't mean that it's cursed. The Indians had a lot of superstitions and used to give names to lots of things they didn't understand. It doesn't matter what they call this area, we have the knowledge that we are going to be delivered safely home. We have the promise of our Lord. We have faith. That's something that the Indians didn't have."

"You do know how to pray don't you?" asked Phil.

"Yes, sir," said Weber "I do. I just thought that it might be prudent not to test the Lord." The others were listening turning their heads from speaker to speaker.

"First of all, we're not testing the Lord. The trail we're following has been well traveled and we haven't made any plans on veering from that path. Just hold true to the promise of our Lord and know that He is with us always, until the end of time," said Phil.

"Hey, I recognize that verse, I had to memorize it for confirmation. It's from Matthew, one of the last verses in that book!" said Buck.

"Very good, Buck. You did learn something from my classes after all," laughed Pastor. The rest of the dinner was filled with light conversation.

A few of the fellows disappeared into the woods from time to time until they all ended up sitting around the lanterns as darkness set in, talking about the day's events. The conversation turned to talk about their fathers.

"Yeah, I have been blessed," said Mark, "my dad's cool."

"Mine too," said Weber, "he's always around helping me with my computers and spending time with me."

Zach spoke up, "I don't think my dad or mom worries too much about spending time with me. In fact, I think they're happier when I'm not around."

"Sorry to hear that," consoled Quinton, "my dad works so much he doesn't spend as much time with me as I would like, but when he does we have a great time."

Pastor and Phil listened intently to their conversation.

"Well," said Dolton, "my dad is gone so much that we don't see each other hardly at all." He paused for a moment and then added, "He told me that one of these days he would start taking me with him on his trips. I suppose that's something to look forward to."

About half-way through Dolton's explanation Buck got up and walked away. They all noticed and Zach asked, "Is he okay?"

"He never knew his father so he doesn't have anything to talk about" said Mark.

"Aw, man. I didn't know. I'm sorry, I should go apologize," offered Zach.

"Me too," added Dolton.

Phil stood up and stopped them from going after Buck. "I'll go talk to him," said Phil. He glanced over at Pastor, who gave him a slight nod, and started off in Buck's direction. Pastor let everyone else know, "They need privacy, let 'em go." Then, wisely, he started a new conversation.

Phil's Promise

Buck sat down on a large rock that looked out over the valley below. It afforded a perfect view of the night sky, which was filled with stars. Buck never appreciated, until the moment he looked up to admire them, just how many stars there really were in the sky.

"Quite a few of them; aren't there?" asked Phil, who sat himself next to Buck on the rock.

"Yeah, I never knew. Guess you can't see them so well in the city because of the lights. They kind of get washed out in the background," replied Buck. They sat in silence for a while.

Phil leaned over and nudged Buck with his elbow, "What's troubling you?"

Buck shrugged his shoulders, "I'm not sure, I guess I just don't want to hear their conversation tonight. Maybe I'm getting tired of them and their stories; always trying to outdo each other. Dunno, just. . . ," he trailed off.

Phil noted the break in his voice. He recognized the need for Buck to be able to converse without getting too emotional. After all, Phil had a lot for him to hear tonight. "Could it be the subject matter?" asked Phil after a short period of silence.

"Yeah, I guess," said Buck. By his tone, Phil could tell that he had composed himself again. "I just don't know much about him. I don't know; it's like Mom is ashamed of him or something. I just. . . ," he trailed off again.

"How much about your dad do you know?" Phil asked.

"Not much really. . .his name. . .his face. I have a picture of him, but it's from before they were married so he looks really young. I carry it with me all the time. Wanna see it?"

"Sure," Phil replied, a bit surprised.

Buck reached into his back pocket and pulled out his wallet. He moved some papers and carefully removed the old, wrinkled photo of his father, Bart Bond. He looked at it for a moment then handed it to Phil. "It's all I have of him. I really wish I'd had an opportunity to know him. He looks like he was a really nice guy. I think I would have liked him," said Buck.

Phil took the photograph and looked at it for a while. Slowly and purposefully, he took a deep breath. "Buck, I have no doubt that you would have loved him. He was an exceptional human being and one of the best friends I ever had."

Phil heard Buck take a breath, "You knew my father?" he asked in disbelief.

"Bart was my best friend. I loved him like a brother. I was never closer to another human being in my life," said Phil. He could feel the adrenaline begin to flow. He hadn't thought that he would be this nervous when it came time to tell Buck of his father. The memories began to cloud his mind and he realized that it was his turn to take a moment to regain his composure. What he was about to share with Buck hadn't been spoken in a very long time and it was important that he know the truth in its entirety—impartial and unbiased. Buck needed to know how much his father loved him.

"Your father wanted me to wait until you were 18, but I believe that you are mature enough and strong enough to hear it now." Phil paused and reminded himself to breathe. "Your father was my best friend. There wasn't a time when we weren't together. When your father and I finished college we both went to work for The Company. It's an organization that takes care of the work of a higher power. You could call it a maintenance service. We were assigned as partners and worked very well together. So well, in fact, that we were the fastest promoted team in the history of The Company. As we became more important to The Company we were given more elevated clearances until we had reached the top level of security. We were assigned the most sensitive cases and given the most, shall we say "adventurous" assignments. I can't tell you much more than that except that we did very well for ourselves. We were wise with our money and never had to worry about finances, but we loved the job so we never left.

"Before long, Bart met your mother. She was amazing; smart, funny, beautiful and a heart as big as all outdoors. He fell madly in love with her and she with him. Whenever he wasn't with me, I knew that I could find him at her house. She naturally fit into our lives, but more his life than mine."

"He wanted to marry her and asked me to be his best man. I told him I couldn't believe he even had to ask. The night he proposed to her, I was the one who made all the arrangements. I reserved the restaurant, set up the violinists, and chose the dessert, the champagne, and the music. They were both fond of the old-fashioned music. You know, the romantic and corny stuff, but it moved them, so the night was perfect. He picked Becky up in a full stretch limo. They had a picture perfect dinner complete with strolling violinists and the best service money could buy. After dinner, he got down on one knee and asked for her hand in marriage in front of all the people in the restaurant. She didn't hesitate for one second. The words had barely finished coming out of his mouth and she said yes. You should have seen it, Buck. It was the happiest moment in all our lives."

"How did you know all of this?"

"I was watching from the kitchen. He was like a brother to me, do you think I'd miss a moment like that?" he chuckled. "Almost immediately after they were married, Becky announced that she was pregnant. You never saw a more proud and happy man. He was a very doting husband. He did everything for her. Wouldn't let her lift a finger. He even sang to her belly so the baby could hear and appreciate the music that meant so much to the both of them. If you didn't know better you would have thought that he was a little kid. He was so excited about having you. It didn't matter to either one of them whether you were a boy or a girl. All that mattered was that you were part of the both of them. When the blessed day came and you were brought into the world, Bart was there to pull you from your mother's womb. There was no part of the pregnancy that Bart wasn't a part of. He wanted to be there for every moment, and he was. He was there. . . ," Phil heard his own voice break, "until he wasn't any more."

"What do you mean, he wasn't?" asked Buck.

After another deep breath Phil continued, "I mean that he wasn't." He took a few more moments before speaking again, when he did Buck noticed that his tone was very different. He sounded a little angry and sad at the same time. He knew this was big. Unconsciously he shifted his position and turned toward Phil.

"About a year after you were born we were assigned to one of the biggest cases that The Company had seen in a very long time. Something went very wrong. There was no warning, no sounds, nothing that could have tipped us off that we were in mortal danger. I didn't even know what had happened until I woke up in the hospital. I had been shot in the face and the hip. It was two days before they told me what happened to your father. We had been set up. I think it was someone on the inside, but I didn't stay around to find out.

"He was my best friend and there was nothing I could do—nothing I could have done! I had lost my brother. My only family." He paused again, this time for a long time. As Buck examined his face he could see the tears running down Phil's cheeks. He knew that this had been a hard thing to talk about. *Why is he telling me now*, thought Buck? *Lord, be with Mr. Phil*, Buck prayed. *Pastor always said that popcorn prayers would come in handy, guess now is the time.*

"I didn't stay with The Company. I was in the hospital for six months. They said I would never walk without a limp. The damage to my face was extensive. When I was finally given a mirror I didn't even recognize myself. I was a different person, inside and out. After I was discharged from the hospital I just didn't go back to work.

"I found out that your mom had taken you and left the area. Our friends said that it was just too much for her. Everything and everyone reminded her of Bart. I had to find you. I had to keep my promise. I sold everything. With my looks changed, I changed my name and went looking for you. About 12 years ago I finally found you. I had promised your father that if anything happened to him I would take care of you and your mother and that's what I was going to do. When I came here I found out that Becky was having a hard time getting a job that paid enough to support the both of you. I arranged for her to "find" a couple of jobs that weren't too taxing and would meet your needs. I took up residence here and found that it was very easy to watch over you because you two were attending the same church I decided to become a part of. I guess God really knows what

He's doing. He brought us all here to a place where we could grow in Him and watch over each other.

"I ran into your mother on a number of occasions but she never recognized me. It's better that way. She was always a proud woman and never wanted charity. That's why she moved away from The Company. They would have taken care of her but on their terms and not hers. Anyway, once I found God, I found my place in your life. I've kept the promise I made to your father and, between you and me, that's saying a lot."

Phil wasn't ready to let Buck respond so he continued, "There was another promise I made but I'm not going to keep to the letter of it. I promised I would give this to you when you were eighteen. I see no reason to wait," he said as he reached into the inner pocket of his vest. He pulled out something that looked like a passport and handed it to Buck. "Your father and I did quite well and he thought that when the time was right you would find a good use for this."

"What is it?" asked Buck.

"Only way for you to know is to open it," said Phil.

Buck opened the small booklet and a piece of paper fell out. "Read it," said Phil. Buck could feel his hands shaking. This piece of paper was from his very own father. Written by his own hands. Written to him.

Dear Bucky,

If you are reading this then I'm probably dead. Don't worry; I knew what I was getting into when I took the job with The Company. I figured that this day would come. I just hope it's not too soon in your life. Regardless, Wes promised to look after you the day I married your mother so you are probably with him now.

Buck paused from reading and mouthed the word "Wes."

Part of the wedding vows that we said on our wedding day were for him; the pastor was pretty perplexed when I told him that I had a vow to make with my best man before my bride. But that's another story for Wes to tell you about. Save it for a time when you can talk about me without being sad, because it's a happy story and obviously has a happy ending. There isn't another man in the world that could take my place except Wesley Philip Carter, my best man and best friend.

"Mr. Phil, I thought you were my dad's best man," inquired Buck.

"I was. Keep reading," he replied. Buck thought for a minute and Phil could see that he was working it all out in his mind. Buck continued and as he read he could see that it now made sense to him and he understood what he had been telling him.

Bucky, don't be sad because I have kept my promise to you too. When I held you for the first time I promised that I would take care of you. The little booklet you are holding belongs to you now. It represents all the investments I have made over the years. None of it is illegal or improper. It was money earned, invested and saved. I'm hoping that this will help you through your years of higher learning. But, really, it's for you to use however you see fit. Know that no father loved you more than I did and I'm so proud to call you my son. My love for you will go on forever. Never forget that. Do well in life and know that no child was ever loved more.

Love, Your father, Bartholemew Bond

The tears were now falling from Buck's eyes. "My father said he was proud of me. He said he loved me. All my life I never knew that he ever felt that way." Buck was shaking, trying to stay in control.

Phil put his arm around Buck's shoulder and said, "Buck, if you believe nothing else, believe that. He loved you very much." They sat for a long time in silence.

When Buck had shed the last tear, they both wiped their eyes and looked at one another. "The day you were born, your father made me promise that if anything ever happened to him, I wouldn't tell you about his work or the money until you were 18. He handed me that book and also made me promise that I would make sure you and your mom were taken care of. I've been watching over you and your mom since I found you. My only regret is that I didn't make myself known to your mom. I guess I'm afraid that it will bring back the hurt that she left behind when she moved away."

They sat in silence for a while.

"You haven't looked at it, Buck," said Phil gently. Buck slowly opened it. He rubbed his eyes. He was sure he wasn't seeing it correctly due to the darkness. He looked again; he pointed his finger to the figure that was on the page before him. "What's this?" he asked.

"It's a investment book. They used those before they had electronic account tracking. This is what your father left you," replied Phil.

Buck began counting the digits to the left of the decimal point. "There's a lot of money in this account!" said Buck incredulously.

"Actually, there's a fair bit more. That bankbook hasn't been stamped in over 16 years. The interest on that account is pretty high. I think the amount may have doubled since then. This is only part of it. That bank has a safe deposit box with your name on it filled with stock and bond certificates of some of our investments. The key is taped to the back cover of the bankbook. It's all yours, Buck," said Phil.

"You mean to tell me that I'm rich?" asked Buck in almost a whisper.

"Well, if you mean do you have the money to make things happen in your life from this time forward? Then yes, you are rich. But be careful when you use the word rich. It means many different things. You can be rich in money but it could cost you your soul. You have to remember which is the most important, earthly riches or heavenly riches." Buck looked at him inquisitively.

"This is a tool for you to use and improve your life. It's not meant for you to use frivolously. Don't get me wrong, Buck. I'm not saying it's not all right to have money. All I'm saying is to not let it go to your head."

"Oh, you don't have to worry about that, Mr. Phil. Or do I call you Mr. Wes? What am I supposed to call you now?"

"Buck, I don't think you should tell anyone about the information that I have shared with you. It might not be a good idea just yet. Keep calling me Mr. Phil like you have for all these years. All will be known in good time." They sat again for a while in silence.

"Oh, I have one more thing for you. This is the picture that *I* carry around. I'm giving it to you now." Phil took the picture from his wallet and handed it to Buck. "It was taken the week before he died. It was the last picture he ever took," said Phil.

Buck looked at the picture carefully. He marveled at how much he looked like his father. His smile, the color of his hair and eyes, even his chin was the same. He figured the rest must be from his mother. *Funny*, he thought, *I never looked at her that way before.* He looked at the others in the picture, Wes. . .Mr. Phil. . .Wes, and his mother. *The cheeks. . .the forehead. . .the ears. . .yes*, he thought, *I got those from her. I'm a perfect combination of the both of them. I'm really part of a family.* He could feel his eyes filling again. "I wish I had known him," said Buck to Phil.

"I know, son. I know," replied Phil gently. They sat there on the rock on that beautiful night listening to the crickets and the frogs for a long time. Finally Buck put the picture carefully into his wallet in front of the picture that he had carried for such a long time. As he put his wallet back into his pocket he looked at Phil and said, "I think it's time we get back."

The air of authority in Buck's voice gave Phil a warm feeling. A feeling of pride and love. *If I had ever had a son I would have wanted him to be just like Buck,* he thought. *He's grown up in less than an hour tonight. All the pieces of his life's puzzle have finally come together and he took it like a man. Bart would have been so proud.*

They got up off the rock and found themselves standing face to face. As though they had the same thought at the same time they threw their arms around each other in a manly embrace. They patted each other on the back and started back to the campsite.

"Where were you guys?" asked Dolton, "We thought you got lost or something."

"Yeah, we were just getting ready to send out a search party," teased Mark.

"Everything okay, Phil?" asked Pastor Mike as he looked up at them.

"Everything's just fine. Thanks," said Phil.

"Yup, just fine," echoed Buck.

Phil and Pastor Mike exchanged knowing glances as Phil and Buck sat down around the lanterns. "So, what hails this fine nocturne around the blazen center?" asked Phil to the boys.

"Huh?" "What?" "In English!" came the responses.

"What's going on tonight around the lanterns?" said Phil.

The boys noticed that Buck had a glow about him and a smile that made all of them wonder just what went on with him and Phil. Noticing the time and not wanting an inquisition to occur, Pastor said, "I think it's time to go to bed."

"Oh, Phil," said Pastor, "we took care of the food and that so you don't have to worry."

"Thanks very much, Mike," he replied gratefully. Everyone climbed into their tents with their jackets on since this night was a little chilly, and Phil turned out the lanterns and climbed into the tent with Buck. They lay there for a time when Buck whispered, "Are you sleeping?"

"No," said Phil, "but you should try, we have another big day ahead of us tomorrow. Good night and enjoy your dreams."

"Thanks, you too."

Fourth Morning – Bear Trouble

Around 4:00 a.m. noises awoke Phil from a dead sleep. The others were awakened along with him. As Phil crawled from his sleeping bag he warned everyone, "Stay in your tents and don't come out until I tell you it's safe." He searched around in the dark for the flashlight that he had left in the corner of the tent by the door. As quietly as he could he unzipped the door to the tent and without turning on the flashlight peered out from the top of the tent door.

It was just as dark outside as it was in the tent. The night sky was black and the clouds had come in while they were sleeping and extinguished all the natural lighting. He heard the other tents starting to rustle with movement and again instructed everyone stay in their tents. Phil called for Pastor, "Mike, grab your flashlight and slowly look out your tent door without turning on your light."

The noises grew louder and sounded closer. He looked around in front of the tent and saw nothing. He strained to see in the dark and moved his head and shoulders out of the tent. A loud crack and a thud sounded, this time very close and he dove back into the tent.

"What was that?" whispered Buck obviously shaken.

"Quiet, no talking," demanded Phil as he grabbed a knife from his pack and started towards the door again. Rustling and voices from the other tents were growing louder. Phil was concerned that the noises might irritate the unwelcome visitors.

Pastor Mike was so startled at the cracking and thudding noises that he took a step backward in the tent and fell over Mark. The two of them became so tangled that they were about to knock over their tent. The commotion had now wakened everyone else.

Phil heard, "What's going on?" "What's all the noise?" "Shh, somebody's in our camp." ". . .or some *thing*." "Mr. Phil said to be quiet."

Curiosity to see what was going on was building. Weber was still in his sleeping bag, trying to keep Zach from opening the tent door. "Zach, it's not safe, let Mr. Phil handle it, it's too dangerous," he warned as he tried to find his glasses in the dark.

"Don't worry, Webmeister, I just wanna see what's going on." But Weber tried to grab Zach's arm and pull him in.

Dolton and Quinton got out of their sleeping bags at the same time and unzipped part of the window. Dolton tried to see what was going on while Quinton grabbed his camera and opened the front of the tent.

Ripping, tearing, growling, rustling, breaking of branches and crunching of leaves on the ground were heard and continued to grow louder. Phil knew he needed to take action and started out the doorway of the tent. A flash of light blinded him!

Quinton's body was sticking a third of the way out of the tent and he had his camera in front of his face. He was so excited that he kept hitting himself on the forehead with the camera. Every time he did that his finger kept pushing the button on the camera. After the second flash went off, the rest of the group had all poked their heads through the doors of their tents to watch the photo strobe-light show that Quinton was directing. Even Dolton had squeezed alongside Quinton to see what was going on. With their mouths hanging open and Quinton flashing, shooting and hitting himself, the boys watched frozen as the photoflash showed four bears in the process of stealing and robbing their backpacks.

When Quinton first started the light show the bears got startled. They dropped what they were doing and raised themselves up on their back two feet, their front paws trying to block the light flashes. Then they dropped back down on all fours, turned and lumbered away. When the bears finally ran off Dolton grabbed Quinton by the arms to calm him down, "It's okay, Doc, you chased them away. They're gone now. You're a hero!"

Pastor Mike and Phil came out of their tents and turned on their flashlights to assess the situation.

Pastor Mike nervously checked to see if everyone was okay. "Weber, Zach, you two all right?"

"Yes," said Weber with a shaky voice.

"I'll be okay," said Zach, "as soon as Weber lets go of my arm!" With that Weber noticed that he was still holding onto Zach's arm and let go, slightly embarrassed.

"How about you two?" Pastor asked Quinton and Dolton. Dolton was rolling around the tent laughing, almost in hysterics. Quinton was still standing in the doorway of the tent with a "deer in headlights" look on his face. He turned to Pastor and just nodded yes. Dolton popped up next to Quinton and said between laughs, "We BEARly escaped with our lives!"

Phil who was inspecting the area looked up at Dolton and smiled as he shook his head. But it was too late. The jocularity had begun. A second later Zach was laughing and said, "It's a good thing we weren't BEAR naked when they attacked." They laughed all the harder. Quinton had sufficiently calmed down and found that funny and laughed.

They all left their tents and the banter lasted a while longer. When the laughter finally died down and Pastor Mike said, "It's too dark to be out and about. It'll be light soon and we can see what the damages are then."

"I'm not tired."

"I won't be able to sleep."

"What time is it anyway?"

"A little after 4."

"The sun'll be coming up soon."

While they were resisting, Phil walked over to Pastor and whispered in his ear, "We were very lucky, but it looks like they got our packs and food."

"All of them?" asked Pastor realizing the impact of such a loss.

"I don't know," said Phil, "I can't tell right now but I think so."

Pastor turned around and said, "All of you in one tent."

They eagerly crawled into one tent. They were slap-happy so the roughhousing started. Phil looked at Pastor curiously at the command. "Safety in numbers; besides, I want to know exactly where they all are for the rest of the night," he explained.

The mayhem was already starting so he leaned in to scold them and decided not to. Putting the six of them in a two-man pup tent was just asking for a wrestling match. After about ten minutes Pastor said, "Okay, all of you out here now and get off Weber."

As they climbed out the sky was starting to lighten, even though it was still dark on the ground. Dolton, who was the last out of the tent, looked up and noticed the sky. "Look, it will be light soon." He turned to Mark and slapped him on the arm, "Hey, did you hear that?"

"Hear what?" said Mark.

"The crack," said Dolton. By now everyone was listening and nervously looking around. "The crack of dawn," said Dolton in a most serious voice.

It took a moment because of the scare they just had, but when it sunk in, the dogpile was on. Mark, Zach, and Buck jumped on Dolton and back into the tent they went rolling. Pastor Mike and Phil just shook their heads. Quinton was tapping his arms. Weber was watching Mark, Zach and Buck give Dolton a roll for his bad joke.

"Hey, guys, we could use your help," said Phil. "Get your flashlights and help pick up what's left in the immediate area and put it in a pile over there by the tents. Don't go too far—I'm sure the bears are gone but I want to make sure no one gets lost in the early morning hours. Got it?"

"Yeah, sure."

"No problem."

"I'm there."

"Zach, will you get off me already!"

Phil started picking up a few pieces of backpacks, food, and clothes that the bears had spread over the forest floor. He directed the rest of the group to spread out and pick up whatever they could find. It was beginning to get lighter out. That made the retrieval a little easier and allowed for a wider area in which to search. Pastor Mike pulled Phil under the tree where the packs were hung. "Sorry Phil, this is my fault," said Pastor, "Apparently I didn't get the Bearmuda Triangle lesson right."

Phil put his hand on Pastor's shoulder, "I'm thankful to God that everyone is alright. It could have been much worse. I'm not sure you could have done anything about the bears coming into camp. If they hadn't gotten the packs they might have gone looking for food in the tents."

He gazed at the disarray. "I don't think were going to have much to carry back," Phil confided in a whisper. "I just hope we have what we need to *get* back."

Phil called the group over. Then turned to Pastor, "Let's sort the things as they bring them in." He turned back to the group, "It's getting lighter so we can cover more ground. You need to pair up. Go and collect anything you can find, even if you don't think we can still use it."

They were eager to help and, of course, still pumped up from all the excitement. As Dolton walked away, he said, "We BEARly have any provisions left."

"We were stripped BEAR," Buck chimed in.

"I can BEARly take this," teased Weber.

"Well, the thought of this happening again is unBEARable," added Zach.

"Oh brother," sighed Phil as they left the area.

Soon they had picked up everything they could find within a hundred feet of where the packs were hung. By the time they finished bringing what they found back to camp, they were starting to figure out that breakfast could be a problem.

"Okay, let's see what we have," Pastor Mike announced, "let's gather around."

Phil had been trying to separate the items that were salvageable as they brought them in. As they started going through all the gathered-up items Phil was shaking his head. He stood up, "Men, the bear attack last night has created a little problem. We may not have the food we need to finish the trip, so just know that we are going to have to ration it. Don't worry, we should be okay. We'll supplement what we have by foraging and fishing. Doc, keep a sharp eye for edible berries and whatever else you recognize as safe. Zach, we will be coming up to a lake later today so your skills will be utilized then. I want you all to spread out further and see if you can find anything else. Pastor and I will continue to inventory our gear and provisions. We'll know better where we stand after we have collected all we can."

They followed his instructions. As they were walking away, Weber told Zach, "I guess I'm lucky I slept with my pack. But I'm feeling a little guilty that I wasn't carrying any food."

"Naw, little man. The equipment you have is going to get us home," Zach replied.

"What do you mean?"

"Didn't you see Mr. Phil's pack? His was torn to bits and most of his stuff hasn't been found. Chances are that the map and compass are lost too. Your electronic gizmos are going to get us to where we need to go."

"I hope you're right."

Phil and Pastor Mike collected and organized the remnants of the seven packs. Two had been taken, three had been destroyed by the bears, and two were able to carry food and equipment. "I'll finish up here, Pastor. Why don't you start cooking? Get the water going for breakfast." Phil started to repair a third pack to carry food and equipment. As the pairs brought fewer things back, the jovial spirits that they'd had were beginning to wane. They figured out that their situation was serious and they were becoming concerned.

Breakfast that morning was oatmeal and dried milk. Pastor Mike offered the morning blessing over the meager breakfast that was salvaged, "Most Gracious Father and Protector of all, we thank You this beautiful morning for the blessings You have seen fit to give us on our adventure."

Dolton and Zach shot each other a questioning look. Zach mouthed "Blessing?" Dolton shrugged his shoulders in questioning acknowledgment.

Their exchange didn't escape Pastor Mike's keen vision. He continued, "We thank You for our good health, the fellowship we have shared on this trip and the food You have provided us with. Your hand of protection in the early morning attack is a testament to the love You have for us and we acknowledge Your complete authority over all and are grateful for Your enduring love for us. Please continue to guide and protect us as we continue our journey with lighter burdens and more challenges. Provide us our daily sustenance. Bless the food that we are about to eat. May it be health and nutrition for our bodies as Your Word is nutrition for our souls. We thank You, and we ask and pray all of this through Christ, Our Lord. Amen."

As he concluded, he shot a glance to Zach and Dolton, who returned the glance, now understanding the initial "blessing." "Remember, in all things give thanks and praise," said Pastor. "You never know what's waiting around the corner, but you can be sure that coming from God it's got to be good!"

Everyone nodded their heads in agreement as they began eating what might prove to be the first of many meager meals on the remainder of their trip. After breakfast they cleaned their plates and utensils with water from their bottles and collected them to be put in one of the packs. Zach and Mark wandered off still looking for anything they could find when Mark saw a glimmer of gold. As he bent over Zach said, "What is it?"

"Oh, thank God, it's my dad's communion set."

"His what?"

"Come on!" and Mark took off in a run with Zach on his heels. "Dad, Dad!" said Mark excitedly and half out of breath, "Look!" and he held it out for Pastor to see.

"Thank God, thank God," said Pastor," it didn't get lost or destroyed! Thank you Mark," and Pastor gave him a big hug.

"What was all that about?" Zach asked Mark. "It's dad's communion set. He never goes anywhere without it. It was one of the last things that my mom gave him before she died. It's pretty important to him."

"Oh, so. . .what's a communion set?"

"Well, when you're clergy, you never know when you will have to administer communion to someone. You can't bring the fancy chalice or plate that we use in church on Sunday with you when you travel so they make one that's smaller, more compact and you take it with you when you need to travel."

"Hey, you learn something new every day," responded Zach.

Phil had them gather around the center of the camp to get their orders for the day. "There were only four packs that survived the attack. One was Weber's because he was sleeping with it. Pastor and I will carry a pack each and the rest of you will carry the rest of the gear in turns. We need to break camp and I'll have to show you how to pack and carry it without packs. We have to make it to the lake before tonight and we have some serious ground to cover, so let's get started."

Pastor packed up the two packs that he and Phil were going to carry and Phil instructed the youth on packing of the rest of the gear as they broke down each tent. It took more time than usual to get everything packed up and mounted on their backs. When they started out Buck and Zach chose to carry the gear first. Weber had his and the other three decided that they would carry the water bottles and jug. "All right," said Phil, "grab your walking poles and let's go."

The Visit

Deacon Dave Dillon was sitting at Pastor Mike's desk reading his Bible and enjoying the quiet of the morning. *What a beautiful morning,* he thought; *I'm so glad this week has been quiet.* So far his week had consisted of opening up the church in the morning, walking the grounds, collecting the mail, and answering an occasional phone call.

About an hour into his morning he heard a car pull into the parking lot. He wasn't expecting anyone so he got up to see who it was. Three large black SUVs had pulled up just outside of the office. This probably would not have been strange except for the fact that the windows were blacked out and the SUVs pulled across the parking stalls instead of into them. Dave was curious now and kept watching as two men, who were dressed in black and wore sunglasses, exited from the rear SUV. One hurried over to the front SUV, looked around, opened the passenger door and a large man slowly climbed out. He buttoned his coat and walked directly toward the office with the two other men in tow. "Hmm," said Dave, more than a little curious about their manner.

Deacon Dave decided not to take whatever was to come too seriously, so he sat back down at the desk and waited. The door opened and they walked in.

"Good morning, gentlemen, the Lord's blessings on you. What can I do for you?" he said trying to sound casually in charge.

The large man removed his glasses and stood in front of the desk directly across from him. Dave got a good look at him. He was about six-foot-two with gray hair cut high and tight in a military fashion. His face was pitted and slightly wrinkled from years of stress. He had bushy eyebrows that hovered over deep-set dark brown eyes. When he looked at you, you felt as if he were looking into to you, not at you. He wore a very expensive suit.

"My name is Marshall Redwing," he said as he drew a badge from his coat pocket and flashed it at him. Marshall spoke in a low gravelly voice that demanded respect and attention. He was obviously a man who got what he wanted when he wanted it. "Are you Pastor Mike Miller?"

"Oh, I'm not the pastor, he's away." He started to say in his cocky manner, "I'm Deacon Dave Dillon but you can call. . . ."

"Where *is* the pastor?" Redwing interrupted. He spoke every word slowly, with authority, and before Dave could even think he blurted out, "He's on a hiking trip with the youth."

"And. . .*when* do you expect him to return?"

"Friday, he'll be back Friday," Dave responded surprised by Marshall's boldness.

"Are you in contact with him?" he asked and moved one step closer to the desk. His actions made Dave sit straight up in his chair.

"No."

As Marshall slowly put his hand inside his coat one of the lackeys began to speak, "Sir, the shepherd. . ." and was interrupted by Marshall lifting his hand for silence. When he did that his coat moved in such a way that Dave caught a glimpse of a holster and a gun. Dave could feel himself begin to sweat. He looked at Marshall's lackeys, then the door, then Marshall again. *Oh my goodness,* he thought, *I'm going to die.*

Marshall pulled his hand out of his coat and was holding a picture. "Can you tell me if Wesley Philip Carter is with him?" Relieved that his worst fears had not come to fruition, Dave leaned back, sighed, and answered, "I don't know anybody by that name."

Marshall leaned over the desk and held out the picture. "Do you recognize this man?" Dave leaned in and reached over to look at the picture, acutely aware that Marshall was scrutinizing him with his deep stare. Dave tried to take the photo but Marshall did not release his hold. For one awkward moment both hands were on the picture, and both men were intently looking at each other. Dave relinquished his hold and felt himself turn red as he returned his gaze to the man in the photograph while Marshall held it up.

"No, no I don't believe that I do. Who is he?"

Marshall retracted the hand with the photo in it and with the other handed Dave a business card. "If you do see this man call me at the number on this card immediately. It's in your best interest to do so," he instructed clearly. "I'll be watching." In one motion, he had his glasses on and was walking out the door with his gargoyles in tow. Dave leaned back in his chair now fully aware of the sweat dripping down the back of his neck and his forehead. *What in the world was that all about?* he wondered. He got up and went to the window and watched them return to their vehicles and drive away. *So much for my quiet day,* he mused.

Sharing

Despite the trials of the early morning hours, the youth felt confident enough to lead the way out of camp. Phil and Pastor Mike took up the rear. Phil moved in close to Pastor and said, "I didn't want to say anything in front of the others but I don't know how long the pump and water filter will last. It's not in good shape and I'm afraid it'll break before the end of trip. Maybe even today."

"Are you sure?"

"Yes," said Phil, "I can only leave it in God's hands. Pray that we'll find water this morning."

"Well," said Pastor, "God will provide us with what we need, He hasn't failed us yet." He paused, "I take it God answered your prayer about your promise."

Phil gave Pastor a wink and a smile and said, "Yes, I was able to tell him everything."

"Everything?" asked Pastor excitedly.

"Everything plus," said Phil. "Hey, we should be the ones leading the group. All right fellows, make a hole. Old guys comin' through." They made their way to the front of the pack and picked up the pace. As Pastor Mike passed Quinton, whom everyone was now calling Doc, he noticed that he had started hitting himself again with his walking stick. *That poor soul,* he thought, *doesn't he know how much he's worth yet? Maybe by the end of the trip he'll finally know his value.*

With the lighter loads, they were able to move faster and cover more ground. While Pastor and Phil continued their conversation, the youth were having conversations of their own. As they left the camp area, the trail was wide enough to allow the group to walk together rather than one by one. They weren't in a hurry so they lagged behind a bit. Mark reached over and tapped Buck on the forearm and said, "Buck, it's killing me, you're still glowing, even after everything that happened last night. What did you guys talk about?"

"I promised not to tell," said Buck smiling.

"Oh man, come on," said Mark, "I'm your best friend, I won't tell."

Dolton pointed to his chest and said, "Me too."

Zach added with a smile, "You said we're all your friends."

Buck turned his head and looked Zach straight in the eyes and smiled even bigger.

"Okay," said Buck, "but you have to swear on a Bible that you won't tell anyone. . .and I don't make that demand lightly. *No one,* got it?"

Mark reached into the pack that Zach was carrying and pulled out a Bible and handed it to Buck. He took the Bible, stopped walking and said, "Okay, everyone touch the Bible." They stopped and crowded tightly around him and touched the Bible.

"Do you swear that if you tell anyone about what I am about to share with you that it will damage your soul forever? Everyone has to agree or I don't talk. One at a time." So one at a time they said, "I swear." Buck paused and handed the

Bible back to Mark and started walking again. Mark pleaded, "Come on."

So Buck began telling them all that transpired after he left the group the night before. When he arrived at the part about whom Mr. Phil really was, most of them gasped. Zach rationalized, "That's why he knows so much about everything," and Buck continued. Dolton's mouth dropped opened and he became uncharacteristically quiet when Buck got to the part about the money. The others were stunned.

"So. . .you're rich?" asked Quinton. Buck pulled out the booklet for them to see, and then told them about the letter that his dad had written and the safe deposit box filled with stocks and bonds. Not wanting to alert the men, they all mouthed silent wows.

"Remember," said Buck, "you swore an oath; you can't tell anyone." They became quiet and ungrouped as they continued hiking. They had been rendered speechless; no one talked for quite some time as they processed the news. Noticing the extended period of silence behind him, Phil turned to check. They were fine but when he made eye contact, they gave him strange smiles. Phil turned back and leaned over to Pastor, "They're up to something."

"That doesn't surprise me in the least," said Pastor, "considering what happened this morning. They are coping, they need to deal with it their way," he explained, and they walked on.

"No, I think it's more than that," Phil answered, more to himself than to Pastor.

The morning sky was partly cloudy. The air was fresh with a hint of rain. The trail headed through another forest where the trees started to thin and rocky boulders popped up between them like mushrooms. They walked briskly for a few hours when Phil stopped them just before the trail headed down a slope with very few trees and wound between large tall boulders.

"Let's rest here," said Phil. He turned to Pastor and whispered, "Don't you think something's going on with them?"

"I do," said Pastor, "I haven't heard a peep out of them all morning. Maybe I should take up the rear?"

"Good idea," Phil answered.

Unlike the other days, this day had not warmed up. It was cool and the wind had started whipping over the rocks. There were few trees to provide a barrier from the wind. They all felt the nip from the wind and climbed into their jackets. After Phil got his jacket on he spotted, off in the distance, what looked to be a portion of a small body of water and said to Pastor, "Look over there, I think it might be the lake we need to get to."

"Are we supposed to be going that way?" asked Pastor.

"Well, if I remember correctly, this is the direction we need to go and according to our timetable we should arrive at a lake by the end of our hike today."

"It's unfortunate that we lost the map and compass, but very fortunate that you were the one who plotted our course and have such an excellent memory for details. Whenever you're ready, oh fearless leader," teased Pastor.

The hike down the slope was quite a bit easier than the grade down to the giant forest. After about forty-five minutes it leveled out and the trees thickened. Phil stopped and pointed out a trail marker that was on a rock as opposed to a tree, which had been the case on the first portion of their trip. "Oh, thank goodness," said Phil, "I was hoping that we would find a trail marker."

The youth were still unusually quiet but smiled every time Phil looked back to check on them. They walked on for another half hour and he stopped the group, "We may not be able to stop for a regular lunch. We need to reach the lake by tonight. If anyone is hungry you'll need to eat a trail bar as we go. Is everyone all right with that?"

Nods all the way around. Pastor came up alongside Phil and sat down and spoke with him, "Something's wrong with them." Phil and Pastor both turned to look at the boys and as they did, they saw them looking at them and instantly, as if a switch were turned on, they all grew smiles.

"Yep, something is definitely going on." Phil turned for another quick look at the youth.

Dolton, still smiling, asked, "Are we headed Wes?" Buck gave him a punch to the shoulder.

Phil smiled back and said, "No, we're going south."

Phil turned back to Pastor and said, "They know."

Pastor chuckled and said, "Well, they're a pretty close knit group now. You have no one to blame but yourself."

"They're good guys," Phil conceded, "but for now I'm not going to worry about it. We need to concentrate on getting them out of here safely."

Pastor agreed with a nod and started to say something when Weber interrupted, "Excuse me, sir, if my calculations are correct the water that you saw from the top of the grade should be the same lake I saw on my computer last night."

"Thank you Weber," said Phil, "Then it was a lake that I saw. Fellows, if we don't find a stream we have to head for the lake. I'm sure that this trail is going to it. Look, I'm going to lay it on the line with you because I think you should know. Our food supplies may not be enough to get us back. We have damaged equipment, which means that water will be an issue for us. And the loss of our map and compass means that everyone will need to watch for trail markers and any signs that will keep us going in the right direction. Do you understand?" They all nodded that they understood.

"Okay," he turned abruptly, "if everyone's ready, let's go," and they started off.

As they wound through the pine trees and up and down the small rises and falls of the trail, Mark caught up with Buck to talk. "Well," said Mark, "Mr. Phil knows we know."

"I think so," said Buck.

Dolton, joining them said, "Umm, Buck, I just, uhh wanted to, umm apologize for saying that back there. I need to put a lock on my lips sometimes."

"Dolton," responded Buck, "I forgive you, but now he knows I told you. I hope he's not mad at me."

"Sorry," said Dolton, "sorry."

Pastor watched as they talked. Before long they were starting to bump each other going down the trail like nothing in the world was wrong.

Thousand Island Lake

The clouds in the sky had finally started to thin and the sun was at full strength in the afternoon sky. Phil checked his watch: 3:10 p.m. He was starting to get worried. He paused for a minute and then stopped the group and told them to take a knee. He walked to the back of the group, "Pastor," he said, "we should have found that lake by now."

Dolton tapped Quinton and said, "I'll be back in a second. Don't let them leave without me," and stepped off the trail and behind a tree.

Pastor looked up and noticed that Dolton wasn't with the group. "Where's Dolton?" Pastor asked worriedly. Quinton responded quickly, "He had to use a tree."

Pastor relaxed and continued talking with Phil. When they finished, Phil returned to the front to wait for Dolton. He came running out from behind the tree like he was shot out of a gun.

"Mr. Phil, Pastor!" he shouted, "I found it! It's over there!"

"What is?" said Phil.

"The lake! It's over there! C'mon, I'll show you!" The group followed Dolton as he led them back toward where he'd come out of the trees. As they reached the spot he'd told them about, he pointed his finger. There it was, about two hundred feet off the trail through the trees.

"Thank God!" exclaimed Pastor. "Thank God."

The guys were high-fiving and slapping Dolton on the back and Zach gave a loud whistle.

They headed for the lake and exited the trees about fifty feet before the water's edge. Spotty patches of grass about four inches tall, and white and gray sand replaced the forest floor. It was beautiful! The lake was about a half mile or more wide and just less than that across. Directly across the lake was a sheer rock cliff that stretched up at least two hundred feet. There must have been hundreds of landmasses breaking up the beautiful blue body of water.

"Wow!" said Quinton, "it looks like there's a thousand islands out there."

"Hold on," said Weber in a worried tone, "didn't Noah warn us about a place called Thousand Island Lakes?"

"Yeah," said Quinton now worried too.

"Well there's nothing we can do about it now. We're here," said Phil. "We need the water and we could use a fish or two."

Zach let out a loud yahoo.

"First things first," said Phil, "let's find a place to set up camp."

Pastor spotted an area where there were three logs around a firepit, "How about there?" he said.

"That's great," Phil responded. "Good job! We're going to need that pit tonight with only one lantern and one usable stove."

They went to inspect the firepit and Phil spotted an area for the tents not too far away in the trees, "Perfect," he said as he pointed, "Let's set up the tents over there." The boys started setting up the tents and had them up in minutes.

Zach asked excitedly, "Now, how 'bout them fish?"

"As a matter of fact, that's a great idea," said Phil, "We need you all to try and catch something or dinner is going to be real light. Zach, help them make up as many stick poles as you can and teach them whatever they need to know."

"Okay, Mr. Phil!" Zach turned to Weber and said, "I need your gear. Some of my stuff was broken last night." Weber went to his pack and retrieved the equipment and gave it to Zach.

Weber asked Phil, "Sir, would it be okay if I try to send a e-mail to my folks?"

"Sure, Weber," said Phil, "and send a message to Dave Dillon to get hold of Nolan to meet us with some supplies."

Weber took off, grabbing his pack and heading for a clear area. Phil looked at Quinton, "What're you waiting for? Weber'll need help." Quinton smiled and took off after Weber.

Zach found some small trees with branches that could be used for poles. He showed Mark, Buck and Dolton how to make them and set up for fishing. "Okay," said Zach, "tie the string at the end of your stick like this. Good, now take this piece of wood and tie it about eighteen inches up from the bottom of the line for a float and then tie the hook on the end." The boys followed the directions to the letter.

Buck said, "What're we using for bait?"

"Well," said Zach, "one of you go get the shovel and we'll get some live worms. In the meantime we can use the plastic ones we have left." Dolton was off to get the shovel and back in seconds.

"Let's go," said Zach to the others and off they went. Dolton said, "I'll dig," and headed to an area between the trees and the water where the bushes were thick.

Pastor and Phil were off in the forest gathering firewood. Weber and Quinton set up the laptop and were on their third location when Weber in frustration said to Quinton, "I don't understand, it should work. I have power, an open clear area. I don't know." Quinton talked Weber into trying two other areas before giving up.

Phil and Pastor finished gathering firewood and got the pit set and ready to start their fire. They sat to rest when Pastor said, "Phil, when we arrived here Weber and Quinton said something that made me think of something."

"What would that be?"

"The day we left for this trip, Quinton's mom told me that she had a dream. She said Quinton was having fun up until he got to the islands."

Phil was about to inquire further when he looked up and saw Weber and Quinton come walking back into camp with their heads hanging down.

"We can't get it to work," said Quinton.

"I can't figure it out," added Weber, disappointed.

"It's okay, we'll give it a shot tomorrow. Let's go see how the fishing is coming along, maybe you can lend a hand there," said Phil.

They walked up to see the other half of the group fishing. "How's it going?" asked Phil.

"Not so good," said Zach, "we haven't even had a nibble."

"What are you using for bait?"

"Plastic worms. Dolton is digging for some real ones," said Zach.

Pastor turned to see Dolton digging off in the distance. "I'll go see how he's doing and give him some help," offered Pastor.

"I see you made enough poles for everyone," said Phil and bent down and picked up three, handing one to Quinton and Weber and keeping one for himself. Quinton stared at it. Phil noticed that neither had started to fish.

"Look, it's easy. Just take the pole and give the end a little whip and let the line go out in front of you. Like this," he said as he demonstrated; and plop, it landed out in front of him. They moved into their own areas and mimicked Phil's actions.

"Finding anything?" asked Pastor as he walked up to Dolton.

"No, I thought by now I would have loads."

"Maybe we should try here instead," directed Pastor as he walked over to another area. Dolton followed him and brought up the first shovel-full. Four worms were hanging out of the soil.

"Wow!" said Dolton excitedly, "how did you know where to dig?"

"Well," said Pastor smiling, "I haven't always been a fisher of men. I love to fish, too." They collected as many worms as they could and headed back over to the fishing area.

"How many have we caught?" Pastor asked.

"None," came the reply.

"Well, Dolton and I have come bearing gifts," and Pastor held out a cup full of worms. Everyone eagerly pulled in their lines and made their way over to them. Weber and Quinton were the closest so they grabbed theirs and Quinton watched Weber carefully and copied exactly what he did. Excitement was unusually high as they put their bait on their lines and returned to their fishing spots.

"Praise God" yelled Pastor and the echo repeated. Mark looked at his dad along with the rest of the group and after a thought yelled out, "Amen" and the echo repeated.

Just as the echo ended, everyone had a fish hit their line, and the game was on. As Buck, Mark, Pastor, Quinton, Weber, and Dolton were trying to pull in their fish and keep them from flopping back into the lake, Phil and Zach were running from person to person unhooking fish and throwing them onto shore. After unhooking Pastor's fish, Phil looked at Pastor and said, "God is good, He provides."

"Amen," said Pastor, "He gives when His children are in need."

"I'm going back to get the fire started," said Phil. "Zach, could you show the fellows how to clean these?"

"Be glad to," said Zach and Phil handed him his knife and left.

Pastor said, "I think we have enough time to catch at least one more fish before you do that." With a large smile, Zach grabbed his pole and followed Pastor.

Phil went back and started the fire. He set up the remaining stove and started the water for cooking. After about 20 minutes Pastor, Weber, Mark, and Quinton came back, all smiling.

"How did you do?" asked Phil.

"Well," said Pastor slowly, "we had to stop because we were catching too many."

"Great," said Phil, "I have everything ready so we can start cooking as soon as they bring in the catch."

No sooner did he finish his sentence than Zach, Buck, and Dolton came back into camp, each with the prepared fish hanging on sticks through their gills and mouths. Phil had no idea that they had caught so many more fish. "Whew! When the Lord provides, He doesn't mess around," he observed.

Pastor lent him a hand in cooking and they were done in another half hour. Thumbs were already up when Pastor offered to do the blessing. "Gather around and hold hands," said Pastor. "Dear Father, You have looked down on us, Your children, and provided what we truly needed. As You draw us together and closer to You please continue to offer us Your blessings and protection. Bless this feast and make it health and strength for our bodies. This is asked through Christ our Lord. Amen."

Dinner truly was a feast! They ate without speaking except for the occasional, "Can I have more?" Going without lunch made the meal of fish and pan bread that much better. The sun was just starting to set as everyone finished. They sat back with full stomachs and stared at the sunset. The colors were particularly brilliant and clouds behind the rock cliff made it look like a beautiful pastel painting.

<{{}}><

"So did you check in on our boy today?" Karen asked with a smile.

"Well, I didn't want to worry you until after dinner, but since you asked, I tried several times today and couldn't get a visual lock on them. I was able to track their progress today and they seem to be on course, but it bothers me that I wasn't able to get the satellite imaging working. Before you get worried, it's possible that because of the area they're in, the satellite isn't picking up enough of a signal to lock in for visual. However, as I said, I was able to use the other programs to lock onto their location. They're still moving so that's good. Did you happen to get an e-mail?" he asked.

"No, I was hoping that you had," she replied, now concerned. "Well, perhaps tomorrow they'll move out of that area and we'll get a message from him. Stanley, please be careful about using The Company's programs to track Weber. I know that you're as concerned as I am but it's not worth the risk. Okay?"

"Don't worry, honey," he paused, "but you're right, it's not worth the risk. Would you pass the pepper?"

Attack

The sun finished setting and they all had full bellies. This was the happiest they had felt all day. They cleaned up and sat back to enjoy the fire. Since there wasn't any wind they had drawn up logs and spread themselves evenly around the pit.

"I like this much better than the lanterns. It really feels like we're camping," said Zach.

Pastor, who was reading a Bible, looked up and said, "Yes, but it's much harder to read by firelight."

There was a lull in the conversation so Phil asked, "Well, boys, what are your plans for the future?"

Buck smiled at this question and a few of the others looked at him and smiled too. Not wanting to acknowledge the knowing glances, Pastor asked, "Zach, why don't you go first?"

He just shrugged his shoulders and said, "I don't know, until this trip I hadn't thought about it, but the idea has crossed my mind to be a coach."

"Really? What kind of coach?" inquired Phil.

"Not too sure, really. Maybe for high school. Dunno, I'm gonna have to give it some more thought."

"I think I'd like to be a doctor," offered Quinton, not waiting to be asked.

"Yeah, Doc, you're a natural," encouraged Dolton.

Mark cleared his throat and turned to his dad, who was sitting next to him, "Umm, I was thinking that I would follow in my father's footsteps and become a. . . ."

Without warning, before he could finish, the fire exploded into a ball of flames reaching higher than their heads. Then it exploded in eight directions at the same time. It was as though the flames reached out trying to engulf them. The fire surrounded them! Then, the middle of the pit became a fiery face. The flames seemed to form not only a head and fiery hair, but they formed hands with long slender fingers that reached out trying to grab their throats! The face followed the hands coming right at them all passing through them screaming in unearthly tones, "Nooooo!"

Then it ended, as quickly as it started. The group had fallen back and all were lying on the ground in stunned silence for a second before getting up. They were too shocked to speak but the terror on their faces said it all. Pastor and Phil looked around to see if anyone was hurt. They slowly started getting up.

"It's okay, it's okay," said Pastor.

Phil began to comfort them when an unearthly noise took his attention and he turned in the direction of the lake. They all heard the sound. A combination of high-pitched shrieking and clicking and a leathery slapping sound was getting closer. They all looked at each other and turned toward the lake in time to see a dark cloud closing in on them from just above the surface of the lake. As the cloud got closer, Phil yelled, "Duck!"

Everyone dropped just as a swarm of bats swooped through the camp. There were thousands of them. It took a while for them to pass the camp area, all the time shrieking and diving at the group as they tried to hide under the logs. After the last of them flew away, Pastor and Phil stood up, not saying a word, to survey the area.

The air was still and dusk had turned to night. There were a few dead bats lying on the ground and the fire was burning as though nothing had happened.

Phil got up and stepped over the log. The rest of the group began to stand up, very slowly. Pastor started to speak again. Before he could even get a word out, hail, the size of peas, started crashing down around them. Phil yelled, "Head for the tents."

They ran for the tents as fast as they could, wondering if the thin cloth would offer any protection at all. A loud crash of thunder sounded and shook the ground as if a bomb went off. A bolt of lighting hit behind them lighting up the sky as if it were day. Without looking back, they dove into their tents, zipping up the doors behind them. The hailstorm lasted several minutes, pelting the tents, accompanied by more crashes of thunder from time to time. Suddenly, as if someone turned off a faucet, the hail stopped. The air was completely still. Then it began to rain. Not a violent rain, but a gentle one. It sounded like each raindrop was caressing the recently ravaged area. It continued for a few minutes and quit as fast as it started. No one knew what to say after all that had just transpired. It was several minutes before anyone spoke. Then Mark asked, "Dad, what's going on?"

He didn't get an answer right away but when he did it was almost a whisper. "The light rain we just received was a comfort measure or a reminder given to us by God that He sees everything and is here. But the other. . ." he paused and found himself catching his breath. "Well, it wasn't from God. I would say that some evil is not happy that we're here and certainly not happy with the protection we are being afforded by the Lord. It's over now and the Lord has sent his angels to protect us. Let's try and get some sleep."

"Mr. Phil," said Buck nervously, "what was that all about?"

"I don't know, Buck," answered Phil quietly, "maybe Pastor Mike can tell us something in the morning. I'm sure he is going to pray about it, we should too. Pray and try to get some sleep."

Weber had crawled into his sleeping bag and slid down and was making some strange sounds. Zach leaned over patted the lump and said, "Hey, Weber, it's okay, I won't let anything happen to you." Quinton and Dolton didn't say a word. They lay in their bags staring at the top of the tent. It was not a restful night. The unnatural sounds that came from the forest would, at times, bring the ones who had fallen into restless dozing back to stare wide-eyed and frightened into the darkness.

Fifth Morning – More Trouble

When it became light enough to see, everyone had the same idea and crawled from their tents. It was like an alarm had gone off because they all came out at the same time. Pastor and Phil had come out of their tents and walked up to talk to each other - both began talking at the same time. They smiled at each other and Pastor spoke, "Phil, I've never in my life seen or been involved in anything like that. I can tell you that we had the hand of the Lord protecting us last night."

Phil didn't speak right away. He shook his head and said, "Mike, I think the best thing for us to do is to get out of here right away. We can eat somewhere else down the trail."

Pastor nodded his head in agreement and turned to inform the group when he noticed that they had already heard what Phil said and without a word had started packing up the campsite. Phil and Pastor decided to go pack up the cooking area. They had only taken a few steps when they both stopped dead in their tracks.

"Oh my," said Pastor as they stood staring at the sight before them.

Phil didn't quite know what to make of it all and said, "Well, I guess we won't be using that firepit any more." The large crash of lightning they had heard hit behind them as they went dashing into their tents the night before had struck one of the large trees at the edge of the woods and split the tree right down the middle. The largest half fell across the cooking area directly over the firepit, completely destroying it and the stove that was next to it.

Pastor looked more closely and said slowly as he made his observation, "Why didn't it catch the tree on fire?"

"I don't know," said Phil, "all I do know is that it's a good enough reason to get out of here. There's too much I can't explain about this place." He headed over to retrieve the food sack. It was stuck pretty tightly under the stove, but he managed to remove it. Phil opened the it as he picked it up and shook his head, looking at the area around him.

Pastor saw his concern and asked, "What's wrong?"

Phil looked up and said, "The food in the bag is ruined and the stove is trashed." Phil looked again in the food sack and his shoulders drooped and he hung his head.

"What are we going to do?" Pastor worried.

"We're getting out of here now," said Phil with determination, "Let's get the group and go."

Pastor made another observation, "Uhh, Phil, weren't there dead bats lying around here last night?"

Phil looked around and said, "Yes. Not only that," he paused, looking around again, "it really doesn't look like it rained or hailed either. The only evidence that anything happened last night was the food and stove with the half a tree on them. Everything else is covered with morning dew."

They were silent again for a few moments. Then Phil said firmly, "Let's go."

The youth packed up the equipment quickly and had already donned the remaining packs when Phil and Pastor returned to the tent area. Pastor said, "Let's gather for a quick prayer."

They gathered quickly and held hands. Pastor began, "Dear Father, we thank You for Your hand in the protection You afforded us last night. Deliver us from any further evil on our trip and gain us safe passage today. We ask that You provide us with sustenance on our way and remove the fear and uneasiness that is within us this morning. We ask this through Christ our Lord. Amen."

The sound of wings flapping overhead and a loud screech sounded at the end of the prayer and Phil said decisively, "Grab your walking poles and let's get out of here." They fell into line, moving down the trail at a rapid gait.

They walked rapidly for about 20 minutes when Weber, huffing and puffing said, "Are we going to keep up this pace up all day?"

Phil slowed down and apologized, "I'm sorry, fellows, I have a lot on my mind and wasn't thinking. Let's rest a minute."

No one up to this point had said very much. Zach finally spoke and asked, "Are we out of that area yet?"

"I don't know," said Phil, "but as soon as you all catch your breath we should get moving. I'd like as much ground between me and that place as possible." They all nodded in agreement and got back on the trail.

They hiked along without noticing the trail or the surrounding environment as they had on previous days. Everybody was lost in their own thoughts and fears. Zach, who usually stayed behind Phil, had slowly moved his way to the back of the line to speak with Pastor.

"Pastor, can I have a word?" said Zach and they slowed to let the rest get out of hearing range.

"What's the problem, Zach?" asked Pastor.

"Well," Zach hesitated, "umm . . ."

"Go on," said Pastor, "whatever you tell me will be between you and me."

"Well, last night I, ah, well, I've never been afraid of anything and last night, well, that scared me and I don't know what to do about it."

Pastor gave Zach a pat on the shoulder and said, "Zach, if in your life it took something like last night to scare you for the first time, then you are the bravest person I know. I don't know if will be any comfort for you but I was scared and I knew that we were being protected by the Lord. I believe last night we witnessed a battle between good and evil. Evil lost and wasn't happy about it. The only thing that protected each one of us was our knowledge that God was there. In other words, our faith protected us. I believe that your faith, although young, must have been strong enough to have the protection you and the rest of us received last night. That thought alone should be enough to give you comfort. Don't worry too much about what scares you. Although it was the first time, it won't be the last. Keep your attention focused on what helps you through. Keep your eyes on the Cross."

"Yeah, I remember, be Cross-eyed." Zach looked at Pastor for a second and said, "Mark doesn't know how lucky he is to have a man like you for a father."

"Thank you, Zach," Pastor said as he put his hand on the back of his neck, "I believe he might. He started to say so last night."

Zach smiled and walked a little taller; he said, "Thanks Pastor," and headed up the line. Pastor smiled to himself and thought *that young man is going to make a good warrior for the Lord.*

It was late morning and Weber, Buck, and Mark were not feeling well. Their stomachs had been bothering them all morning but they thought it was because they hadn't eaten.

Phil stopped abruptly and turned around, "Has anyone seen a trail marker of any kind?"

They all shook their heads. It had been about thirty minutes since their last stop and Phil had not seen any trail markers.

"Well," said Phil, "let's have something to eat and then we'll go looking." They took off their packs and found a place to sit. Phil took the food sack out and emptied it on to the ground, "I was hoping that there was something left."

They didn't know that the food was ruined and they all stared at the pile on the ground. Reality set in and their stomachs growled even more. Dolton heard a moan and looked around to see a pale-looking trio. He turned to Phil and said, "Weber, Buck, and Mark aren't feeling well."

Phil walked over to them, "What seems to be the problem?" asked Phil.

Buck responded, "I don't know, my stomach is hurting. I thought it was from not eating."

"The three of you feel the same?"

They nodded yes. Phil stepped over to Pastor.

"Mike, we may have a very serious problem here."

"Why? Are they getting sick?"

"I don't know for sure but, if they are, they are going to need water and I think that the water pump and filtering system is failing."

"Phil, let's not lose our heads. We all ate and drank the same things yesterday and only three of us are getting sick. There must be a reason."

Quinton stood up and cleared his throat, "Excuse me, Mr. Phil, Pastor, I believe that I know how to help them and maybe find some food at the same time."

They stared at Quinton and Phil said, "You do?"

"Yes, sir, the forest we are standing in is a virtual smorgasbord *and* it's full of medicine." As Quinton explained and described his plan, everyone stared at him in disbelief, amazed that he knew so much about these things. Phil smiled and said, "Okay, Doc show me and teach me."

"We should start looking for the stuff that will help Weber, Buck and Mark first and then get some food," Doc instructed and he and Phil took off into the woods.

Confrontation

They were gone a long time, so Pastor was pacing the trail back and forth. Soon Zach and Dolton got up and started wandering around. Zach slowly wandered down the trail, hoping to find sight of Phil and Doc. Dolton followed him and said, "What's the matter tough guy, worried?"

That was the last straw. Zach was hungry, tired, and concerned about their current situation, not to mention that his newfound friends were getting sick and no medical facility was around. He was in no mood for Dolton's smart-aleck remarks. Zach whipped around and grabbed Dolton by the front of his shirt collar and pulled him close.

Pastor Mike spotted the confrontation and headed towards the two as fast as he could. Face to face Zach and Dolton were finally at it. "Hey, let go of me you street punk."

"I should kick your rich little butt."

Pastor split them up, "This isn't how we take care of things. Fighting isn't the answer."

Dolton straightened his shirt, "It was my fault, Pastor, I provoked Zach. My mouth sometimes says the dumbest things. It gets going before my brain is in gear."

The look of astonishment on Zach's face at the confession said everything that Pastor needed to know. He told them, "Shake hands as friends and brother Christians." Dolton held out his hand to Zach and said, "What I said was out of line and I hope that you would give me a chance to show you I am not a spoiled rich kid and to be a friend."

Zach stared at Dolton for a moment and then he smiled that smile that he showed just before he takes on a foe. He took Dolton's hand and started squeezing hard, "You know what you're asking?"

"Probably not," said Dolton, starting to wince at the pressure in his hand. Zach gave Dolton's hand just a little harder squeeze and a shake and continued to stare into Dolton's eyes. Then he said, "Friend," and let go of his hand.

Pastor sighed with relief and said, "Good," and walked back to check on the others. Dolton followed him, shaking his hand trying to get the blood back into it. Sounds of footsteps in the forest brought their attention back to their current situation. Pastor lowered his head in silent prayer when his attention was suddenly drawn to his right by a subtle sound. *Thank you, Lord!* His spirits were high as he greeted the returning party.

Phil and Quinton came walking out of the forest excited that they had found the remedy for their stomachs. "What did you find?" asked Pastor excitedly.

"We found the leaves that should help their stomachs," said Phil. Then turned to Quinton, "Okay Doc, would you take care of this while I talk to Pastor?"

Quinton took the leaves and asked Zach and Dolton to help prepare them.

"Okay, just grab a bunch and rub them together in your hands. We need to break the skins so the juices get into the water. We have to make a kind of tea with 'em," Quinton instructed.

"These smell good, what are they?" Zack asked.

"They're bay leaves." They continued in silence.

Phil took Pastor by the arm and started walking down the path. "I didn't want them to hear this but we need to keep moving. We're too far behind schedule to meet Nolan at the pickup point when we said we would. He's going to be worried when we don't show up today. We also need to be on the lookout for trail markers and food. I'm not certain we're still on course and the food and water situation, well. . .I don't need to tell you about that. I'm hoping that we'll come upon some hikers going in the opposite direction to help us and get us back on course and lead us to a water source."

Pastor agreed, "I know our current state is not good, but we've been helped all along. Don't forget to take *everything* to Him in prayer."

"I know you're right, Mike. Thanks for the reminder."

"By the way, you never asked if I found anything."

"Oh," he said, a bit confused, "did you find anything?"

"Yes," he replied with a sly grin, "Look to my right and out a little ways."

Phil aimed his gaze to Pastor's right side and out aways and his eyes suddenly opened very wide. "Water!" he shouted taken completely by surprise. "Get me what's left of the water filter."

They all gathered in a semi-circle to watch Phil filter the water. Weber was a little slow on the uptake and got left to the back of the pack. There was no shortage of thirst in this group. Phil tried to manipulate the filter the best he could, "It's no use. This isn't going to work. We'll end up getting sick from the water. I'm so sorry fellows," he surrendered.

Just then Weber made his way to the front of the group and saw Phil holding the damaged water filter. "Hey, I have one of those," he said, surprised at the realization of its importance.

"You do?" they all replied.

"Yeah, I opened up my pack the first night we were on the trail and didn't know what it was so I stuffed it in the bottom," he explained as he emptied his pack to get it out. "Here it is!" He gave it to Phil, who was speechless, and he pumped water into his water bottle and proceeded to fill everyone's in record time.

It took a while for Doc to prepare the remedy but as soon as it was done he gave it to his friends and told them, "It'll take a few minutes for it to start working, but we need to get going."

"Thanks, Doc," said Buck, as the others nodded their heads in thanks. They all got up and continued down the trail at a little slower pace than before. Everyone was looking for trail markers and anything they could eat. They had gone along for about forty-five minutes and the forest was getting thicker and the trail narrowed. The ailing stomachs started to feel better.

"Stop!" yelled Quinton, "There's berries. And wild onions!"

Phil stopped the group and made his way back to Quinton, "Where, Doc?" he asked excitedly.

"Over there." Quinton pointed to a hillock a fair distance away.

"The rest of you, rest here," ordered Phil. He and Quinton left the trail to collect some food.

Everyone had unloaded and sat on the side of the trail. Pastor kept a close eye on the patients as they guzzled from their water bottles, "Easy on that water. We're not sure if that's what gave you boys a bad stomach."

Weber, who'd been uncharacteristically quiet since the night before, spoke, "Excuse me, Pastor."

"Yes," said Pastor, "are you ok?"

"Yes, sir, I am now, thanks to Doc, but, umm, I was just wondering about what happened last night," and he started to shake.

"It's okay, Weber," said Pastor as he came over and put his hand on his shoulder. "Maybe I should explain what I think happened last night."

Quinton and Phil rejoined the group with arms full of wild onions and a bowl full of berries. Without interrupting Pastor's conversation, they got the rest of the group to help wash off the berries with their water bottles and they passed them around. They ate as they listened.

"It's my opinion that last night there was a fight between good and evil, and evil lost. Evil wasn't happy about it but it wasn't about to give up. However it didn't have a chance because we had already asked our Lord for protection which he afforded us completely last night."

Quinton interjected, "But why weren't we burned when the fire went around us."

"Good question," said Pastor.

Before he could explain further, Mark explained, "It was because of the protection the Lord gave us. Remember the story of Shadrach, Meshach, and Abednego? When King Nebuchadnezzar had them thrown into the fire because they refused to renounce the Lord? They were unharmed because they knew the Lord and He protected them. Their faith saved them from the fire."

"About the fire," said Dolton. "I saw a face and hands that looked liked they were trying to reach out and choke me."

"Yeah," said Buck, "what about that?" The others nodded except Quinton, who looked like he was busy with his own thoughts.

"I don't have a clear explanation about that, but if you'll remember the last thing that happened after the hail stopped suddenly. The gentle rain fell. I felt as if, well, it were a cleansing rain. . .as if the area were being caressed tenderly. That would have been God healing the area after evil's little tantrum," explained Pastor.

"So He was watching over us," replied Buck.

Pastor and Phil smiled proudly. "Yes," said Pastor, "exactly. I believe that we are being watched over right now and we are on a mission, not just a hiking trip, and our faith is the key that will get us through. Our faith will help us to grow stronger in the Lord and stronger in our love for each other."

Dolton and Zach glanced at each other. Pastor heard the rumbling in his own stomach and said, "Pass me some of those berries, Phil." Given a handful, Pastor lifted his full hands up and said, "Lord, You have shown us that you are with us in good times and in bad. You have taught us that we don't need to rely on ourselves for life. You have provided life for us in the beautiful surroundings we find ourselves in. Thank You for these fruits of your creation to sustain us. Bless this food and bless our journey. Thank you Lord Jesus. Amen."

"Amen," echoed the group in a particularly heartfelt way.

After eating and a short rest they were ready to start off again. Zach helped Weber don his pack and stand up. *Where would I be if Zach weren't here to help me?* thought Weber.

"Okay, fellows, it's time to face the facts," said Phil." We need food and water, we may be lost, and the only thing we have going for us is the sun. I'm not sure we're on the right trail and we are not on schedule, other than that we're fine."

"And the bad news would be. . . ?" said Dolton; then he shot a quick look toward Zach, "I did it again, didn't I? Sorry."

"Let's not lose our heads," said Pastor. "As long as we remain calm and rely on the Lord we'll be fine."

"Don't worry, Mr. Phil. I'm feeling a whole lot better," said Weber.

"Me too, and I'm full from those berries," added Buck.

"Who would have thought that such a little snack could be so satisfying?" observed Zach. Mark and his dad exchanged knowing glances.

"So, let's get moving," ordered Phil. Everyone started off down the trail with a renewed outlook and uplifted spirits.

Memento

Pastor took his place in the rear. As they hiked along he began thinking about what Mark had started to say the night before. Pastor reached out and tapped Mark on the shoulder as they walked and said, "Mark, I was thinking about what you started to say last night."

"Yes?"

"I was wondering."

"Yes?"

"Are you sure you want to follow in my footsteps? I mean, are you sure this is what you want to do and not what you think I want you to do?"

Mark turned his head and answered, "Yes, Dad, I'm sure. I've thought about it for a long time and whenever I think about my future that's the first thing that pops into my mind. So, yes, that's what *I* want to do." They hiked along in silence for a while.

"I was thinking about your mother and you and what you said last night and I think that your mother would want you to have this. It may not be the appropriate time or place to give it to you but I think it's the right thing to do and I'm not waiting any more." Pastor hastened his steps and grabbed Mark's hand, stopped him and put something into it then closed his fingers around it. "Here," said Mike, "this is for you."

Mark could tell this meant a lot. He could hear the emotion in his dad's voice. Mark opened his hand to see a gold cross on a gold chain. It was unlike any other cross he had ever seen. It was a silhouette of the risen Christ cut out of the middle of a gold cross. "Your mother had it made for me, when I graduated seminary, from her old jewelry. We weren't very well off financially but she wanted me to have something special so she took all of her gold jewelry and had it melted down and designed this cross. She told me that she was proud of me and I think that she would agree that you have this to reflect our pride in you."

"Dad," said Mark and he could say no more. This was so unexpected and so touching that words escaped them both for the moment. Pastor gently took the chain from Mark's hand and placed it around his son's neck, and then he grabbed his son and gave him a tight hug. A tear ran down Pastor's cheek and when they separated from the embrace, Mark had one in the exact same place.

"We'd better catch up," said Pastor as he cleared his throat, "We don't want them to get worried about us too." They took off at a slow run and resumed their place in the back of the group.

They had been hiking for the better part of the morning when the trail started to go up and the trees, once again, started to thin. Phil stopped the group. Before them was a divide in the trail. Pastor made his way up to Phil, who was staring at the trails and pulling on his beard in thought.

"Well," said Pastor, "which way do we need to go?"

"I don't know," said Phil indecisively. They stood there for a moment and Phil said, "I think I'm going to take a page out of Dolton's book."

Pastor stared at Phil, confused.

"Let's pray about it and then take our best guess," said Phil.

Pastor smiled and gathered the group. "Fellows, we have come to a split in the trail, and I don't remember which way the map indicated us to go, so we are going to follow Dolton's example and pray. Bow your heads." After a few amused looks they complied. "Dear Father, You have been faithful and we have no doubt that You are with us now. We have come to what we will call a crossroads and are uncertain which direction to choose. Please clear our heads and direct us down the right path. We ask this through Christ our Lord. Amen."

"Okay, fellows, which way do we go?"

"I went left," said Dolton.

"Okay, then left it is," and Phil started off down the left trail.

The trail proved to be an easy hike. The trees thinned and the trail widened and the sun shone brightly through the woods. They hadn't passed another water source and most of the group had run out of water. They shared what they had, but the situation was about to get serious if they didn't find some soon.

Phil waved Pastor to the front, he obviously wanted to speak with him again as they walked. "Pastor," said Phil, "I pretty sure we're not going to make it back to meet Nolan tonight, we're moving too slowly. I think that we're going in the right direction but without the map and the lack of trail markers I just don't know. Not only that, we need to find water soon."

Pastor responded, "I hope Nolan knows what to do when he realizes that something has happened when we don't show tonight."

"He will," said Phil.

"I have a feeling that everything will be okay," said Pastor. "We are being guided by a higher source and He's helping you deliver us." Pastor drifted back toward the rear of the line again and as he passed Buck he heard them talking about the all the noises of the forest. The birds were singing more noticeably and they seemed to be enjoying the hike again. *Praise God from Whom all blessings flow. You are so wonderful to lighten their hearts in the midst of our trials. Thank you Lord,* prayed Pastor as he finally took up the rear.

<{{}}><

"Stanley, since you decided to take the afternoon off, I have a surprise for you," said Karen coyly.

"Oh, really?"

"Yes, we are going to have dinner in front of the monitor tonight."

"Oh," he replied a little disappointed, "I thought you had something else in mind."

"I know." She walked over to the computer armoire and opened the doors. On the screen was the youth group. She explained that she had tapped into the satellite program and enabled the automated visual tracking programs and had been watching them for a good portion of the day.

"We have Weber-vision," she teased.

"Why, you little vixen!" he shouted, "You haven't lost your touch. You are still the best hacker The Company ever had. You never cease to amaze me."

"I know," she said as she slipped her hand into his. She led him to a chair in front of the armoire and took the seat next to his and watched the group as they traversed the wild.

"Too bad we don't have audio," lamented Stanley.

Weber's Adventure – Zach's Transformation

Phil reached the crest and stopped in utter disbelief at the sight before him. It was by far the most spectacular panorama he had ever gazed upon in his life! The rest of the group made their way to him and stood in silence as they took in the beautiful landscape. From where they were standing they viewed a panorama that was unequaled in any movie or TV show they had ever seen. The side of the hill below them was covered in green grass, as in the meadows they had previously seen, but the wind was blowing in such a manner that each blade of grass moved in harmony with another. It was as if God threw down a carpet of green silk and added a gentle breeze to invite them in.

Just beyond the grass, which dramatically halted halfway down the steep hill, was, in marked contrast, a rocky area that looked like it didn't belong. The rocks were not like the rocks they had seen along the way. These were more like river rocks. The rocks they had seen up to this point were jagged, brown and gray, and looked like they had broken away from bigger rocks; the kind usually found in these mountainous areas. The rocks in this area were smooth, shiny and colorful. There was almost a gentleness to them, if such a thing could be said about a collection of rocks. Compared to the terrain and rockiness they had seen so far on their trip, the smoothness and color of these rocks were a welcome sight to their eyes.

This was a most unlikely site but even more surprising was the fast-moving stream that was just below the rocks. It appeared to them rather suddenly when their eyes moved down past the rocks; almost as if it had been playing hide and seek with them and didn't want to reveal itself until just that moment.

"It's like a garden," said Quinton.

"Like the Garden of Eden," Mark corrected him.

"That's got to be the snow melt," said Phil almost inaudibly. "There was no stream on the map in this area that I can remember." Just as he said it his eyes followed the path of the water downstream and saw, off in the distance, a rushing river. "There must be many runoff streams and they're gathering in that river over there," he said pointing it out to the young men who had now formed a semi-circle with Phil in the middle.

"Wow," said Dolton, "you can even hear the rapids from here. Listen." They stood there in silence for a moment and listened. The birds were active in this hilly oasis as well as the buzz of the flies that were now their constant companions. A frog made his presence known by his croaking song. Off in the distance they could hear the roar of the rapids as they pummeled the rocks and the shore. They began to notice that this area seemed cooler than where they had just been. It was a welcome contrast for the hot, thirsty group. They removed their packs and sat down. They had been traveling for too long without water. Most of them had headaches and were nauseated and weak from dehydration. Weber, Quinton, and Buck put their jackets on.

Pastor Mike and Phil looked at each other and walked together away from where the others were resting. "Phil, we need water in the worst way. Do you think we should chance going down to the stream to get some? It looks pretty steep and I'm not sure I can make it down there."

Phil thought a moment; it was hard to concentrate. The need for water affected his thinking. "I should probably do it. I have concerns about those rocks. They look like a rock-slide just waiting to happen. If I started sliding down I'm pretty sure I would end up in the stream. From here, it looks like the current is pretty strong. The water is flowing down-hill toward that river. I'll be the one to go."

They had tried to keep the youth from overhearing and were surprised when Weber stepped up to them. He had been listening from a distance. "No, Mr. Phil," Weber said with authority, "I'll go down there. I'm the lightest one and the rocks don't bother me. Anyway, no one else has a water filter left. I'll fill up the collapsible jug and bring it up for everyone. Okay?"

Phil looked at him and saw the resolve on his face. He prayerfully considered Weber's request. Weber had not volunteered for a single physical task on this trip and Phil knew that he was feeling inadequate about it. He realized that it was important for Weber to participate. This was his chance to prove to himself that he was as worthy as all the others on this trip. *Lord, be with Weber and keep him safe,* he prayed silently.

"All right then, but go slow and be careful," said Phil.

Weber turned around and ran back to where he was sitting. He took his jacket off and gave it to Zach. Then he hoisted his pack onto his shoulders. Zach helped him get it into place and gave him a slap on the top of the pack to let him know he was done. He turned around, grabbed the jug and nodded thanks to Zach. Then he began his descent.

Weber slowly and carefully inched his way down the hill as the others watched from above. The pack was making it even more difficult than usual to keep his balance. The descent was more slippery than he anticipated but he made his way down the grassy area without incident. Weber stood before the rocky area for a few moments surveying the next leg of this treacherous trek. He tried to determine where he should go down over the rocks and where he would end up if he slipped. He walked parallel to the stream for a few minutes and then started to make his way down over the rocks.

Phil commented to Pastor Mike, "He made a good decision. If he starts to slip he'll land on that large flat rock that's sticking out over the water's edge over there and won't end up in the stream."

Weber tottered under the weight of his pack as he made his way down through the rocky area. Phil could barely hold himself still with worry. When Weber reached the water's edge he started down the hill himself. "I shouldn't have let him go alone, what was I thinking?" he told Pastor has he left. He slid to his rear on the grass. *What was I thinking? He didn't need to bring his backpack. We should have looked for a safer place to access the water. How could I have been so stupid!*

Meanwhile, Weber slipped his backpack onto one arm and opened one of the outer pockets. He reached in and got the water filter and his water bottle, zipped up the pocket and put the pack back on his shoulders. *After I fill the jug I'll fill my water bottle. Thank goodness the bear didn't destroy my pack*, thought Weber; *I don't know where we would be without all my stuff. This should only take a few minutes, then we can all get something to drink. Too bad this is so hard to get to. I sure would like to wash up.*

Weber got down on his knees and carefully leaned over the edge of the water and put the tube into the quick moving waters below him. Remembering how Phil had taught him to hold both the water jug and the pump at the same time, he correctly positioned his hands and began pumping. The water splashed up onto his arms and face. It felt cold and smelled fresh. He was very thirsty but he knew he had to wait until he had put the water through the filter. He really didn't want to have problems with diarrhea. The guys already made enough fun of him, especially Zach, and they were seriously low on toilet paper.

Phil regretted his decision to let Weber go on his own. As he made his way down the steep, grassy part of the hill, using the same path as Weber, he chastised himself for not thinking the plan through more thoroughly. *I know I'm dehydrated but I can't believe I let him do this.* In his haste to act, he began slipping down the grass. He didn't stop until he had almost reached the rocks.

Weber looked up and saw Phil coming down and noticed that he wasn't having such an easy time as he'd had himself. Phil wasn't as sturdy on the decline as Weber had been. *Maybe I really am more athletic than I give myself credit for*, he surmised as he could see Phil slip time and time again. *Guess I'm not such a geek after all*, thought Weber. *Well, anyway, after I bring them water I'll be the hero—geek or not!* He pumped vigorously to fill the jug as fast as he could. When it was full, shouted as he stood up, "Hey! It's full, I'm comin' up!"

But Weber stood up so fast that he couldn't balance the load of his backpack and the full water jug. He stepped back to steady himself but slipped off the side of the rock and tumbled into the water.

Just as Weber hit the water, Phil took a large step down the hill and lost his balance. He started sliding down, feet first, to the edge of the grass and the beginning of the rock-covered slope. He rose, took a panicked step into the rock area and continued his slide all the way down the rocky area to the place where Weber had been. When he hit the bottom, he fell forward landing on his hands and knees on the large rock jutting out over the stream. But he was too late to grab Weber's hand and he could only watch as the boy drifted away in the rapid current. He could see that Weber was struggling to stay afloat under the load of his backpack.

"Get your pack off!" he yelled.

"I – I can't!" screamed Weber.

The rest of the group stood at the top of the hill in utter panic and disbelief! They didn't know what to do. Their friend was being swept down to the river and it looked like Phil had hurt himself when he fell. They were helpless to do anything. All they could do was watch.

Zach looked down at the water and the grass and then the rocks. Then he looked at the landscape in the direction that Weber was headed. His head cleared all of a sudden and he was sure he saw a place in the distance where he could safely access the river. If he were able to get there before Weber he could grab a hold of him and get him out. The rest of the group had their eyes locked on Weber and Phil. No one saw Zach run off.

Phil yelled again, "Get your pack off! You have to get it off!"

Weber went under again.

He saw Weber's feet surface, then the pack, then his head. "Help!" panicked Weber. It was clear that Weber was in big trouble.

Phil looked at the terrain along the stream. There was no shoreline on which to run ahead and get to him. Phil realized that the only chance Weber had was if he went after him. He pulled off his boots as fast as he could and jumped into the rapid water. It was faster and colder than he thought. The shock of the cold water made him very alert and he put his body into action. As the currents drove him into the rocks that jutted out of the water, he wondered how Weber had gotten this far without getting seriously hurt.

The others at the top of the hill were yelling at Weber for him to get rid of the backpack. It didn't matter that Weber couldn't hear them. They kept on shouting – they needed to do something! They began to edge along the terrain atop the hill in the direction that Phil and Weber were being swept. All they could do was watch in horror as their friend disappeared from the water's surface time and time again only to reappear in distress and be quickly forced toward the mouth of the river rapids ahead.

Weber couldn't believe that he had fallen off the rock. The water was so cold. The backpack was very heavy in the water. It felt like an anchor. As Weber heard Phil yell for him to get rid of his pack, he thought, *I just can't let my pack go! Everything I have is here. If I lose it now there won't be any way for us to get out of here alive. They need me and they need my stuff.* The water pulled him under once again. Everything was blurry this time.

"Oww!" he yelled under water. Whatever he had just hit forced most of the air from his lungs and he just barely made it up to the surface and gasped. "Help!" he heard himself yell. *What am I doing?* he thought, *I'm gonna die!* The pack got heavier and heavier and it was clear to Weber now that if he didn't get rid of the pack he was going to drown under its weight. He tried to get the straps off of his arms. He went under again. This time he was tumbling under the water. His head hit the bottom of the riverbed. His left shoulder really hurt. He was pretty sure he wasn't coming up this time. Somehow he struggled back to the surface and gasped for air once again. *This isn't good,* he thought. *I can't breathe and I can't get my pack off. If I go under again I won't have the strength to get back up to the surface again.*

Phil was close enough now to see the panic on Weber's face. *I'm not sure he can take much more of this*, thought Phil. *He's not that strong a swimmer and it looks like he's hurt. I've got to get to him before he goes under again.* Phil swam harder than he had ever swum before. All of his muscles burned and strained as he pushed through the water with all the strength he possessed. *I have to make it! I have to get to him!*

"He's not going to make it!" yelled Quinton. "I think he's hurt."

"Quiet, Quint!" said Pastor Mike tightly. "He's going to make it. The Lord won't abandon us. Remember that."

"Hey, where's Zach?" said Dolton.

For a moment they all looked around for signs of Zach. "There!" said Quinton, pointing down toward the river.

Zach had made his way downstream over the grass and rough terrain and was now making his way to the river. It was clear that Zach's plan was to cut off Weber from getting into the rapids of the big river up ahead. The boys began to cheer Zach on and tried to let Phil know that help was on the way.

Mark looked over at his father, who stood quietly and was obviously in prayer, so he followed his father's example. He turned his head upward and folded his hands in front of himself and began praying out loud, "God, I know we aren't supposed to make deals with you." As he prayed, the others heard him and slowly bowed their heads and offered up their own silent prayers. Mark continued, "So I won't, but I want You to know that I would like it very much if you would please save Weber and please make sure that Mr. Phil and Zach don't get hurt either. Thank you."

Pastor Mike put his hand on the shoulder of the young man standing next to him and with pride said, "I couldn't have said it better myself, son."

The water was moving Weber faster now toward the rushing rapids of the big river. There was little time before he reached the mouth and was pulled into the violent waters and crushed by their forces. Phil was desperate! The water temperature had started to seriously impede his efforts. It wouldn't be long before he and Weber would be affected by hypothermia. This was a concern that kept Phil focused. He had promised Stan to look out for Weber and keep him safe, a promise he intended to keep if it was the last thing he did! He was almost within arm's reach of Weber and saw the real struggle he was having. His left shoulder had become dislocated, probably the last time he went under. He wasn't going to be able to loosen the backpack by himself. If Phil didn't get there to help him, Weber was going to drown.

Weber could see that Phil was almost there, but there was nothing he could do to help himself. He still couldn't get the pack off and every time he tried he would start sinking again, not to mention the pain in his shoulder. His strength was waning and it was all he could do just to keep his head above water. The current was turning him around again and he was facing the mouth of the river. He could see the rapids rushing and the rocks jutting up out of the water. He also saw how hard the water was hitting the rocks. *That's it, then,* he said to himself. *I'm going to get knocked out and drown, or I'm going to pass out and drown. I guess I'm not a hero after all.* Dejected and almost out of strength he said a little prayer, *God, please don't let it hurt when I die and please don't let my parents be too sad that I'm gone. I know that Mr. Phil has put his life on the line for me, so rescue him and get the group home safely. I guess I'll be seeing You face to face in a few minutes.*

No sooner had he finished than a big rush of water thrust him up against a huge rock. That was it. As the rest of his strength left him he felt himself slip into unconsciousness. The darkness started to fall and his knew his eyes were closing for the last time. He heard his name called, "Weber. Weber, I'm here!" he heard. *That must be my guardian angel,* he thought as he felt himself being lifted up. The heaviness of the pack seemed to disappear and he could feel the pain in his shoulder no more. His burden was finally being relieved. *So this is what it's like to die,* he thought. Then everything went black.

<{{}}>＜

Stanley and Karen were frozen to the screen watching their son struggle. "No," whispered Stanley. "C'mon Web, hang on."

Karen started to cry. "Weber," she said, barely able to get the words out. "Can you zoom in any more, Stan?" she asked as she put her hand on his forearm.

"Not with this equipment. The equipment at the lab can, though. I can still get you in. Do you want to come?"

"No, but please don't leave yet," she said.

"Honey, the signal is fading. Increase the signal booster over there, will you Karen?" he said. "That's better, thanks honey."

"Don't worry," he continued, "the boy will be all right."

"I know," she replied as she put her head on his shoulder.

"Look!" he said suddenly, pointing to the screen. "There goes Zach! Who would have ever thought. . . ?" He let his surprise trail off.

<{{}}>＜

In an office on one of the top floors, Marshall sat glued to his monitor. He had been ghosting the Deerfields' transmissions and documenting their illegal use of Company resources. Although, at the moment, that was much less important than the object of Marshall's attention. "C'mon, Wes. Let your instincts take over! I just found you again and

240

I'm not going to lose you again to a bad decision because you were dehydrated! C'mon!"

Just then, the door to his office opened and his secretary poked her head in, "Did you call for me, sir?" she asked.

"No!" he replied forcefully. He thought for a second and said again, "No. Thank you." He never took his eyes off the screen.

The secretary backed out and silently closed the door.

<{{}}><

Phil had just reached the spot where Weber had gone under for the last time. He took a deep breath and dove down. He went under just in time to see the force of the underwater current make Weber hit his head on the rock. *If I can't get to him he isn't going to make it*, thought Phil as he used the last bit of energy to fight the current and get to Weber. *I can't let him get caught in that river current. This stream is bad enough. C'mon Weber, hang on, I'm almost there*, he willed his thoughts to Weber.

He reached Weber just as the river rapids began to draw them both in. He grabbed Weber's pack and tried to lift it off his shoulders, but before he could get it entirely off, he saw an arm reach down into the water from the surface and grab it. The arm of a savior! It began to lift Weber to the surface. Phil, following the lead of the savior, pushed Weber up out of the watery enemy. Just as he pushed through the surface for air he saw the determined face that belonged to the arm of the savior. Zach had somehow made his way down the hill, braving the treacherous terrain to save his friend.

"I gotcha, man! I gotcha!" shouted Zach as he pulled his friend onto the rocky shore. This was the only spot that was accessible to the stream before the river took them.

Weber had already lost consciousness and wasn't breathing.

Phil pulled himself up on the rock next to Weber on the other side of Zach. He was out of breath and strength and could only watch.

"Hold on, Web!" said Zach.

In what seemed like one movement, before Phil could even catch his breath, Zach removed Web's backpack and got him in position to give mouth-to-mouth. Zach leaned on Weber's chest to remove anything that might have been lodged there. "C'mon, man, BREATHE!" he shouted. He leaned over and pinched Weber's nose, lifted his chin and breathed as much air as he could into Weber's mouth.

All of a sudden, Weber spewed a geyser of water up into Zach's mouth. Weber began coughing and spitting up as Phil rolled him over on his side.

"Gross!" yelled Zach. "Aww, man! I didn't know he was going to do that!"

Phil held Weber's head gently as he expelled the rest of the water from his lungs and stomach. It wasn't a pretty sight, but to Zach it was the best thing he could have ever seen.

After Weber regained some control over his bodily functions, Phil helped him sit up. No sooner had Weber looked up than Zach grabbed him in a hug and wouldn't let go. Phil fell back on his knees and watched the touching sight. These two boys, who had tormented each other from the time they met, were locked in an embrace of relief and love.

"Web, man, I thought I was going to lose you. Don't do that again!" cried Zach.

At that moment, Weber realized what had just happened. The one person he had prayed for the most had just saved his life.

A couple years back, when Weber went to Pastor Mike to complain about Zach and how he always picked on him and teased him, he was told that he should love his enemies and pray for the ones who persecute or tease him. Zach, who, for all these years, Weber thought had hated him, was his savior, his angel.

In that moment of revelation, Weber's heart turned all the way around for Zach. He felt the warmth of tears forming in the corners of his eyes. He was losing control and shook under the sobs of joy and love and relief that followed. "Zach, I'm sorry, man. Thank you so much for saving my life. Thank you *so much*," cried Weber.

Exhausted and filled with emotion, Phil found himself wiping a falling tear from his cheek as he mouthed a silent prayer, *Thank you Lord for keeping Your promise.*

"Oww!" yelled Weber. At that moment, the feeling in his body came back, "My shoulder is broken!"

Phil acted quickly, "It's not broken, it's dislocated; Zach cover your ears."

"Hunh?" he said.

Phil had already grabbed Weber's arm and was lifting it enough to get his own under Weber's armpit. At the same time, he lifted his arm and lifted Weber's and put the joint back in place. This elicited an unexpected flash of pain far over and above the underlying pain he felt from the dislocation.

"Agghhhhhh!" echoed all through the valley.

"Cool!" said Zach as he watched the deformed shoulder return to its normal state.

"Aww, man, that hurt!" yelled Weber at Phil, "Why did you do that?"

"I had to set it as quickly as possible to prevent further injury. Sorry, but if you saw it coming you might have tensed up and unknowingly prevented the set. You're okay now, Weber. You'll probably be sore for a couple of days. We are definitely going to have to lighten your load. Where's your pack?" asked Phil as he looked around.

Lost

Meanwhile, the rest of the group had taken a slower, safer route to get down there. Mark, Buck, Quinton and Dolton arrived and formed a little semi-circle around the trio. Pastor arrived last and pushed his way inside the group, "Thank God you're all right," he said gratefully as he panted from the trip down.

Phil looked up and said, "He'll be sore for a couple of days, and he could use some rest."

Pastor asked, "Weber, how do you feel?"

"Everything is a little blurry, but I'm fine, sir," said Weber.

Quinton suddenly noticed, "Where's your glasses?" He had never seen Weber without them on.

"Down river, I suspect," Phil said sadly, "and we lost our only good water pump and filter too."

"No," said Weber, "it didn't go in with me. I'm pretty sure that I dropped it and the jug on the shore where I fell in."

"Come on, Zach, help me get Weber to his feet," said Phil and they got him up. He was weak and his legs were wobbly. Zach put his arm around him and held him up, "It's okay, lean on me."

"Buck, Dolton, Mark, you need to make your way to where Weber fell in and see if the pump and filter and Weber's water bottle are still on the shore, and be careful," Phil instructed. "Pastor, would you and Quinton go back up and find a place to camp for the night? Once you find a place to set up camp, send Doc back our way to see if we need help. But get it started and prepare a pit for a fire."

Pastor frowned at him, concerned about the nearness of the woods. Phil understood and responded, "It'll be all right. There are places far enough away from the trees that it'll be safe for a fire." They all left for their assignments. Zach and Phil slowly helped Weber get moving.

Buck, Mark, and Dolton started making their way over to the "drop in point" as Dolton was now calling it. Mark stayed above the rocky area. He wasn't as sure about the rocks as the other two. As they reached the area where Weber fell in, Buck found the filter lying alongside a rock. "Oh, no," he said, "it looks like it might be broken." But he picked it up and he slid it down into his shirt.

"The jug's over here!" Dolton shouted. "When Weber fell in, the jug must have landed on the rock. Most of the water's gone. There's still enough for everyone to have a drink, though." He picked the jug up and took a drink. He walked over to Buck and handed him the jug.

"Oh, man, I needed that!" Buck sighed in relief after taking a mouthful.

"Come on, Buck," Dolton urged, "let's get this stuff back and maybe Mr. Phil can fix the pump." As they reached the top of the rocky area they handed the jug to Mark.

"Ahhhh. . .the elixir of life." Mark tipped the jug up, drank and sighed as he pulled it from his lips, "The anointed waters, the well-springs, the living waters."

"You're starting to sound like Dolton," said Buck.

"Yeah! Who are you? Me?" Dolton teased.

Pastor and Quinton had found a place back at the top of the hill not too far from where they all had stood and watched Weber go in. The ground wasn't as level as the previous places they had set the tents but it provided cover for the tents and an open area for a fire. Pastor watched Phil, Zach, and Weber coming back up the hill. They stopped every few feet to let Weber get his bearings. The other three boys made it back to the top of the hill and headed to Pastor and Quinton to help set up camp.

They gave Pastor the news about the pump and filter, he just shook his head and said, "Mark, you stay here and give us a hand. Buck and Dolton can go see if Mr. Phil and Zach need help with Weber."

Weber was doing very well and was almost to the top of the hill and the campsite.

"Let me help," said Dolton to Phil and they traded places. He nodded at Zach who returned his smile.

Buck said to Zach, "Want a rest, Zach?"

"No, it's okay, I've got him."

"Okay," and Buck turned and followed Phil up the hill to the camp. They had all but one tent up by the time Phil and Buck came walking into camp.

"Oh, great! Good job," said Phil, "they should be here in a few minutes. Doc, would you please pull out sleeping gear for Weber and set up a cushioned area by that rock so he can sit down?"

"Sure, but don't you think he'll want to sleep it off?" asked Quinton.

"I'm sure he'll be tired, but we can't let him go to sleep. He's suffered a head injury. We have to be sure he didn't get a concussion. If we let him go to sleep after sustaining a concussion, he could lapse into a coma. No, we need to get him comfortable and keep him awake."

"Phil," said Pastor, with disappointment, "They found the pump and filter but it looks like it's broken."

He handed it to Phil, whose shoulders drooped on receiving the news, "I'll look at it later."

The rock was ready when they got Weber into camp. "Put him over here," said Pastor and Weber sat down to rest. Phil called Quinton over, "Okay Doc, I need you and the boys to go find something to eat, do you think you can?"

"Yes, sir, I think that area there has what we are looking for," as he pointed to the other side of the meadow area, "and we may have to check by the river. Don't worry, we'll be safe."

"Take Dolton, Mark, and Buck to help," said Phil, "and be careful! Stay in pairs." They left with Quinton in the lead.

"Come on, Zach," said Phil.

"What about Web?" said Zach.

"He's okay for the moment. Pastor'll keep an eye on him." Phil turned to Pastor and said, "We're going to back-track the trail to get some wood for a fire. We'll be back soon," and they left.

Pastor told Weber to relax. He explained that it would be a little bit before everyone returned. He felt like he needed to be busy while everyone was gone so he started to set up a ring for a firepit while Weber rested.

"Pastor, do you remember I came to you when I was little and asked your advice about Zach?" Weber asked.

"I remember. You were pretty upset. I seem to recall that he was always picking on you and teasing you. That day, you were particularly unhappy."

"Yeah. I thought you were crazy when you told me that we should pray for those who persecute us. As a matter of fact, I didn't pay attention to your sermon the next Sunday because I thought you were just giving me a line to get rid of me. About a week later, Zach was really getting on my case and I decided to use your advice as a last resort."

"Really?" he laughed.

"Yeah. I've been praying for him ever since. And, you know, it seemed that every time I prayed for him, his teasing bugged me less and less, until one day, I realized that he was teasing me because I had something that he didn't."

"And what was that?"

"Love."

"How do you know that?"

"Well, I never saw him with any family member. He was always alone. His parents never came to church or any school event."

"Hmm."

"I never figured that he would like me; in fact, I expected the teasing to continue and get worse."

"Did it?"

"No. It was pretty much the same, but it didn't bother me too much after that. I mean, pretty much all the kids tease me. I know I'm kind of a nerd. I don't care, I like who I am. But here's the really surprising thing. Today, when I realized it was Zach who rescued me, I knew that it was God telling me that I had done the right thing all these years."

Pastor looked at him in amazement. This awkward little boy had just become a Christian man.

"I have a feeling that Zach and I are destined to become great friends. When we get back, I think I'll invite him to dinner."

"That's a wonderful idea, Weber."

Out in the meadow, as the others were following Quinton looking for edible plants and berries, Buck saw something and said, "Look over there," he said, pointing. "Come on, let's check it out."

Dolton said that he would stay with Doc to keep looking for food so Buck and Mark hiked across the end of the meadow.

"What do you know," said Mark astounded, "it's a trail."

"Come on," said Buck, "we'll tell Mr. Phil when we get back. Right now we need to go help Doc and Dolton."

Phil and Zach had walked back quite a way into the woods. It was proving difficult to find good wood and kindling to use for a fire. "Wow," said Zach, "this stuff is getting heavy."

"Yes, and I'm sure we're feeling it more because we're tired and hungry. I think we have enough here for the rest of the day and this evening. We should start back. We don't want Pastor to worry. We've been gone a little longer than I wanted," said Phil as they started back with full arms.

Meanwhile, Quinton's group found everything they could. "I think we have enough food here to keep us going through the night."

"I *hope* you don't mean *going*," joked Dolton.

Ignoring him, Doc continued, "These onions'll make a great soup, and the berries we found should suffice for dessert. We should get back, they'll be getting worried."

"Do you really know what all this stuff is? I mean, do you *know* what you're doing?" asked Dolton.

"Sure, you're holding the bulbs from lilies. They're nutritious and tasty and should provide substance for the stew. The leaves we picked from that young tree we found are bay leaves. Your mom uses them in soups and stuff. It's the same stuff you buy in the store. The red berries are currant and their flowers and stems are filled with vitamin C. Buck, you have the dessert. Those are blackberries."

"And for all these years I thought you were a geek. I'm impressed," said Dolton.

Pastor was pacing when Quinton's group came strolling back into camp. They carefully laid out the fixings for one of the strangest soups they ever heard of.

A moment later, Phil and Zach came into camp and threw down the firewood. Both looked exhausted. "How'd you do?" asked Phil turning to Quinton.

"We did great! Look," said Quinton.

"Great!" said Phil as he examined the fixings. "Go ahead and get to work preparing the soup and I'll get to work on getting us some water."

They started on the food as Phil gathered up the retrieved pump and filter and the old pump and filter to see if he could combine them to make a good one. After about ten minutes Phil had rigged together a functional pump and filter. "Buck, Mark, Dolton," said Phil, "take this down to the river where we came out of the water and get all the water bottles and the jug filled. Hurry, but be careful, it's going to get dark soon."

"Is there anything I can do to help?" asked Pastor.

"We need to get the fire going," said Phil, "can you help me? You two can help too," he said to Zach and Quinton. They began placing wood into the pit as Phil directed and gathered up tinder and kindling to start the fire. Phil took a dry piece of wood and made a groove in it with his knife. Then with a second piece of dry wood he started rubbing it in the groove as fast as he could. Weber watched intently. From where he was sitting, he had the best vantage point.

Phil instructed Zach, "Lay some tinder in the groove." Zach put some dry grass in the groove as directed and after a moment it ignited and turned into a small flame.

"Whoa! Did you see that?" said Buck excitedly.

"Yeah!" said Dolton.

Phil then added a little more tinder, which started a flame. He carefully brought the burning tinder to a small pile of kindling. Once that was burning, he positioned it to start the logs burning.

"I have *never* seen a fire started that way," said Quinton completely amazed. "I've heard about starting a fire by rubbing two sticks together but I didn't think I'd ever see it done. That was amazing, Mr. Phil."

"Thanks, Doc, not too bad if I do say so myself. Now, what say we get the rest of the dinner finished."

"You bet, Mr. Phil," and off Quinton went to finish preparing the vegetables.

"Mr. Phil?" asked Weber.

"Yes. Hey, how are you feeling? Got a headache?"

"No, but my shoulder is sure sore. Do we have any pain relievers?

"No, I'm sorry, buddy. That was in my pack which left with the bears. Maybe, Doc can fix something up for you. I'll ask him."

"Sir, before you do, can you tell me how you learned all this stuff? That fire was pretty interesting. I did a lot of research about camping before we came on this trip and I never saw anything like that on the Internet."

"Oh, I've been around the block a few times. You learn one or two things along the way. Let me go talk to Quinton and see if there's anything he can do for you. Okay?"

"Okay. Thanks, Mr. Phil."

At the river, Buck stood watching as Mark and Dolton did the pumping. Mark said, "Mr. Phil sure knows a lot about a lot of stuff."

"Yeah," said Mark, "he did a great job fixing this pump and filter."

Dolton looked up at Buck and paused a moment, "I know you don't like talking about your dad Buck, but I think that he must have been a lot like Phil."

Buck stared at Dolton for a second and then slowly said, "Yeah, I think so too."

They finished up and headed back. When they returned to camp they found the rest of the group sitting around a blazing fire. Immediately they all got their own water bottles and drank as quickly as they could.

"Easy fellows," Phil advised. Drinking so quickly could make you pass out. The water is here now and there's plenty of it so just a little at a time. Besides, dinner's not too far away. I'm sure you don't want to spoil your appetite."

Phil and Quinton got up, took the large plastic jug and their own water bottles, and started the water for the soup. As it started to boil, Phil added the vegetables. Pastor jumped to his feet and retrieved one of the packs and started digging in it. After a few moments he pulled out a small container and handed it to Phil, "I just remembered that I brought this!"

Phil looked at the container and said excitedly, "Great! Salt and pepper," and added them to the soup.

The sky was now scattered with clouds and it was starting to turn dark. The sun was setting and the air was cooling. One by one they put on their jackets. Zach got Weber's jacket and also grabbed his backpack and brought it out with him.

"Hey Web," said Zach, "maybe we should empty this out so it can dry." Weber nodded so Zach opened the pack and empted the contents on the ground between himself and Weber. He started emptying the pockets. Zach pulled out a case and held it up so Weber could see and asked, "What's this?"

It took a moment for him to focus then he shouted in joy, "All right! My dad packed a spare pair of glasses!"

Zach handed them to Weber who pulled them from their case, cleaned them and put them on. He looked straight at Zach, gave him a big smile and a grateful, "Thanks." He paused for a second, still looking at Zach, smiling but looking like he might cry, and said, "I'll never forget what you and Mr. Phil did for me today."

Zach was surprised. He'd never even given a second thought to what he'd done, it was a natural thing for him do to. And he sure never expected to receive thanks for it. All of a sudden he felt a little warm in the face and said, "I'm glad I was there for you." He put his hand on Weber's shoulder. "You're welcome."

Weber then turned to Phil and said, "Thank you."

Phil just winked at Weber and said quietly, "You're welcome."

The soup was now cooking and filled the air with a wonderful aroma. Everyone was eagerly waiting for it to be done.

While they were waiting they talked about the catch of the day and began to tease Weber about the one that almost got away. Dolton teased, "Yeah, Zach caught one this big," as he stretched out his arms as wide as he could.

"Weber was quite the catch," Quinton chimed in.

"Maybe when we get back Martha Sue will ask *him* out," chided Mark.

That comment made Dolton sit up straight, grab his chest, and make a face like his heart was breaking. They all laughed.

"I think dinner's ready," said Phil, and turned to find everyone with smiles on their faces and their thumbs up, except Weber. He was smiling.

"Weber," said Phil in a puzzled tone, "why didn't you put your thumb up?"

"Because, sir, I *want* to say the blessing, I have a lot to be thankful for."

Phil glanced at Pastor, who sat down and smiled with pride as if Weber were his own child. They all held hands as he started to pray. "Our Father, who art in heaven. . . ."

"Hey, that's the Lord's Prayer," interrupted Dolton.

This time it was Zach that corrected him, "Let him pray any way he wants."

"Thank You for bringing us all together on this trip and for the way You made everybody become friends. Even more than that, thank You for making us a family. For the food that You provided for us in this beautiful meadow, we thank You and ask that You bless this meal. Personally, I'd like to thank You for sending my angel to save me this afternoon." On the word "angel" he squeezed Zach's hand, and to his surprise, got a squeeze back. "For all this we thank You through Christ, our Lord. Amen."

"Amen." Buck, Mark, and Quinton shot questioning glances to each other and mouthed the word "angel." Zach and Weber saw the glance and looked at each other – they knew what it meant. They smiled.

Everyone loaded their bowls but no one started to eat. They just stared at the food. It seemed to smell all right but it looked pretty bad. It was green and stringy.

Phil noticed this and said, "All right, you big scaredy cats, I'll try it first," and took a mouthful. "Ahem" as he cleared his throat and then "mmm," as he tried to make his face look like it had tasted good. Everyone laughed and took a taste for themselves.

"Oh," said Pastor.

"That tastes like. . ." and Buck stopped in mid-sentence.

Quinton shook his head and said, "Wow."

Dolton gave a large smile and said, "It tastes like my mother's cooking when the cook's on vacation."

Weber half gagged and kept eating. Zach's mouth turned into a frown and he too kept on eating, forcing it in. Mark didn't say a thing; he sat there lifting spoonful after spoonful and dropping it back into his dish, almost afraid to take a second bite. Not much was said after that as they all struggled to make their way through the dinner. The meal didn't last long, even though everyone was famished. They all had a good laugh when Pastor tried to get them to have second portions.

After cleaning up, Pastor and Phil started talking about what Nolan was probably doing since the group had not shown up at the designated time, and whether or not he would go to the authorities. As they spoke, Phil confessed that he was worried that they might not find the trail, since it had ended at the river. Buck interrupted enthusiastically, "Excuse me Mr. Phil, but Mark and I found a trail on the other side of the meadow and it looks well traveled."

"Praise God," said Phil and Pastor at the same time. They looked at each other and started to laugh and that made the boys starting laughing with them.

As the laughter started to die down a loud screeching sound came from the direction of the meadow down by the water. Several of them hit the ground with hands and arms covering their heads. Pastor said quickly, "It's okay, believe me, it's okay."

Pastor, Phil, and Zach had been the only ones that didn't duck. The rest of them were getting up and brushing themselves off, all with worried looks on their faces. Weber was shaking, his nerves on end and his voice almost a squeak, "Wwwhat was that?"

Zach reached down and helped Weber up. "It's okay Web, it's only an owl." For the second time on this trip Zach had known something that the others didn't know.

"Don't tell me," said Buck, "TV." Zach just smiled.

Pastor said, "I don't think we're going to have a problem tonight. Besides, it feels more like, what'd you call it Mark, a Garden of Eden." They started to relax again.

They talked for a while longer then Phil said, "We should all get some sleep. Tomorrow could be a long day."

They headed for their tents and climbed into their bags. Phil and Pastor sat in silence watching the fire die out. Phil poked at the coals until all that was left were the embers. He looked up and admired the sight for a moment. The moon illuminated the valley and surrounding areas. It was almost as if a muted sun had come out. He could see details of the landscape, the mountains of the area, and the treeline. It was a strangely beautiful sight.

"You know, Mike," said Phil after a while, "When I saw Weber go under for the last time, and I went under after him,

I got really angry at myself. Here I was, spending every last amount of energy I had to save this child, who is somebody's baby, and the child of *my* heart has been out of reach for his entire life. I realized that I'm no longer content just sitting back and lending a hand now and then."

"I was wondering how long it was going to take you to start talking about it," replied the Pastor.

Without responding, Phil continued, "I've lived the last 12 years on the sidelines. I've watched the two people I ever really cared about. . . ."

"Cared about?" interrupted Pastor.

"I've ever loved," Phil corrected himself, "live, grow, and struggle and I've done nothing. I haven't been a part of their lives."

"Well, I'd have to say that's not true. Who secured the apartment they're living in right now? Who got Becky the job she has when no one was hiring? Who got Buck out of trouble a couple of years ago when he started going down the wrong path? Phil, you've been there for them. You've *kept* your promise. From the sidelines, yes, but the promise has been kept. Buck and Becky are well."

"They should be more than well. When I promised Bart that I'd take care of them, it didn't mean from afar. Mike, I need to face the past now. I need to get this all behind me so I can move forward. I need to be in Buck's life. Full time! I don't want to be on the sidelines anymore. I don't want to watch from a distance. I want to be right in the middle of things. I want to take care of Buck and Becky the way they deserve. I want to be there for Buck in the morning when he wakes up and in the night when he goes to sleep. I'm not going to let the rest of my life go by and not be involved anymore. I'm done running and I'm done hiding.

"You know what you're saying?"

"I do!"

"Are you prepared to face the past in order to move on?"

"Only God knows for sure, but I'm stepping out in faith. I can't stand another day of living without the two people that fulfill me."

They sat for a while in silence.

"Phil, the Lord is with you on this one and so am I. When you came to me and revealed yourself, I knew that there would be a time when I would see you on the other side of the darkness you carried. This is your time. As you face your past, you will not be alone. You've got God. . .and me."

Phil looked up at Mike. Words were unnecessary.

<{{}}><

Nolan came driving up the road and stopped a little too fast. The noise made Ryan and Irene come running out of the cottage.

"What's wrong, Nolan?" asked his brother in Polish.

"They didn't show up at the meeting point," he anxiously answered back in their native language, "I got there mid-afternoon and waited. They didn't show up, so I got my chair out and read until it was getting to dark too read. I looked at my watch and got pretty worried. I started down the trail and called for them. I used my whistle and made noise for them to follow if they were close enough to hear it. I think that they've run into trouble. I need to use your phone."

"Certainly, certainly, come in," Ryan told him.

"I'll get your search and rescue pack ready," offered Irene.

"Thank you," Nolan replied as they all hurried in.

"You know, there isn't anything that you can do tonight. It's too late for you to go out there on the trails. You should stay here and leave at first light," suggested Ryan.

"Good idea, but there *is* something I can do." Nolan sat down and dialed a number.

Deacon Dave put down his book and got up to answer the phone.

"This is Dave."

"Dddave, iiit's me," stuttered Nolan in English, "Ttthere's bbbeen sssome trouble."

"What's happened?"

"Ttthey dddidn't ssshow up ttthis afternnnoon."

"I knew it was getting late. Most of the parents are here in the Youth Hall. I'll let them know but what do you want me to do, Nolan?"

"Wwwell, fffirst thing is ttto pray. Ttthen you nnneed to ttttell ttthe ppparents. Mmmy bbbrother wwwill lllet you kkkknow wwwhat's gggoing on. I'm gggoing after ttthem at fffirst light."

"Nolan, I know you're upset, but you're stuttering more than usual. Let me make sure I've got this straight, you can just answer yes or no. Now, the Youth Group didn't show up today. You waited a long enough time for them before assuming that they may be in some trouble."

"Yyyes."

"Okay, the praying thing is an absolute. You're going to go after them as soon as it gets light out."

"Yyyes."

"Okay, have your brother call me and when you find them you let me know. I'll have the parents come to the church then and we can decide what to do from there. I'll keep them informed as your brother calls. Does that sound all right?"

"Yyyes."

"What's your brother's name and number?"

"Rrryan, ttthat's R-Y-A-N. 555-2343."

As Dave took down the information he said "Nolan, you have done all you can tonight. I'm sure they'll find their way back tomorrow. You be careful yourself and try to get some sleep tonight. You need to be clear-headed tomorrow, okay?"

"Ttthank you ssso mmmuch. Iiii'll bbbe sssure to do ttthat, Dddave. Gggood night."

"Good night, Nolan, and God bless your efforts." Dave hung up the phone and headed to Youth Hall. Dave knew that Nolan was an experienced hiker and that he knew that area like the back of his hand. He was sure that they would be found tomorrow. After he finished informing the families and leading them in prayer, he slowly walked back to Pastor's office and sat down in his chair. He leaned back and prayed for a little while longer before he went home.

<{{}}><

Thrashing, tossing, and screaming woke Zach. His eyes wide open, "Web, Web," said Zach as he grabbed Weber by his shoulders and gave him a shake, "Web, wake up!"

Weber sat up in a sweat, his eyes open and half panicked, "No, no, don't bite me, fire!" It took a moment but he looked at Zach and asked, "Where am I?"

Zach spoke softly in a brotherly voice, "You don't have to worry anymore, Web. I'm here, and I'm not going to let anything happen to you, it's okay." Weber grabbed Zach in a bear hug tightly and wouldn't let go. Then Zach said gently, "I thought your shoulder hurt." After a moment Weber let go and Zach could tell that he had been crying. "Go to sleep Web," said Zach and laid Weber back down and watched him until he fell asleep. Zach lay there awhile thinking and staring at the top of the tent and then fell asleep himself.

<{{}}><

"Stanley, do you think he'll be okay?" asked Karen.

"I'm sure he will, just keep him and the rest of the group in your prayers," he answered reassuringly.

"Oh, that's a given. I don't think Phil should have let Web go get the water alone," she said bitterly.

"No, I think he did the right thing. You know Weber. He always feels like he has to prove himself. He needed to do what he could to help out and that was his attempt. Besides, when have you even known Weber to change his mind once he had it made up?"

"I guess you're right," she said after she thought about it for a moment. They sat watching the monitor, which showed mostly darkness. The embers of the dwindling campfire were the only things clearly visible. The outline of the tents blended into the campground floor. The moon provided enough light to make out some of the shadows.

"I don't want to sever the link. We won't be able to get the visual again. All he has now are his spare glasses. They only have a simple tracking chip. It doesn't have the strength for the visual tracking capabilities of the satellite to lock on. I've done all I can. I wrote a program to overlap the tracking of satellites as one moves out of range and the next one picks up where it left off, but even with that there's a chance that they'll be out of communication just long enough to lose the signal," Karen said, concerned.

"Well, I have another surprise for you."

"Oh, really?"

"Yes, do you remember in the parking lot when I went up to Phil just before they left?"

"Yes, you said you were going to ask him to look out for Weber."

"Well, I did and while I was speaking to him I straightened his collar."

"You didn't!"

"I did. I planted a tracking patch just inside his jacket collar. I was afraid of something happening and I just figured

that Phil wouldn't let anything happen to their outerwear so.
. .there you are," he said, proud of his sneaky efforts.

"Well," she said as she got up, "you solved that one."
She gave him a kiss on the cheek and a hug. "Here is another
problem that we haven't discussed. They're lost and seriously behind schedule. What are we going to do to help?"
she asked.

"There isn't anything we can do."

"Oh, come on!"

"No, I mean it. If we say anything to anyone they'll ask
how we know. We would have to explain our, shall we say,
"indiscretionary" use of Company resources for personal
advantage. No, we can't say anything. Besides, the phone
call from Deacon Dave tells me that Nolan is sufficiently
alarmed. He's been hiking the trails up there for years. He
knows what could happen and what to do if anything did
happen."

She looked at him in disbelief.

"You don't think that I didn't research all the people
involved in our son's affairs before I let him go off and do
something this adventurous, did you?"

"Stanley Deerfield! You *never* cease to amaze me."

"And you, me," he said affectionately, "Why don't you
come back to work at The Company? I miss not having you
there every day."

"Stanley, we agreed, not until Weber is old enough."

"He's old enough now. You've procrastinated long
enough. You're the best hacker programmer The Company
has ever had. We need you there. *I* need you there." He
leaned back and gave her the pout and puppy-dog eyes. She
laughed gently.

"I'll think about it, but let's not forget about the problem
at hand."

"There is nothing more we can do tonight. Let's shut it down and go to bed. Tomorrow is another day and I'm sure things will have worked themselves out."

"Okay, but if you're wrong. . . ."

"I'm *never* wrong," he interrupted.

"Yeah, right," she said as she shut down the program.

<{{}}><

In an office on one of the top floors of The Company, Marshall Redwing and his team were still working. He and five agents were sitting at the conference table across the room going over the information they had collected so far.

There was a knock on the door and a man came in and dropped a note on Marshall's desk and left immediately. One of the agents got up, took the note off the desk and read it. "Sir, I think you should see this," he said as he walked over and handed it to him.

Marshall read the note and sat back in his chair. "It looks like the sheep will be returning to his flock soon. When it goes down, we'll have to move fast. Anything more from the Shepherd?" he asked.

"No, sir," one of the agents answered.

"Okay, I want everything we have on Nolan and his brother and I want to know the minute you get anything from the pastor's phone on their return. I want satellite-tracking information on their location updated every 30 minutes after the sun comes up. Operation Shepherd is officially in full swing," he commanded. The room got very busy.

Sixth Morning - Found

Early that morning Phil climbed out of his tent with the darkness of the early morning turning to light. As he stood at the firepit he decided that starting a fire wouldn't be a good idea and sat down to watch the sunrise and reflect on the trip and what the new day might bring. As the sun started to brighten the partly cloudy morning sky, Pastor and Mark emerged from their tent followed by Buck and Zach.

Zach sat down, greeting everyone with half a yawn, "Morning."

Phil responded, "Morning. Didn't sleep well?"

"No, not at all," replied Zach, "Web had a nightmare last night and it was hard to go back to sleep."

"Well, we've all been through a lot," said Pastor. "I hope that Weber will be okay to travel."

Zach chuckled and said, "His legs are doing fine, he kept kicking me last night, but I'll be glad to carry his things for him." Quinton and Dolton came stumbling out of their tent and over to the firepit.

"What? No fire?" said Dolton as he rubbed his eyes.

"No," said Phil, "nothing to cook, and besides we need to try and get out of here before Nolan gets any more worried."

"Mr. Phil?" said Quinton.

"Yes, Doc?" said Phil.

"I saw some bushes with berries on them over by the river yesterday. Would it be all right if we went and collected some for breakfast?"

"Yes, of course," said Phil with a smile, "take someone with you and be careful."

Before Quinton even had an opportunity to ask, Dolton, Mark, and Buck were standing and walking towards him. He smiled as he pointed and led them off. Weber lumbered out of the tent just after they left and sat down by Zach. It looked like someone had forgotten to iron him. His clothes were wrinkled and his hair looked like something from a scary movie.

"Morning, Weber," said Phil. "We heard you had a rough night. How's the shoulder today?"

Weber lifted his head and slipped his fingers up under his glasses and started rubbing his eyes, "A little sore but it's working, thank you. Where is everybody?"

"Doc and the 'gathering committee' went off to get us some berries for breakfast," explained Zach.

"Hey, Zach, give us a hand breaking camp," Phil said as he and Pastor got up. "Weber, I think you should sit this one out." They all nodded in agreement as they stood and headed to the tent area to start packing up.

Just about the time the tents were packed the gathering committee came back and headed straight over to help finish packing. Once that was done they joined Weber at the firepit to eat and, as they sat down, their thumbs were popping up.

"Looks like it's me," said Zach, and the group gathered hands so Zach could give the blessing. "Lord, I'm not as good with words as some of the people here, but You know

266

what's in our hearts today. We'd like to get home and, if it's not too much trouble, without any more excitement. Thanks for creating this family for us on this trip and by Your grace, keep us as close as we are today. Bless this food and get us home. Amen."

It only took about ten minutes to eat up the collected berries. As they were getting ready to go, Phil asked Buck if he could take the lead and get them to the trail. Pastor had everyone gather for a prayer to start the day's walk. "Father, once again we take up our yoke and we ask that You bless our steps and get us going in the right direction. Lead us to safety and keep us free from all harm. We ask this through Christ our Lord. Amen."

They geared up and started off with Buck in the lead. He slapped Mark on the back of his shoulder as he passed him saying, "Come on!" and Buck and Mark led the way through the meadow to the trail they had discovered.

When they arrived Phil said, mostly to himself, "I wonder why we didn't see this many tracks on the trail at the split."

"You have to admit, this hasn't been a normal trip," said Pastor sarcastically.

"Well, by the sun we're going southeast and that's the direction we need to be going," Phil admitted. They headed down the trail away from their Garden of Eden. The morning sky had cleared and the air was warmer than it had been for the last few days. The hike itself was pleasant and uneventful until the trail turned and headed back down into the pine trees. Phil stopped the group and had everyone gather around. "Well," he sighed, "we haven't seen a trail marker or another hiker all morning, keep your eyes open. We'll stop in another hour and start looking for lunch."

They took a few minutes to get some water and trade off packs. Zach handed Weber his water bottle and he took a drink. All of a sudden he gasped and breathed in the water, he spit it out and it went through his nose. He got excited and tried to speak. Zach started patting him on the back thinking that he was choking. Weber pointed his finger and through the coughing said, "Look!" They turned to see a trail marker.

"Praise God!" shouted Pastor.

"How'd you see that?" asked Zack.

"I saw it when I tilted my head back to get a drink!"

They came alive with the thought that they were going to be okay. Phil didn't even have to ask. They were all ready to continue hiking. Pastor noted that not a single one of them had a problem keeping up. They all walked with a bit of a spring in their step. *Thank you, Lord for answering yet another of our prayers,* he prayed silently.

Phil decided not to stop for lunch after an hour. But after another two hours the group started to think that they had celebrated a little early. The sun had passed over the halfway point in the sky and the water was starting to run a little low. The trail came out of the trees and alongside a cliff where there was a river flowing about one hundred feet below them. They stopped to view the river. Dolton looked down he pined, "Water. . .water. . .water. Boy, that's a long way down."

"Yes it is," said Pastor, "and we're not going down there."

"No more water adventures for me," said Weber.

Phil smiled and started them off again.

Nolan To The Rescue

They hadn't gone far when Phil spotted movement on the other side of a small meadow and stopped the group. "Look," Phil said in hushed excitement, "someone's coming." The look on Phil's face changed from concentration to recognition, then to joy, excitement and surprise, "It's Nolan!"

The rest of the group looked intently as Nolan came into view. They took off running and surrounded Nolan whooping and hollering and hugging him. Phil and Pastor followed behind and each gave him a welcoming hug and handshake. Nolan handed everyone a full water bottle and a couple of trail bars.

"Nolan," said Phil, "how did you find us?"

"Wwwhen yyyou dddidn't ssshow up lllast nnnight, sssomething wwwas tttelling mmme Iii nnneeded to cccome to yyyour rescue. Iii knnnow these wwwoods pretty wwwell so Iii wwwas able to rrrun a gggood dissstance up the tttrail. Iii fffigured out ttthat you ppprobably took a wwwrong turn aaaround the rrrun-offs."

"How's Triple D doing?" asked Pastor Mike.

"Dddon't wwworry, Iii cccalled Dddeacon Dave. He said ttthat it's bbbbeen cccrazy and hhhe's pppraying ttthat you mmmake it bbbback and he wwwill nnnotify the ppparents and kkkeep them up ttto date."

"Thank you, Nolan, we can always count on you. Let's go," said Phil to the group and they started off with Nolan leading the way.

"Nolan," said Phil, "how far is it to the van?"

"Iiif we hurry wwwe ssshould mmmake it bbby dark," said Nolan.

"Ok, men, you heard him, everyone is worried and we need to let them know that we're okay," said Phil, "Let's step up the pace."

With Nolan in the lead, for about an hour they walked under pine trees that had briefly turned into bushes and formed an arch tunnel before turning into the pine tree forest again. As they exited the archway tunnel Phil asked Nolan, "How did you know where to go? I haven't seen any trail markers."

Nolan said with a smile, "Nnno mmmarkers, Iii lllleft mmmy own marks," and he pointed to a tree that had a fresh notch in it that looked like a elongated triangle that was pointing the way. Phil just looked at Nolan, smiled and gave him a thumbs up.

It was dark when the van finally came into view. As Nolan opened the doors to the van, Dolton gave it a hug, and the others were patting the van as they waited for the side doors to open. Pastor said, "Thank God," gratefully as he gazed up.

Phil said, "We have been blessed and our prayers answered. He sent Nolan to bring us home safely." Nolan didn't even get around the van before everyone was in and buckled up. He got in, said a quiet prayer for safety, and pulled out. When they reached the main road, he looked back to see that everyone was fast asleep except Phil and Zach, who were each staring out their windows. After a few moments Phil came out of his thoughts. He turned to Nolan and asked, "Where're we going?" Pastor sat up to listen.

"Iii am tttaking yyyou all ttto mmmy bbbrother's house to eeat aaand rest. Iii'll tttake you hhhome tomorrow. Iiit's too lllate ttto get ttthere tonight."

"I can't tell you how grateful I am to you, Nolan," said Phil very seriously, "thank you."

Pastor laid a hand on Nolan's shoulder and confirmed Phil's notion, "God bless you and thank you."

Ryan and Irene Trendovich

In no time at all, the van pulled up in front of Ryan's house, and Ryan and Irene came running out the door.

"Thank God, Nolan, you found them," said Irene as she held her hands up to her mouth.

"Ttthey nnneed to eeeat and ggget cccleaned up," said Nolan, "iiit sssmells lllike a gggym lllocker in there."

Pastor and Phil laughed and gently nudged the sleeping beauties from their slumber and got out of the van. Slowly they filed out and were led through a white archway, covered with vines and flanked by a white picket fence that surrounded a manicured yard, to a house that looked like a European cottage. All the way up to the entry door Irene kept telling them, "Come in and make yourselves at home." Once inside Irene headed to the kitchen. Ryan directed them to the sitting room to relax. All the while Ryan and Nolan were speaking to each other in Polish. Pastor and Phil asked to use the phone so they could get a message to Deacon Dave.

The brothers finished their business so Ryan went into the sitting room to hear about their adventures. They group was having fun with the fact that Nolan and Ryan were perfect doubles and the only way they could tell the difference between the two was by their clothes and when Nolan spoke in English.

Dolton asked, almost teasingly, "Nolan, how come you don't have a speech problem when you speak Polish?"

Ryan laughed and Nolan looked embarrassed. Ryan explained, "He's done that since we came here as young boys. They told us that Nolan's stuttering comes from the fact that his brain thinks faster than the words can come out. In fact Nolan has a very high IQ. He retains almost everything. I think that's called a photographic memory."

Mark laughed and teased, "He sure remembers all those Polish songs."

Everyone laughed and Nolan turned red again. Mark looked at Nolan and said, "Only kidding, we love you Nolan. We're never going to forget you're our hero."

Then Dolton started chanting, "Nolan, Nolan," and they all joined him.

Pastor came in and said sternly, "Keep it down, fellows, Phil's on the phone."

Ryan invited Pastor, "We have two bathrooms and you are welcome to use them so you can freshen up."

"Thank you, Ryan. Okay," said Pastor, "we'll take turns getting clean, who wants to go first?" and they all stood up.

"Weber and Dolton, you can go first," he directed.

Ryan stood and walked over to Pastor, "I have clothes for everybody if you would like. They may not fit but they're clean."

"That's so kind of you," said Pastor gratefully. While they got cleaned up, Ryan and Nolan heard all about their adventures.

In the kitchen, Irene was busy cooking and the aromas started to drift into the sitting room. By this time, everyone was fully awake and anxiously waiting to eat.

Dolton came out from taking his shower and said with gritted teeth, "I don't think that this rash from using those leaves is ever going to go away." Everyone sitting around started to laugh.

Ryan still chuckling said, "I have something that will help. Come with me." Weber had finished his shower and came out still rolling up pant legs and sleeves. The shirt Ryan gave him hung on him like dress.

Just as Pastor walked out from his shower, Irene called everyone to eat. Phil had not had the chance to shower, but Irene insisted that he eat before he did.

The dining room table wasn't large enough to hold everyone so Irene used it to serve the food. "Wow! Mrs. Trendovich, did you cook all of this yourself?" asked Dolton.

"Of course," she said.

"It would take my mom and a cook two days to get this much food done!" he said, surprised that only one woman could cook so much food. It all smelled so delicious.

Everyone gathered around the table and Pastor held up a thumb along with the rest of the youth. Phil chuckled as Nolan, Ryan, and Irene stared at them in confusion. He explained what the thumbs meant and Ryan thought it was a great idea. Nolan excitedly offered, "Iii'll sssay grace."

Ryan reached over and wrapped his arm around his brother and said to the group, "You gotta love this guy," and then turned to Nolan and said, "I'd be honored to do it, Nolan."

Nolan just smiled and nodded his head. Ryan began, "Dear Father, thank You for returning Your precious children safely. Thank You for letting us share a meal with them and offer them comfort and rest. You have continued to bless us and our family and friends and from the day we decided to follow You, You have never left us. For this we are eternally grateful. Now we ask that You bless this food and the hands that have prepared it. We ask all this through Christ our Lord. Amen."

"Please eat and get full," invited Irene. They didn't need a second invitation. They started digging in, loading their plates with everything Irene had made. Dolton grabbed a sausage and held it up with his fork and asked, "Is this a hot dog?" and without waiting for an answer dropped it on his plate. When they had finished loading their plates Phil, Pastor, Nolan and Ryan looked at what was left and laughed. "Well, it looks like we get what's left," said Phil with a smile.

Irene was beaming as she said, "Those boys must be famished."

There was hardly a word spoken as everyone ate. They were scattered throughout the house. There wasn't a morsel of food left at the table. As they finished eating they brought their dishes into the kitchen and without direction started cleaning up. Irene kept insisting that they should all go and rest, that she didn't need help, but with all the help the mess was cleaned up in no time. Six young men in the kitchen cleaning, drying, and putting away was quite a sight for her. When they finished, each one of them kissed her on the cheek and thanked her for the food as they left the kitchen. Nolan called them out to the van to retrieve their sleeping bags and what was left of their gear. After everything was settled they started looking tired and before long Ryan spotted them, throughout the house, fast asleep.

Nolan, Ryan, Irene, Pastor, and Phil had settled down at the dining room table and were talking about the trip when Phil said that he should probably get cleaned up. Irene reached over and grasped a handful of Phil's hair and said, "I could give you a trim. In my younger days I used to be a hairdresser."

Phil looked quizzically at Pastor and Pastor winked. Phil said tentatively, "There's something that you should know about before we get to that." They sat there and listened intently as Phil told the story of how he came to Jamestown and what he had revealed to Buck on the trip. It took quite some time for Phil to finish relating the story. When he was done he confessed, "So I guess I'll have to face Becky before long, but no one else really needs to know the details."

Nolan stood and gave Phil a hug and said, "Yyyour sssecret is sssafe with me."

Ryan and Irene agreed that they would say nothing. "One more thing, I'd appreciate it if you keep calling me Phil. That's who I am now." They all agreed and Irene took Phil by the arm and led him to the bathroom and said, "It's time to shed your disguise."

It was a while before Irene appeared again and she joined the men as they were chatting. A little while later Phil came in. There wasn't a closed mouth in the room. "Wwwow!" said Nolan. Ryan just stared and Pastor extended his hand and with a smile said jokingly, "Hi I'm Pastor Mike Miller."

Phil smiled and said, "Nice to meet you, I'm Phil Thomas." He was completely clean-shaven and his hair was short and neat. He was indeed a handsome man and now looked considerably younger. "You look great," said Ryan, "Irene did a great job."

Nolan said, still amazed, "Yyyou lllook lllike a dddifferent person."

"Well, thank you," said Phil, "if you don't mind, the delicious food and shower has made me a bit sleepy. I think I'll get some rest. Tomorrow's going to be an interesting day."

Going Home

Morning light shone through the window. Irene was already cooking breakfast and the smell was again drifting through the house. The aroma fueled hunger and Phil awoke. He stood up and stroked his beard and at first was surprised that it wasn't there any longer. Thoughts of the previous evening returned. For the first time in many years he felt the skin of his face. He stood up and stretched and realized that the toll of the last six days had caught up with him. He felt a little sluggish and sore and his head was just a bit fuzzy. He figured that the stress of the last few days was the cause and knew that a cup of coffee would help immensely. He yawned as he walked into the dining room and was surprised that everyone else was already up. For the first time since the beginning of the trip he had slept later than anyone else.

Dolton was doing his fair share of talking and was the first to see Phil enter the room with his hair cut and his beard shaved off. He stopped in mid-sentence and stared. Of course, when he stopped talking, everyone else in the room

279

had to turn to see what could have made Dolton silent. In a moment all eyes were staring at Phil standing in the archway to the dining room.

The entire room was silent until Pastor said very calmly as he stepped from the kitchen, "Phil, would you like a cup of this delicious coffee?"

They turned back and looked at Pastor, who wasn't shocked by Phil's appearance and then back to Phil, who felt himself smile from ear to ear as Nolan, Ryan, and Irene crowded into the dining area.

"Good morning everyone" said Phil exuberantly. They were stunned to hear Phil's voice come from this stranger's face.

Irene broke the tension and informed them, "Breakfast will be ready in ten minutes," and quickly left again to the kitchen. Phil held up his hands and said, "Before you start asking questions I have something to say. I know that all of you know that my real name is Wes Philip Carter. I know that Buck told you." Phil looked at Buck, "I would have done the same thing if they were all my friends too." Phil looked back at the group, "When I came to Jamestown I gave my life over to the Lord, changed my name, and became Phil Thomas, and that's who I plan to live as. I'm asking you to keep my secret and honor my wishes."

They nodded their heads and said, "Yes . . . Sure . . . You can count on me . . . Me too."

"I'm sure," he continued, "that in time all of this will come out, but I'm not prepared for that to happen just yet. Feel free to ask me anything you want but, please, when you do, make sure you do it confidentially. I don't want anyone hurt by any of this. Okay?"

"Okay," they all replied.

Irene interjected that they all needed to clear out of the dining room so she could put breakfast out if they wanted to eat, and handed Phil a cup of coffee. As breakfast was being set out the youth moved into the sitting area and discussed Phil's transformation. "Wow!" said Zach.

Dolton, who was most amazed, kept saying over and over, "Can you believe that?"

"I think he looks great," said Quinton.

Buck said, "He looks older," they looked at him a bit confused.

"He gave me a picture," and Buck pulled it out and showed them.

"Is this your dad too?" asked Mark.

"Yeah," said Buck.

"You look just like him," said Quinton.

"You think so?" he said.

"Yeah," confirmed Mark.

"It's amazing," said Zach.

"What?" asked Weber.

"Well, after everything that we went through this week and all of the stuff we found out about him, that Mr. Phil is still the same guy."

"What do you mean the same guy? It's Mr. Phil," said Dolton.

"Yeah, but people are going to find out who he used to be. Don't you think he must be nervous about that?"

"He won't have to be if we all keep our mouths shut," said Mark as he looked straight at Dolton.

"Hey, don't worry, I'm a vault," replied Dolton.

"But Buck, how're going to keep this from your mom? She used to know him and when she sees him with all his hair gone, looking like the guy in that picture, she'll recognize him. Don't you think people are going to find out then?" explained Zach.

"Well, he did say that it would all come out in time and that it would be all right. I've gotta believe that. I don't think that he would lie about that," said Buck.

"You're right, if we've learned anything we've learned that you have to take some things on faith," concluded Zach.

"I trust him," said Buck.

"Me too," said Zach, and they all agreed. Pastor walked in at that moment and said, "Time to eat, come on."

They adjourned to the dining room and started to raise their thumbs. Phil said, "I think that I need to give the blessing for this meal." They all held hands in a circle around the dining table and Phil started to pray. "Dearest Father in Heaven, we have so much to thank You for. For bringing us home safely and for the shelter and hospitality we have been afforded in the house of Your servants, our new friends, Irene and Ryan. Thank You for our guide, Nolan, whom you gave the presence of mind to come looking for us and bring provisions when we had lost our way. Thank You for our families back home whose prayers helped us as we ventured far from them. Thank You also for the challenges You gave us on our journey. They have made us stronger in mind and body and have drawn us closer as a family and confirmed our knowledge that at no time did You abandon us. For the sustenance we have before us now, prepared and provided for us by our new friends, we thank You and ask Your blessing upon them. May it be strength and nutrition for our bodies as You and Your Word are nutrition for our souls. For all of this, we thank You and ask this in Your Son's most precious name, Jesus Christ. Amen."

For the first time since they began their journey, they did not break the circle right away. They held their hands tightly, opened their eyes and looked at each other with new eyes. They had been changed and they knew it. They felt it. Nothing would be the same from this point on. "And the old order of things has passed away," observed Pastor.

"Amen," they all said, one at a time.

Gently Irene invited them to eat, "Please, feed your-selves. Your day is just starting and you still have a drive ahead of you."

You would have thought that they hadn't been fed the night before by the way they attacked breakfast and the sizes of their portions. Irene continued to fuss over the group as though they all belonged to her. "Boy, Mrs. Trendovich really knows how to cook," said Zach.

Dolton nodded his head, his mouth completely full. Weber was just about to get up to get more to drink when Irene gently pushed him back into his seat and refilled it for him. Buck and Quinton were eating as though they were in a race with each other, hardly taking time to breathe. Phil and Pastor did their fair share of packing it away, too.

Breakfast lasted a long time and slowly came to a close, with everyone laying around like bears stuffed for hibernation. Irene had cooked enough food to feed a small army and they did a good job of making sure there was little left over. Phil came out of the kitchen and said, "Okay, Mrs. Trendovich needs helpers in the kitchen. Let's show her how much we appreciate her and her cooking."

They did their best to jump up but the best they could do was a saunter into the kitchen. Quinton took two tries to get out of the chair he was in. Weber and Dolton were the first to enter the kitchen, shortly followed by Buck. Pastor stopped Zach, Quinton, and Mark and asked for help outside, "I think Mr. Phil needs help loading the equipment into the van." They headed out of the house towards the van.

Nolan had taken everything out and had it piled on the ground and was putting everything in separate piles. The three helpers said in unison, "Hi, Nolan."

"What's going on? Can we help?" asked Mark.

"Iii'm fffixing ttthe load," said Nolan, "wwwould you mmmind gggetting the sssleeping bbbags fffrom ttthe house ssso Iii can fffinish pppacking the van?"

"Sure, no problem," replied Mark, and they went back in to get the sleeping bags and the rest of the gear. It didn't take long with everyone pitching in to get everything done. Everyone except Pastor had gathered out by the van and talked about the week and the prospect of finally getting home. Pastor Mike was inside on the phone with Deacon Dave. He wanted to make sure he had an estimated time of arrival. When he was done he came out of the house laughing. Phil asked him, "Is everything all right?"

"Yes," he chuckled, "that Triple D makes me laugh. He's making sure that all the parents will be at the church when we get there. Are we about ready to go?"

Phil announced, "It's time to go." Pastor walked up to Ryan and Irene, put out his hand to Ryan and, as they shook hands, Pastor pulled Ryan into a hug and said, "I can't tell you how much your hospitality has meant to me. Meant to us."

Ryan smiled and returned the hug, "It was our pleasure to help. Anyone who loves Nolan the way you all do is welcome in our house any time, day or night. Go with God, my friend."

"May the Lord be with you," Pastor replied. Then he turned to Irene and said gently, "Irene, thank you so very much. You and Ryan are such a blessing. May God continue to watch over you! I can't thank you enough for the way you have taken care of us." Pastor gave her a small kiss on the cheek, "May the Lord bless and keep you both."

He walked over to the van and let Phil say his good-byes. Phil walked straight up to Irene and gave her a hug and said, "Irene, thank you so very much for everything you and Ryan have done for us and for me. Thank you for your hospitality." Then he stepped over to Ryan, took his hand and pulled him into a hug and said, "If at any time you need anything, and I mean anything, call me and it's yours."

Ryan nodded and said, "God bless and have a safe trip."

Nolan came over and said his good-byes to Ryan and Irene in Polish. Then each of the young men gave Irene a hug and a kiss on the cheek and shook Ryan's hand and climbed into the van. Irene's eyes filled with tears and she held onto Ryan's arm. She was waving as though she was watching her kids leave for the last time. "What a wonderful group of young men. I hope we'll see them again soon."

Ryan yelled to them, "Please come again any time you wish!"

They were hanging out of the windows waving and yelling, "Thank you," along with Pastor and Phil, who was again sitting in the passenger seat. Nolan put the van in gear and they were off; they were heading down the road toward Jamestown and home.

As they settled down in their seats they were quiet. The only sound was the engine of the van. They stared out their windows. After about a half hour Mark, who was sitting next to Buck, said in a low voice, "Buck, can I see that picture of your dad and Mr. Phil?"

Buck smiled and said, "Sure," and he reached into his pocket pulled it out and handed it to Mark. He looked at the photo, "They look so cool."

That comment made Buck smile. For the first time in his life Buck was proud to be able to show off his father. To top it off his best friend thought he was cool. The rest of his friends asked if they could look at it too. Buck was glowing with pride as they continued to talk about his dad and Phil. Pastor turned to see what the boys were murmuring about and noticed the photo being passed around. He reached over and tapped Phil on the shoulder.

Phil had been looking out the window deep in thought. He was startled and Pastor motioned with his thumb to the back of the van, and he turned to see what they were doing. He saw the photo being passed around. Then he saw how happy Buck was. He turned back and gave Pastor a wink.

Pastor smiled and then said softly, "You did a good thing," and sat back. Phil breathed a large sigh of relief and gazed out the window and returned to his thoughts. The conversation continued for a while and then they settled back to enjoy the ride.

Weber had been contemplating something. His face was very stern and his brow was furrowed. Finally he said, "Pastor?"

"Yes, Weber?"

"There's something I don't quite understand about our trip."

"What's that?"

"Well. . .all the time you prayed for our safety and so many bad things happened. We were attacked by the bears and lost our map and compass, then what happened at Thousand Island Lake and then I fell in and almost drowned at the river. Why did God let all those bad things happen to us when we asked him to keep us safe?"

"That's a very good question, Weber. I don't have all the answers but I can tell you this – God did bring us home safely. As He will when it's time to go home to our Heavenly House. That's doesn't mean that our journey won't be filled with pain and suffering. Pain and suffering draws us apart from worldly cares and brings us closer to God. I *can* see that everything we went through on this trip has brought us so much closer to each other in a Christian way, and that glorifies Him. None of us were seriously hurt but we have all been seriously changed – for the betterment of our souls. So, the Lord did answer our prayers—in His way, not ours. Does that explain it?"

"Not exactly."

"Then, let me put it this way. It's kind of like cake," he explained further.

"Cake?" By now, everyone was listening.

"Yeah. Tell me, what does it take to make a cake?"

"Well," started Weber, "there's flour, eggs, oil, sugar and. . .I don't know what else."

"That's good enough. Would you take a cup of flour and eat it?"

"Gross, no way," said Zach.

"What about the eggs, would you put a couple of raw eggs in a bowl and eat them?"

"Only if I were desperate," said Dolton.

"Would you drink a cup of oil?"

"No!" Weber replied emphatically.

"Yet, if you put all the ingredients together in the right amounts and complete the process of mixing and baking, the result is a delicious treat, right? Well, think of all we experienced as the ingredients in the cake. These are God's ingredients. We don't know what it is that He's trying to make, but we know that whatever the outcome, it will be good. In ALL things, give thanks and praise."

Weber was silent for a while. "Thank you, Pastor. I think I understand now."

They all sat there in silence thinking about what Pastor had just said. It had been a while since Pastor had heard anything come from the back so he turned around to see what everyone was doing. Quinton caught his eye and said, "Pastor Mike, umm, I just wanted to say thank you and to let you know that I'll never forget this trip as long as I live."

"I won't either," he replied. He paused for a moment, "I hope that you received more than just a trip through the woods, though."

Quinton smiled, but it was Zach who spoke, "I don't know about anybody else, but I learned a lot from both you and Mr. Phil."

"What might that be, Zach?" asked Pastor.

"Fellowship," he said to everyone's surprise as he put his arm around Weber and Dolton, "and trust."

Dolton said, "Uhh, yeah, and faith."

Weber added his two cents worth, "Strength and the belief that we are never alone. . .no matter what."

"That people may not be who you think they are. . .and not to judge them until you get to know them," said Zach. Then he turned and looked at Dolton and smiled.

Buck chuckled as he looked at Phil, "Yeah, I learned that myself."

Mark said very seriously, "I learned a lot about my dad and me. That I have strengths that I didn't know I had, or at least never recognized them as strengths before. I also recognized how lucky I am to have had the opportunity to be raised by him. I know it wasn't easy for him but I never had a reason to doubt that he would be there for me and I always knew that I was loved."

It was quiet for a moment, then Quinton spoke, "Well, I know this may sound elementary, but I learned that I have value and purpose."

"What do you mean, Doc?" asked Dolton.

"I mean that I started this trip feeling like an outsider, kind of a fifth wheel. I really didn't know any of you too well. I was very aware that the 'Pastor's Kids' Group' was already pretty tight. Zach was kind of a bully and liked to pick on the nerdy guys. I'd watched him pick on Weber for a few years now and always hoped that he never noticed me because I didn't want him picking on me too. Then there was Weber, I knew he was a geek like me but I didn't really know him. But. . .you guys accepted me just as I am. You guys never made fun of me when I was hitting myself and you never made fun of me for being too smart. I felt like I had friends for the first time when Buck gave me the pyrite. Then I felt like I was a friend to all of you when you were hurting and something I knew helped you out. My purpose was to help my friends in need. My value was that I walked into the woods just a guy and walked out part of a family."

Pastor looked over at Phil and said, "Well. . .I think that they've made it."

Phil replied, "I think you're right."

Nolan, who had been partially listening, asked Phil, "Mmmade it wwwhere?"

Phil smiled and looked at Nolan and said, "They made it through a journey. These are not the boys who started on the youth trip. They're gone. The people in the back of the van have stepped into manhood and are coming home Christian men."

Nolan fixed his eyes on the road and smiled, "Ttthe Lllord wwworks in mysssterious ways."

Pastor gave him a pat on the back and said, "Nolan, I could sure use a rest at rest stop, if you don't mind." Ten minutes later the van pulled off into a rest stop. They all got out to stretch and use the facilities. Pastor used the public phone to call Deacon Dave to let him know what their estimated time of arrival was.

It was a while before Nolan got back to the van and as he came up Dolton asked if they could stop for a snack and something to drink. Nolan smiled and said, "Iiirene sssent us ssssome lunch."

Pastor and Phil smiled in surprise as Nolan headed to the back of the van. He pulled the ice chest that Mrs. James had provided at the beginning of the trip. It was now full of the lunch that Irene had sent with them. Nolan took the lunch out, passed out a sandwich, homemade cookies, fruit salad, and a drink to everyone.

"Let's take this on the road fellows. We still have a long way to go," Phil instructed. They piled in the van and Nolan got them back on the highway in no time. They all enjoyed their lunches and then sat back and let their full bellies put them to sleep. There wasn't another sound from anyone until they got back to Jamestown. Except the snoring.

Operation Shepherd

I n an office on one of the top floors of The Company an
agent stuck his head in the door. "Mr. Redwing," he said,
Marshall looked up, "we just received confirmation that the
sheep are returning to the pasture. ETA two hours."

"I want the team assembled and ready to roll in one,"
Redwing ordered.

"Yes, sir," the agent replied and quickly shut the door.
Marshall picked up the picture of Wesley and leaned back
in his chair. He turned toward the window still holding the
photo. *Where have you been all this time and how have you
eluded our searches?* he thought. He rested his arm on the
side of his desk and stared out the window. An hour later he
walked out of the building. There were three SUVs parked
by the curb. Marshall got into the middle one. They took off
and headed towards Jamestown. "Ben," he said to the man
driving, "I want you to take point on this one. There'll be a
lot of concerned parents there and I don't want things to get
out of hand. This will be a smooth, low-key operation and
you'll wait for my mark. Understood?"

"Yes, sir," he replied. Thirty minutes later they arrived at the church. Marshall's vehicle parked on the opposite side of the street from the church. The other two vehicles parked in the street on either end of the church parking lot. They waited. Marshall looked out the window and was lost in thought.

Marshall had been a team leader when he first met Bart and Wes. He'd moved up the ranks faster than anyone in the history of The Company. He was smart, streetwise, and extremely talented in his craft. He was an expert marksman and could negotiate as if he had been doing it all his life. He had a knack for putting people where they needed to be to get the job done and wasn't afraid of confrontation. The Company looked highly on Marshall and used him wisely. There was no doubt in anyone's mind that he would, someday, run the division.

The first time he met Bart Bond and Wes Carter, they were already a team, fast on their way to becoming the best agents in The Company. Bart and Wes had been assigned to him for a field mission and they exceeded expectations. They soon received the toughest and most confidential assignments and gained a reputation as being the best of the best. Not only did they perform well on the job but the three of them became friends almost immediately. When they weren't on the job they could be found at one another's homes. When Marshall's wife, Karen, became pregnant they all went through it together. It was a very happy time for all of them. You never saw a happier man than Bart when Marshall asked him to be the godfather to his child. The three of them reveled in the thought that "they" were going to have a baby. They even prepared the baby's room together; Wes built the baby's crib himself.

It was almost too much to bear when Karen died in childbirth, but Bart and Wes were there for him. They attended the baptism of their baby, which was a happy and sad affair all at once. They were there with him the day he decided to let his wife's sisters raise his baby daughter, which meant her going away overseas. They cried together as they took the baby to the airport to see her off. Then stayed the night and drank together. There were no closer friends - they were family.

"Sir," Ben, his driver, interrupted his train of thought, "we got word. They're just getting off the freeway. They should arrive in ten minutes."

"Very good," he replied, "tell the team to get ready, but wait for my mark." He contemplated the past and the present and could only wonder what the future would bring them.

How *did* Wes elude their searches? If Stanley hadn't been so worried about his son's trip, he would still be on the MIA list. Stanley and his wife, Karen, were the best hackers The Company had ever had. Karen was always a step ahead, but together they were the cream of the crop. Nobody could do what they could together. Marshall's whole staff consisted of the best. Too bad Karen left to have a baby. Weber was old enough for her to come back. She probably liked the home-maker/mother lifestyle. No matter. Stanley's indiscretion in pirating the GPS system had opened the door to finding Wes. If he had used any other tracking program than Shepherd, Marshall never would have known what Stanley was doing. Using The Company's resources to track his son on a back-packing trip was in violation of his contract, but Marshall was willing to overlook that. The result of his indiscretion resulted in locating Wesley Carter, something he had been unable to do for too many years.

It had been hard on both Marshall and Wes losing Bart the way they did. Marshall had already been made head of the department and was on his way to running the division. Marshall secretly spent the following year investigating what happened. His investigation led him to the division head, his immediate boss, who had not been loyal to The Company for many years. Unbeknownst to them, Bart's last mission had been a setup. It was enough to throw them off and divert attention away from his possible exposure, but only for a time. When Marshall finally discovered the true nature of his boss's deception, he brought him down – hard. He would have liked to share that success with his two best friends, but they were no more.

Marshall's friends had been lost: one dead and the other disappeared. He made it his mission to bring the division head out into the open. When Bart's death had been avenged he tried to find Wes, to let him know, but it was too late. He had disappeared and all attempts to locate him failed. Marshall had known that Bart's death hit Wes hard but he had no idea that he wouldn't be able to find him. Wes was good, really good at his craft. If he wanted to disappear, then there would be no finding him. Now, thanks to Stanley, he was only minutes away. This reunion was one he both desired and feared.

"Sir," said Ben, interrupting again, "here they come."

Arrival at the Church

As they pulled off the main highway Nolan gave Phil a shake and he awoke. Phil stretched and leaned over to wake Pastor. When he got his bearings he turned around and said, "Come on, wake up, we're almost at the church."

It took a few moments to rouse everyone, but once they were awake they were excited to finally be home. The church came into view and the whole van started cheering and hollering. Then Phil spotted something that didn't belong. There was a large black SUV with the windows blacked out parked across the street from the church. When they got closer he saw two more at either end of the parking lot. As the van pulled into the driveway of the Church parking lot he recognized the triangulation of the SUVs. *Oh no,* he thought.

A group of people were standing on the sidewalk aside the Youth Hall. It was the parents and Triple D waiting for them to return. They were as excited as the youth to see the van pulling in. As they slowed to stop, Pastor looked over at Phil and noticed that he was staring at some vehicles in the corner of the parking lot, concern tightening his features.

The van parked and Nolan let the youth out. He headed to the back to unpack. Mark followed to help. Pastor and Phil remained in the van. Triple D started toward the van to speak with Pastor.

Most of the group hurried to greet their parents, except for Zach, whose parents had not shown up. Buck ran to his mother and when he reached her they embraced. Buck almost squeezed her too hard and, before letting go, gave her a long kiss on the cheek. "Mom," he said excitedly, "you're not going to believe what I have to tell you!"

Quinton walked to greet his parents. He stood straight and walked slowly and purposefully. As he approached them they watched him curiously. He walked up to his father, looked straight into his eyes and put out his hand and shook it. His father pulled him into a hug. He then turned to his mother. Tears began to roll down her cheeks and she reached up placing her hands on the sides of his face and said," Quint, you've chaynged. You're not 'itting yourself and you're standing. . .well, differently."

"Yes," said Quinton, "I had a great time and I can't wait to tell you all about it." He turned and yelled, "See you guys later!"

As they turned to leave, Buck, Dolton, and Mark yelled, "See you later, Doc!" His parents stopped and looked at him questioningly, "Doc? What's that all about?"

"I'll tell you when we get home. Let's go," and they left for home.

Dolton, who was the last out of the van, went to meet his mother. He casually walked over to her looking straight at her with a smile that conveyed authority.

"Dolton," she said with little emotion, "I'm glad you finally made it home."

Dolton said in a tone of authority that matched his smile, "Thank you. Mom, I think it's time we had a talk." Mrs. James stared at him for a moment and said in a voice unlike her normal tone, almost affectionately, "The way you just said that reminds me of your father. Let's go collect your things and be off. We can speak on the way home if you wish."

"I'll get my things later. Let's go," said Dolton and he led the way to the car.

Weber was the slowest in reaching his parents, and just before he got there, he turned around and went back to get Zach. "Come on," said Weber as he grabbed Zach by the shirt and pulled him, "come on, I want them to meet my best friend."

Zach stopped and Weber looked up wondering what was wrong. Zach said, "I've never had a best friend before."

"Come on," said Weber, "you do now," and started pulling on Zach again. When they met up with his parents, his mother grabbed Zach, hugged him and started kissing him all over his face. Stanley mercifully reached out and shook Zach's hand, pulling him from the kissing machine, and said, "Thank you for saving our son and taking such good care of him."

Zach's face went blank with confusion as he thought, *how did he know that?* Then Stanley took Weber into his arms and hugged him, "Thank God, you're okay."

Weber stepped back from his dad and gave him the bad news, "I'm sorry, Dad, but I ruined all my equipment."

"It's okay, Web," said Stanley, "those are just things. Thank God you're home safe," and hugged him again. Karen, with tears of happiness in her eyes, put her arm around Zach, who was still confused but happy, and they all stood together for a few minutes enjoying the reunion.

Pastor and Phil climbed out of the van and Phil noticed Pastor still staring at the group of cars. "It's okay, Mike, this is something I need to take care of," said Phil as he put his hand on his shoulder.

"Are you sure?" said Pastor, a bit worried.

"Yes," said Phil determined, "it should have been done a long time ago." Phil started towards the SUV that had been parked across the street from the church.

Pastor turned toward Triple D, who was still heading his way. Dave looked worried and kept glancing at the SUVs.

Buck and Becky were still hugging as Pastor and Phil exited the van. Becky pushed Buck back a little and her face turned white as though she had seen a ghost. "Wesley," she whispered.

Buck turned around and realized that his mom recognized Mr. Phil. "It's okay, Mom," said Buck, trying to soothe her. She started to walk towards the van but Buck grabbed her arm and tried to stop her. "Mom, wait."

"What. . .what's going on?" she asked as she kept looking from Buck to Phil. Becky was a strong woman herself, and Buck's attempt to stop her failed. She headed toward the men.

As Phil walked away from the van, the door of the SUV parked across from the church opened and out climbed Marshall Redwing. As Marshall stepped out so did the men in the other SUVs. They headed towards Phil and, almost immediately, efficiently surrounded him. Marshall slowly moved through the men in black and stopped in front of Phil, barely a foot away. They stared at each other for a long time. They made eye contact and examined each other with strong, determined looks on their faces. It was as if one were waiting for the other to make the first move. Neither flinched. "I've been looking for you for a long time," Marshall said.

"Well, apparently you've found me," Phil responded. Marshall took a step forward Phil, grabbed him and embraced him. Phil returned the hug and they locked onto each other tightly. Marshall finally said, "Wes, it's good to see you," as he let go.

"Marshall. . .it's good to see you too," Phil replied, surprised at the words coming out of his own mouth.

"We have a lot to talk about," said Marshall.

"Yes. . .yes, we do."

Becky and Buck passed the van on their way towards Phil. By this time Mark joined them. They reached the circle of men dressed in black suits and were stopped. They weren't allowed any closer. Stanley and Karen came up behind them and they were also halted by the men in black.

Phil turned to Buck and Becky and said, "Don't worry, it's okay. I'll see you soon and we can talk then," and he smiled and winked. Becky watched Wes walk away and then pulled Buck's shoulder and demanded, "What's going on?"

Buck said firmly, "Don't worry, Mom. I think I can explain everything. We can talk at home, c'mon," and pulled her to leave.

Marshall, who was now standing next to Phil, lifted his arm and pointed a finger at Stanley and said in a firm, gravelly tone, "I want you in my office Monday morning at 0700 hours," he paused, "and bring Karen." Marshall then took Phil by the arm and headed towards his SUV, where another agent was standing with the door open. The men who were surrounding them fanned out as the two climbed into the SUV. They got into their vehicles and followed Marshall.

Pastor and Dave met up and came together with hands outstretched. They said in unison, "I guess we have a lot to talk about."

They smiled at each other and hugged, and then Pastor said quietly, "Let me talk to Nolan first."

Dave nodded in acknowledgement, stepped back and followed Pastor. "Nolan," he asked, "would you mind putting all the gear into the Youth Hall? We can sort it out later."

"Nnno ppproblem," he replied and dutifully he brought all the equipment into the Youth Hall.

Becky, Buck and Mark headed back to the van. Stanley and Karen followed a short distance behind. Pastor had waved to Mark to join him. Mark turned to Buck and said, "I'll catch up with you later, okay?"

Buck smiled and said, "Yeah, later," and guided Becky towards their car. She was confused and happy and curious and proud all at the same time.

"Don't worry, Mom, everything's going to be all right. I know what happened and who Mr. Phil is. I'll tell you everything but let's just get home. I want to take a shower and change clothes."

"Of course. . .of course you do," she said as she roused herself from her state of confusion. "Can I drive?" he asked with a twinkle in his eye.

"Do you have your license with you?"

"No."

"Then I think I should drive," she said, finally smiling and enjoying the fact that he was home safely.

"I can't wait to tell you everything that happened on the trip."

"I can't wait to hear it."

Stanley and Karen met up with Weber and Zach, who had wisely stayed behind as all the commotion took place. Stanley walked between them, turned, put his arms over their shoulders looking at Weber and then Zach, "Let's go home and get some dinner," and they headed towards their car. Weber looked over at Zach and smiled, and Zach returned the smile. Not the same smile he used to give, like he was ready to take someone on, but a real smile, a genuinely friendly smile. "Yeah, dinner. Cool," Zach said slowly and he nodded his head.

Nolan quickly finished putting everything into the Youth Hall and waved at Pastor and Dave and said, "Iii'll sssee you Wwwednesday at the ssstaff mmmeeting," and he drove off in the van.

Pastor and Dave stood on the walkway to the office and watched him drive off. Pastor put his arm around Dave's shoulder. "Well," he said.

"Well," said Dave, still a bit confused.

"I guess we have some stories to share, Dave."

"Apparently we do."

"What say we go to my office, pour us a couple of cups of coffee and talk."

"That sounds like a good idea," responded Dave as they turned and headed up the walkway.

THE END

Geoff and Kathleen thank you for joining us on this adventure in Christianity. Please join us on our upcoming adventures!

Soli Deo Gloria

Printed in the United States
85671LV00002B/7/A